TAKE A CHANCE

What Reviewers Say About
D. Jackson Leigh's Work

"Leigh writes with an emotion that she in turn gives to the characters, allowing us insight into their personalities and their very souls. Filled with fantastic imagery and the down-to-earth flaws that are sometimes the characters' greatest strengths, this first Dragon Horse War is a story not to be missed. The writing is flawless, the story, breath-taking"—*Lambda Literary Society* review of *Dragon Horse War: The Calling.*

"*Call Me Softly* is a thrilling and enthralling novel of love, lies, intrigue, and Southern charm."—*Bibliophilic Book Blog*

"D. Jackson Leigh understands the value of branding, and delivers more of the familiar and welcome story elements that set her novels apart from other authors in the romance genre."—*The Rainbow Reader*

"Her prose is clean, lean, and mean—elegantly descriptive..." —*Out in Print*

By the Author

Cherokee Falls Series

Bareback

Long Shot

Every Second Counts

Romance

Call Me Softly

Touch Me Gently

Hold Me Forever

Swelter

Take A Chance

Anthology

Riding Passion

Dragon Horse War Trilogy

The Calling

Tracker and the Spy

Seer and the Shield

TAKE A CHANCE

by

D. Jackson Leigh

2018

TAKE A CHANCE

ISBN 13: 978-1-63555-118-1

THIS TRADE PAPERBACK ORIGINAL IS PUBLISHED BY
BOLD STROKES BOOKS, INC.
P.O. BOX 249
VALLEY FALLS, NY 12185

FIRST EDITION: JULY 2018

CREDITS
EDITOR: CINDY CRESAP
PRODUCTION DESIGN: SUSAN RAMUNDO
COVER PHOTOGRAPH BY EVELYN BRADDOCK
COVER DESIGN BY PAIGE BRADDOCK

Acknowledgments

First and foremost, I have to tip my hat to Bold Strokes Books Senior Editor Sandy Lowe.

Missouri Vaun, VK Powell and I—three unsupervised and over-caffeinated writer friends—were cooped up in Vaun's living room on a rainy Friday, when the discussion of novella anthologies devolved into an entertaining brainstorm for our own collection of novellas. Our ideas weren't serious, of course, because the titles sounded like a bar tab, and the plots were a contest of who could make the others laugh the hardest.

The next morning Vaun told us she'd put our ideas into a proposal and sent it to Sandy. You did what? After ingesting caffeine, we agreed it was a good prank. Despite her affectionate nickname of "the angry librarian," we were confident Sandy would laugh at our little game. We were all surprised, however, when she called our bluff and laid some new cards on the table—serious suggestions, drawn from our silly ideas, for three separate full-length novels. When Vaun read Sandy's ideas to our little group, we sounded like the SNL skit about Alexa for seniors—"I don't know about that." Then we were quiet for a long minute. You know… What if… A third head was nodding. If only we'd known what a difficult challenge we were about to attempt.

Secondly, I have to bow to my writing partners in the three-book Pine Cone romance series. Vaun and VK were the perfect partners for creating a small Southern town full of quirky characters, quaint places, and hot romances.

The most difficult part, overlapping our three stories, was our own design. It was much more arduous than we anticipated, and complicated by conflicting time zones. I was on the East Coast, Vaun on the West Coast, and VK was in Australia most of the summer. Our timeline ended up being a shared spreadsheet. It's a task that can only be undertaken with friends you love and trust deeply, and who can weather the pressure of deadlines and frustration of chapters that have to be rewritten because "my character totally would not act like that."

If you enjoy this book, I hope you'll visit with my characters and their friends in *Take My Hand* by Missouri Vaun, which was released last month, and *Take Your Time* by VK Powell, which will be released in August.

Dedication

This book is dedicated to my cohorts in this Pine Cone caper:
Missouri Vaun and VK Powell. I love you guys.

CHAPTER ONE

"Ouch." Dr. Trip Beaumont grimaced as she slid onto the sun-heated leather seat and reached for the control to cool the temperature of the driver's seat. She loved her new Ford F450 XLT Super Duty and all its high-tech features. It'd been well worth the wait and cost of the custom-built veterinary cabinet for the bed of the heavy-duty crew cab dually. Trip sighed as icy relief seeped through the stretch fabric of her riding breeches. The hot leather of the seat wasn't what stung so much. It was the heat applied as the result of Virginia Hathaway's enthusiasm for role-playing and rough sex.

Trip had been scheduled to pick up two of Virginia's prized Friesian mares to board at her clinic for the final weeks of their pregnancies and first weeks after foaling. It wasn't necessary, but certainly more convenient for Trip to walk down to the clinic barn from her house than to drive to the Hathaway farm when the mares went into labor. And a minimum of four weeks of full board would cost Virginia a pretty penny. Trip buckled her seat belt and squirmed in her seat again, but chuckled. It cost her a little, too.

Virginia had practically purred over the phone. "I have a new stallion just shipped in from Spain that I can't wait for you to see. Wear those sexy riding breeches and boots. I want you to take him for a test spin, and tell me how you think he'll do on the show circuit this summer."

Forewarned by past experience, Trip knew Virginia had a kinky side. So she could have protested that her morning was too booked up, but Hathaway Farms was one of her biggest accounts and Virginia readily accepted that Trip had boundaries—only the two of them, no video or audio recording, and no observers. Besides, sex with Virginia was no hardship. She was a beautiful fiery redhead married to a bisexual husband who Trip doubted gave Virginia the aggressive sex she desired. Virginia had practically drooled as Trip put the magnificent stallion through a thorough workout and gave her stamp of approval, then dragged Trip into the barn office and locked the door. After five minutes of heated kissing and groping, Trip's breeches were around her ankles, Virginia had strapped her favorite dildo to Trip's hips, then dropped her jeans and leaned over the desk begging Trip to take her.

"Ride me, hot stuff. Put that big thing in me and ride like you rode my stallion."

Filled with endorphins from having the stallion's controlled power between her legs only moments before, Trip was only too happy to oblige. Her only mistake was failing to notice the riding crop resting on the desktop well within Virginia's reach.

When Trip slowed her thrusts to dally a bit in Virginia's race to orgasm, Virginia snatched up the crop and laid some stinging encouragement across Trip's bare rump to reach the finish line quicker and more than once. Good Lord, she hoped it didn't break skin. It could leave a scar, and how would she explain that next time she went skinny-dipping or if she ever settled down with a real girlfriend? Ha. Who was she kidding? She wasn't cut out for settling down. She was Fast Break. The CB handle she'd jokingly taken in high school had proven prophetic. Hadn't she lost the one woman she desperately wanted to win by racing to score too quickly?

No matter. She wasn't exactly lonely. She enjoyed some notoriety in her profession as a rising star among equine veterinary surgeons before leaving a huge private specialty clinic in Atlanta and dropping out of the rat race to open her own mixed practice in her hometown. Her colleagues thought her crazy, but she was happy in the small South Georgia town of Pine Cone where the pace was slower, the women beautiful, and her two best friends—Clay Cahill aka Paintball, and Grace Booker, CB handle Glitter Girl—still lived.

She glanced in the rearview mirror as she pulled out of Virginia's drive and stuck her hand out for a farewell wave. Virginia waved back, a white card held tightly between her long fingers. Trip chuckled. Virginia had complained that her Mercedes wouldn't crank that morning, so Trip had given her Clay's business card.

"Give Clay a call. She'll come take a look and tow it to the repair shop if needed," Trip said. "I've known her since high school, and I can vouch that she's honest." She winked at Virginia. "And I know a lot of ladies who can vouch that she gives first class service."

Virginia took the card, her smile predatory. "The Mercedes is fine for the moment, but I'll check with her about coming over tomorrow afternoon to see about it."

Oh, yeah. Clay was going to owe her for this one.

Deputy Jamie Grant stepped out of the Dollar Store and slapped her Stetson on her head. The few other female deputies in the department didn't bother with the hats, but Jamie was ex-military and felt out of uniform without it when outdoors. She scanned the line of shade trees at the parking lot's edge for her canine partner. "P!" The scruffy mutt was engaged in a staring contest with a squirrel chattering from a high limb, but instantly turned to Jamie. After a check for moving vehicles, she flicked a hand signal that brought the dog running.

"Good girl," Jamie crooned, bending to reward Petunia with a scratch behind one half-erect ear. She opened the driver's door of her patrol car, and Petunia hopped in to settle behind the steering wheel. "Over," Jamie said. "Until you get your license, I'm driving."

Petunia scrambled over to the passenger seat, emitting an audible burst of flatulence and a malodorous cloud.

Jamie grimaced and hit the control on the door to lower all windows in the patrol car. "Thank you for that." She instantly regretted her growled remark when Petunia flattened her ears and ducked her head in the doggie equivalent of a cringe. It tore Jamie's heart out that the little dog had been conditioned by someone in her past to expect punishment for a medical condition she couldn't control. She deliberately softened her expression and voice. "It's okay, P. I know you can't help it." She extended her hand slowly and stroked Petunia's rough wirehair coat along her back. "Does your belly hurt?"

Petunia rolled onto her back, presenting her stomach, and thumped her tail softly against the seat in a silent plea for further rubbing. Jamie laughed and complied, then nearly choked when the belly rub elicited another loud emission of stench. She pulled a handful of air fresheners from the bag she'd carried from the store. "Pine, oranges, or coconut?" Petunia sniffed each one, then touched her nose to the coconut. "I like that, too," Jamie said. "But I'm not sure it will go well with your aroma du jour. Let's try the pine scent." She freed the tree from its plastic covering and hung it from the rearview mirror. Petunia sneezed, then jumped into the rear seat.

"Sorry," Jamie said. "Sergeant's orders. It won't be so bad once we get going with the windows down."

Jamie turned the police cruiser toward the old abandoned rail station at the east end of town. She waved, and Petunia yipped a greeting at three homeless men sunning on the porch of the ramshackle building. Two of them were familiar, but the third face was new. Every patrol during the short weeks since she'd come to Pine Cone, she'd slowly circle the small parking lot and then go back the way she came to let them get used to her. Today, she stopped, stepped out of the car, and waited for Petunia to hop out. "Heel," she said softly.

The men eyed her, then Petunia. The new guy was younger than the two familiar men. His face and hands were dirty, but his clothes weren't ragged. His eyes were haunted and his posture defiant. She'd seen the look often on the faces of soldiers serving their second or third tour in Afghanistan. She judged him to be around thirty years old and probably a veteran. Homeless folk always had a story, and a little kindness toward them usually went a long way.

"How are y'all today?" she asked.

One of the men, a wiry fellow with a face leathered by the sun, shrugged and spit on the ground. "We're keeping our heads down and minding our own business."

Jamie smiled. *Like I should be minding mine?* She held her hands up, palms out. "I'm not looking to hassle you. I just wanted to make sure you had plenty of water. There's a heat advisory today, and you need to drink a lot of water if you're out in it."

The two older men looked at each other in silent communication about whether she was to be trusted, but Jamie looked into the eyes of the new guy. "Not as hot as the desert, but humidity here pushes up the heat index and you can dehydrate before you realize it."

He looked away, and she knew she'd guessed right about his military service.

The first man slid off the edge of the porch to stand. "You got water you're giving away?"

"I've got something better than that." She walked to the rear of the car and popped the trunk open. "I've got a gallon of sweet tea from the diner and a bag of peaches from that produce stand out on the highway. My eyes were bigger than my stomach and I bought too many. I'd rather give them away than have them spoil before I can eat them all."

The men looked wary, but licked their lips when she held up the bag of six peaches. Ice dripped from the plastic gallon of dark tea.

"I'm kind of new in town and haven't made any friends to share them with." Jamie waited a long moment while they weighed their desire for the tea and peaches against what she might want in return. "I've been poor and even homeless before," she said softly. She shifted her gaze to the veteran, who was staring at the ground. "I've been in the desert, too."

He jerked his eyes to hers, and she knew he could read the truth in them.

"My mama—before she passed—used to cook a peach cobbler that would make you believe in Jesus." His smooth tenor voice sounded much younger than he appeared. He reached hesitantly, then took the peaches Jamie held out. "Thanks," he said, holding the bag out to the other men to share.

Jamie took four plastic cups from a sleeve of twenty that she kept in the large duffel. She poured a half cup for herself, then handed the other cups and gallon jug to the biggest man, who finally slid off the porch to join them. They waited until she took a big swallow from her cup, then each poured themselves a full cup before handing it back to her. She waved it away. "Y'all keep the rest." Jamie smiled again when they instantly accepted, and then squatted to offer a cup of water to Petunia. She peered up at them while Petunia lapped noisily. "I'm Jamie. You guys got names?"

The big man, his dreadlocks white against his dark brown skin, eyed her for a few seconds, then spoke in a low rumbling voice that reminded her of James Earl Jones. "I'm Toby." He jerked his thumb to the smaller man. "That's Pete."

The younger man chucked his peach pit into the straggle of knee-high weeds nearby. He wiped the peach juice from his left hand on his pants as he offered his right hand to Jamie. "My mother named me Francis, but I was christened Adder—" He shrugged. "You know… over there."

Jamie shook his hand. "Which do you prefer?"

He hesitated, a scowl crossing his face. "Adder, I think."

Jamie nodded. "You sticking around for a while?"

He stared into the distance. "Don't know. I take it day to day."

"I understand." She waved at the duffel in her trunk. "You guys need anything? I've got soap, razors, shaving cream, toothpaste and brushes…all the basic stuff. I keep a stash because you never know when you might need something like that."

"Soap," Pete said. "Lost mine in the river last time we went down there to bathe and cool off."

"Do you have some toenail clippers?" Toby asked.

Jamie shook her head. "Not this time, but I start my patrol here most days. If you're here tomorrow, I'll have some."

"I could use a new razor," Adder said, taking the one Jamie dug out of her bag.

She closed the trunk and opened the patrol car's door for Petunia, who obediently jumped in, emitting another gastric symphony with the effort.

"You guys stay cool, now." She waved once more as she pulled out of the lot and, this time, they waved back. Or maybe they were waving away the blue cloud Petunia left in her wake.

CHAPTER TWO

Hey, Jolene. Does Bud have my lunch order ready?" Trip waved to the five men enjoying lunch at the big round table in the front of the diner. "I parked in the shade, but I've got two of Virginia's pregnant mares in the trailer out there. I don't want them to get too hot."

"I'll go check." Jolene plunked a sweating pitcher of sweet tea down next to one of the men. "Y'all go ahead and pour your own refills."

"Sure thing, Jolene," one of the men said.

"If you've been out to Virginia's place, you must have seen that new stallion she had shipped all the way over from Spain," another man at the table said.

Trip went to the chipped Formica counter and lifted a glass-domed cover to swipe a glazed doughnut from the stack on the plate underneath. "Saw him and rode him this morning. He's plenty impressive. Once she hits the show circuit with him, she'll be raking in the cash for his semen."

"I reckon that will shut Jonathan up. He's been complaining to anyone who'd listen about the cost of flying that horse across the Atlantic." The other men nodded in agreement.

"He should listen to his wife. Virginia knows horses." Trip licked chips of doughnut glaze from her finger and pointed at her conversation buddy. "Her operation is one of the few I know that makes money, rather than just being a tax write-off."

Jolene huffed through the kitchen's swinging door and set a white plastic bag on the counter. "I swear. How long has Bud been the cook here?"

Trip and the table of men shrugged in response.

"Longer than I've been waiting tables here. Do you know how long that's been?"

More shrugs.

"At least twelve years. And he still don't know to put more hush puppies in the fryer before you run out." She began to ring up Trip's ticket. "I'm sorry, hon. It'll be another three or four minutes before your hush puppies are ready. Will the horses be okay?"

"They'll be fine for another few minutes." Trip grinned. "Don't be too hard on old Bud. He couldn't have been the cook here that long, because I know you haven't waited tables here for twelve years. You'd have been twelve years old when you started work because I'd swear you aren't a day over twenty-four."

The men erupted into guffaws, their hands slapping down on the table. A glare from Jolene silenced them, but didn't wipe the smiles from their faces.

Jolene's blue eyes softened when she turned back to Trip. "Sweet talker. You know good and well that I'm old enough to be...well, to be your older sister. And you're a bit past twenty-four yourself."

Bud nudged quietly through the swinging door and nodded an apology to Trip as he slid a grease-stained brown paper bag into the plastic bag holding her order. "I gave you extra since you had to wait," he said.

"Appreciate that, Bud, but you didn't have to. I didn't wait very long," Trip said, smiling to let him know it was really okay. "Tell your mama I said hey, and I'll be by soon to check up on Henry. It's time for his vaccinations."

He nodded and retreated to the kitchen.

Jolene hit the total key on the cash register. "That's ten dollars and twenty-eight cents. Lunch for two?"

It was impossible to keep anything a secret in a small Southern town. This bit of news, however, wasn't a secret. "I hired a vet, Dr. Dani Wingate, to work with me so I won't have to close the clinic when I go out on farm calls. She got into town day before yesterday and is just settling in at the clinic today."

"Where's she staying?"

"At the bed and breakfast for now."

Not as juicy as a new girlfriend but news worth spreading, and Trip had given it to Jolene first. "I didn't charge you for the doughnut you snuck while I was in the kitchen."

"Doughnut?"

Jolene laughed. "Yes. The one that left little pieces of glaze on your upper lip."

Trip swiped her tongue along her lip, then took the napkin Jolene held out and wiped her mouth. "I was going to tell you to add it to my check."

"And I was going to tell you it was on the house." Jolene rested her elbow on the top of the cash register and her chin in her palm, her expression a bit wistful. "It's a good thing I don't play for your team."

Trip winked at her. "I've got horses to look after."

Jolene smiled. "Next time you look to hire somebody from out of town, how about hiring a handsome fellow to come sweep me off my feet and take me away from this luxurious life."

"I'll see what I can do about that."

The rest of Jamie's morning was quiet. Farmers were in the fields. Her new boss, Sergeant Grace Booker, said the annual swell of migrant workers to help plant, cultivate, and harvest tobacco, cotton, peanuts, and other crops was still more than a month away. Most other folks were sheltering in air-conditioned homes, shops, and businesses. They wouldn't come out to sit on their porches until after the heat peaked midafternoon or a thunderstorm blew through to cool things off.

Her first couple of days on the job, Sergeant Booker warned Jamie not to go off half-cocked and arrest half the town. She filled Jamie in on the history of Pine Cone as they patrolled around the eclectic community, "to help Jamie better understand the culture."

The town of Pine Cone's beginning was typical during a time when all you needed was a railroad depot, cotton gin, or a tobacco auction barn to seed the beginnings of a new community. Before you knew it, there was a church, a school, a bank, and a courthouse, Grace explained. Then, as certain citizens prospered, a golf course and country club sprang up because, obviously, you couldn't hold the debutante ball in the high school gym.

Pine Cone, however, took a turn that wasn't typical.

An itinerate artist came through one day and was enamored with the town's rural texture, unique characters, and long sunsets. He settled there quietly, but his paintings of the town and citizens brought an uproar of praise when they circulated through big city galleries. More came—painters, sculptors, potters—to settle among the farmers and townspeople. The influx of quirky creative types was tolerated with a "bless your heart" because, well, Southerners were reared to be polite, and most every family had a crazy Uncle Earl, demented Aunt Edna, or a cousin who was flamingly gay or whispered to be lesbian.

When Interstate 95 paved an East Coast corridor that came within a few miles of the town limits, tourists began to find the artsy enclave an interesting stopover on their way to the sunny beaches of Florida. The "bless your heart" turned into "thank the Lord" as the tourists' money found its way into everybody's pockets. A downside was that drug mules transporting their illegal products from marinas along the Gulf Coast also found Pine Cone a convenient overnight stop while they waited for their handoff to an I-95 runner traveling between New York City and Miami.

That was why Jamie was here. Soon, she'd change to a later shift because the drug mules were like cockroaches. They mostly came out at dusk. But she had another week or two on day patrol because Grace wanted her to get to know the heartbeat and flow of the town and its citizens. So she spent her days writing tickets or the occasional report on a fender-bender.

The highlight of her day would be patrolling with Petunia through the busy parking lot of the truck stop on the outskirts of town that afternoon. Unlike the motel managers who were afraid a drug bust in their parking lot would scare off tourists, the truck stop owner freely gave permission for Petunia to sniff among the trucks and travelers each afternoon.

Until then, Jamie filled her morning by ticketing a speeding tourist out on the highway, stopping a pickup leaving a trail of unsecured trash as it headed for the landfill, and turning on her blue lights to stop traffic while she helped a huge snapping turtle get across a two-lane highway.

The duties of a small-town cop would take some getting used to, but Jamie was accustomed to the military "hurry up and wait," so she'd bide her time until she was switched to night duty.

The sun was high overhead, and Jamie's stomach growled when the delicious scent of roasting pork drifted in her open windows. She inhaled. Pine Cone had a surprising variety of excellent dining options, but nothing beat the downtown diner for lunch. A big old Cadillac pulled out from a parking space just ahead, and Jamie smoothly glided into the space behind a horse trailer. Two sleek rumps were visible over the trailer's ramp. Jamie's jaw tightened. Parked right across from the diner, the truck's driver was probably eating lunch and chatting with friends over tall glasses of iced tea while these horses sweated in the close quarters of the metal trailer. She checked her phone for the outside temperature and humidity, then climbed out of the cruiser, lunch forgotten.

At nearly six feet tall, she could easily see over the lower panel when she raised up on her toes. The horses were nibbling from a full hay net hung below a fan that whirred softly as it rotated back and forth. Their rounded flanks were dry. Not satisfied, she stepped onto the sidewalk and walked to where the front panels were folded back to let air circulate through. The horse on that side paused eating and sniffed Jamie's neck when she leaned in. Their chests were dry, too. The driver had apparently taken all necessary precautions, but if those were her horses, she wouldn't dare stop for lunch and risk them overheating.

Jamie backed up, dodging a bit of Spanish moss that hung a little too low from the branch above. Most of the trees in the heart of downtown were small, flowering dogwoods or crape myrtles, but two huge live oaks still thrived in the small park across from the diner.

That was one lucky driver to snag prime shade for both a large truck and horse trailer. Her gaze slid over the truck, then its familiar logo, and then the fire hydrant by the truck's front tire. Son of a bitch. It wasn't luck. It was that damned arrogant Trip Beaumont parking wherever she wanted, as though she owned the whole town. *Well, she doesn't own this cop.* Jamie whipped out her ticket book and slapped it down on the truck's hood. She clicked her pen and began writing. She'd put so many tickets on this truck that she knew the license plate number without looking. She finished with a flourish and secured the ticket under the windshield wiper. Jamie hated rule breakers, and Trip Beaumont was one of those women who broke every rule she encountered. She'd also broken Jamie's heart.

Trip pushed through the glass door and put her bag of takeout food in the back seat of the truck before peeking in the front windows of the horse trailer to make sure the interior fan was still running and the horses appeared comfortable. She'd been inside the diner maybe ten minutes and the gnarly old oaks had provided ample shade. The mares ignored her as they placidly munched their tasty orchard grass hay, so she climbed into her truck and started the engine. She'd just reached for the gearshift when the flutter of paper caught her attention.

"Son of a bitch." She growled in frustration as she climbed out of the truck and lifted the wiper blade to extract the offending parking ticket. She threw it on the ground and stomped it several times before picking it up again and climbing back into the truck. She closed her eyes and took several deep breaths before stuffing the gritty ticket into the console compartment at her elbow, adding it to the twenty-odd tickets already there.

Yeah, she was parked next to a yellow curb and a hydrant, but everybody knew her truck. If they didn't, Beaumont Veterinary was clearly stenciled on the doors. Horses obviously had to be parked in the shade. Grace had mentioned that they'd recently hired several new police deputies, and this overzealous ticket writer must be one of them. Grace needed to explain to that rookie that Trip was a doctor and could park wherever she wanted. In case there was a medical emergency. That's right. She might be a veterinarian, but people in the South took their animals seriously. Her emergencies were just as important as any physician's.

But it was more than that. Over twenty tickets in just a few weeks? It seemed as though this rookie was deliberately watching for her truck. If that was the case, this little pissant Barney Fife was going to find out exactly who owned that truck. The Beaumonts were one of the founding families of Pine Cone. Not that Trip ever gave any thought to old values such as the family's standing in society. But she did give weight to her value to the community. And, by God, she was an important person in these parts, and she ought to be able to park wherever she wanted.

Trip slid her sleek wraparound sunglasses down from atop her head to cover her eyes and scanned the Main Street square for the rogue cop. Not a hound dog was stirring in the afternoon heat.

Trip shook her head in disgust, then checked her side mirror and pulled smoothly away from the curb, mindful not to let her temper translate into a rough ride for her very pregnant passengers. She wasn't one to dwell on things. If she couldn't charm her way over an obstacle, she just skirted around it. She'd spent her childhood managing her mother's constant efforts to mold her into a proper Southern debutante. The parking violations filling her console were a very minor problem compared to Mrs. Olivia Anne Eastwood Beaumont. So she tucked the irritating ticket writer away into her I'll-think-about-that-tomorrow file, and hummed softly to herself as she drove through the residential neighborhood that would melt into a two-lane blacktop flanked with renovated three-story, hundred-year-old mansions and a few recent replicas situated on picturesque farms with white board fences. One such farm was her home and the location of her clinic.

She slowed to a soft halt at the stop sign next to the Clip 'n Curl, noting the line of cars parked on the adjacent street and absently searching her memory for some special town function that would have everyone rushing for a "do" fix. Had someone prominent died and she missed the newspaper obituary? The whup of tires hitting the curb behind her drew her attention to her side mirrors, and her foot instinctively moved to the accelerator to get out of the way. But the Mercedes had already swerved and bounced over the curb, narrowly missing the back corner of her horse trailer. She watched, frozen in her seat, as it took out the red azalea bushes Connie had planted in honor of her mama being elected the president of the local Red Hat Society chapter, kicked up ragged sprigs of the lush centipede grass as it tore muddy tracks across the lawn, and plowed into the family of deer lawn ornaments before slamming into the corner of the Clip 'n Curl with a resounding bang.

"Holy crap." Trip slammed the truck's gearshift into park. She was barely out of the truck when the door to the beauty salon opened and women began to pour out, looking more like a cast of a horror movie than women in various stages of beautification.

A plump, full-figured woman trotted down the front steps past the gruesome lineup. "Good Lord almighty! I thought we was havin' an earthquake!" Connie, owner of the Clip 'n Curl and head beautician, rushed to the Mercedes and opened the driver's door to peer in. Connie stepped back when the driver extended her arm to point at Trip's truck and horse trailer.

Trip stutter-stepped. Whoa. This day was definitely taking a turn for the better. The beauty looking her way had crystal blue eyes and fifty shades of shining brunette mane that hung straight and silky to just below her shoulders. Trip knew fine bloodlines when she saw them, and she'd be willing to bet this stranger had a pedigree a mile long. The woman was moving and talking to Connie, so Trip surmised she'd suffered no serious injuries. But one could never take these things for granted. *Is there a doctor in the house?* Trip smiled. *Oh, that would be me.*

As Trip neared, she could see the reddening lump on the woman's forehead. Time to take charge. "Connie, is she hurt?"

Connie's brow knitted and her mouth formed a soundless O. She was staring at the woman's forehead, apparently at a loss to evaluate the situation.

The woman squinted up at Trip. "I just hit my head on the steering wheel. No airbags." She fumbled with the seat belt and twisted to get out of the car.

Trip knelt next to the open car door, blocking her exit from the vehicle. "Easy there. Are you all right?" Whatever the prospect of new date material, her concern was real. She looked into the blue eyes—clear but a bit unfocused. She appeared to be moving okay, but she'd have to stand to evaluate any balance problems or muscle strain.

Trip stood and extended her hand to help her new patient out of the car. She was elegant in a sleeveless black dress that hugged her curves in all the right places. The fact that she was also barefoot ran Trip's sex-o-meter all the way to hot.

The woman accepted the assistance, then propped against the side of the car and shaded her eyes with her hand. "I dropped my phone and looked down for just a second to get it. When I looked up, all I saw were horse butts."

"There are a few of those around here." Trip extended her hand again, this time as introduction. "I'm Dr. Trip Beaumont, driver of those particular horse butts."

The woman's fingers were long and her grip was light enough to be ladylike but not limp. Still, she blinked like she couldn't figure out why her hand was in Trip's.

"Connie, did you call Grace?" Trip asked without taking her eyes from the woman's face.

"Lord, no. I just ran out here without thinkin'. I'm so glad you're here to take charge." Before Connie could turn to go inside, an alien with oversized curlers ringing her green face called out to them from the porch. "Grace is on her way!"

"Thank you, Lula May." Connie turned back to their wayward driver. "What's your name, hon?"

"I'm River...River Hemsworth." She withdrew her hand from Trip's. "I'm so sorry about crashing into your salon."

Trip liked River's full, melodic tones. Attractive women with little girl or nasal voices were a total turnoff.

"Now don't you worry about that, sweetie, as long as no one got hurt, that's all that matters," Connie said.

Trip turned when red fake fingernails trailed down her arm, then a warm hand touched her cheek.

"Trip, sugah, are you hurt?"

"No, I'm fine." She raised an eyebrow at the smock covered with dancing piglets and pink bows that Shayla was wearing.

"All the same, maybe you should come to my place later and let me check you over thoroughly."

She could have Shayla's kind of fun anytime, but she wasn't one to burn bridges so she offered what she hoped was a genuinely grateful smile. "I appreciate that, but I'm fine." She gestured to the trailer. "The horses are fine. She didn't even touch the trailer."

"Thank goodness for small miracles." Shayla leaned her head against Trip's shoulder. "My offer still stands, though, if you aren't busy tonight."

Before Trip could answer, the blast of a siren pierced the air.

Grace whipped the black-and-white Ford Crown Victoria up next to the curb and left the blue lights flashing as she climbed out. Trip wanted to smile as Grace predictably adjusted her utility belt and holster before striding over with a large clipboard under one arm. The department had recently repainted their fleet a retro design as part of the city council's brainstorm to rebrand the downtown as a quaint step back in time, and Trip would have teased her with a Sheriff Andy comment if they hadn't been in the presence of such an attractive stranger. Grace could take teasing, but only between close friends—meaning her and Clay. Trip knew that underneath her tough cop exterior and razor wit was a sensitive sweetheart. Grace was the Glitter Girl. A shapely five foot six, her wavy shoulder-length auburn hair and high cheekbones were eye-catching. Grace, however, didn't want to catch anyone's eye. She wanted to capture someone's heart and the kind of love that lasts a lifetime. Right now, she was just a cop about to write up the wayward driver who'd tried to park a Mercedes in the foundation of the Clip 'n Curl.

Grace surveyed the crowd. "Is anyone hurt?"

Trip couldn't resist. "Two fatalities. I'm afraid there was nothing I could do for them." She hung her head and gestured solemnly at the family of fake deer. Pieces of the doe and fawn were scattered across the lawn. She struggled to hold her serious expression as she pointed to the buck that was upended and missing an antler. "But I'm optimistic the injured will fully recover with a little glue and a bit of paint."

Grace smiled as she shook her head at Trip's typical playfulness. Then she glanced at River and shot Trip a questioning look.

Trip grinned and wiggled her eyebrows. "She's the mad motorist who mowed down the unsuspecting deer."

Grace turned to River. "I'm Sergeant Grace Booker. You okay, ma'am?"

River nodded, her stare fixed on the destroyed deer.

"Had a bit of an accident I see."

River focused on Grace. "Yes. I'm River Hemsworth, and I'm afraid it was my fault."

"Well, I assumed the shop didn't pull out in front of you." Grace's all-business cop tone warmed like the melt-in-your-mouth fudge that Jeanie sold down at the Sweet Tooth, and the corner of her mouth hinted at a smile.

Was Grace flirting with River? Wait. Trip had first dibs on the new woman. She was suddenly hyperaware of Shayla's head resting against her shoulder and Shayla's arm entwined around hers. Damn. She was stomping all over Trip's mojo. Trip was contemplating how to extract herself from Shayla the Octopus without damaging any future opportunities, when Connie rescued her.

"Shayla, run fetch Miss Hemsworth a glass of tea. There's a pitcher in the icebox." Connie shooed Shayla in the direction of the front door of her shop. Shayla frowned but sauntered back into the shop with a seductive sway of her hips.

River ran a shaky hand over her perspiring brow. The mention of something cool seemed to deflate her. Now that she was rid of Shayla, Trip cupped River's elbow and guided her to a huge maple. River sagged against it. Trip stretched out an arm to casually prop against the same tree. "It's a scorcher today."

"I see you've got things in hand as usual, Trip." Grace shook her head again, but her eyes were full of affection. Message received. Picking up strangers was Trip's style anyway, not Grace's. "I'll call one of my deputies to come fill out an accident report while we wait for Clay." Grace stepped away from the crowd and spoke into the radio mic attached to her shoulder.

"Who's Clay?" River frowned.

"Clay Cahill drives the tow truck." Trip didn't like the look of the red knot on River's forehead. It didn't look too serious, but would probably produce a headache bad enough to spoil her initial intent of asking this luscious stranger out to dinner tonight. Ah. The concerned doctor plan would work. Find out where she's staying, urge her to go home, take aspirin and nap, then pay an I-needed-to-check-on-you visit tonight with takeout dinner in hand. Worked every time. Just needed to lay the groundwork. "Are you sure you don't need an ambulance, Ms. Hemsworth? That goose egg on your forehead could lead to complications."

❖

"Ten-four. Ten-fifty at the Clip 'n Curl, 518 Oak Street. Unit three is ten-seventeen." Jamie shook the ballpoint pen that suddenly refused to write. Whatever. She drove past that salon yesterday, so she had a good idea where it was. She checked her rearview mirror and made a wide U-turn, then glanced down at her speedometer. The dispatch was the first semi-interesting thing that'd happened to her this week, but she wasn't going in all Barney Fife-like with lights flashing and sirens blaring. Sergeant Booker was on the scene, and this was Jamie's first chance to impress her new boss.

"Damn it." That last turn that Jamie thought was a shortcut had landed her in an unfamiliar neighborhood. She paused at a stop sign to collect herself. Okay. Streets with flower names ran east to west. Streets with tree names ran north to south. She was proud of herself for figuring that out before Grace explained it. Still, it wasn't like a city where streets were numbered so that you could easily figure out if you were headed in the wrong direction.

The sign on the corner read Gardenia Lane. Were gardenias a tree or a flower? Hell, she didn't know. She was trying to find Elm Street. Or was it Maple Street. No. Oak Street. Maybe. She was about to ask her phone for directions to the Clip 'n Curl when a tow truck sped past. Since there was only one garage in town with an actual tow truck rather than a pickup with a winch, it had to be headed for her ten-fifty. "Hold on, P." She whipped a right turn to give the tow truck a police escort...from the rear. She laughed at her justification, and Petunia yipped happily with her.

❖

"I'm fine. Really."

Trip was about to begin her let-me-check-your-vitals routine on River when Clay's big truck roared up, then slowed to ease carefully over the curb to pull up behind the Mercedes.

Clay hopped down from the truck, her faded classic Levi's hanging low on her narrow hips. With scuffed work boots and a white T-shirt that fit snug across her broad shoulders, Clay was a dark contrast to Trip's light. Her tall, lean frame, short, unkempt raven hair, and smoldering brown eyes gave off a definite James Dean vibe.

River appeared riveted as Clay approached. Damn. The playing field sure was crowded today. Then again, Trip didn't mind flaunting her new find in front of her best running buddy. They didn't really compete for women. Trip was bold while Clay had a slower, sensitive approach, and they both observed unspoken "no poaching" rules. You never went after a woman your buddy was dating, without your buddy's consent. Shayla was a prime example. They'd both enjoyed her talents on occasion, but were careful to upend the tiny decorative urn on Shayla's front porch as a signal to the other to try back later. Only Trip hadn't found the urn turned over since Clay returned from New York, moody and more brooding than usual.

Lucky for Trip, Shayla returned with the tea, breaking the spell for a moment. River took the offered drink and gulped down a big swallow, then coughed.

"Now doesn't that taste refreshing?" Connie asked.

"Mmm." River's smile was weak, but she took a few more sips.

Yep. Trip had seen that look before. Sweet tea was an adjustment for any Yankee, and Connie's tea was more like sugar water.

"Thank you, Connie," Grace said. "You've been real helpful. I'll have my deputy come inside when she's done here and get your statement and insurance information. You can get back to your customers in the meantime." She motioned for the other bystanders to move away. "Nothing else to see here, folks."

"Connie believes in having a little tea with her sugar," Trip said, leaning close to whisper as Connie hurried back into her shop. She had to move fast now that she had broken the spell of Clay's entrance onto the scene. She grabbed the only surviving member of the fake deer family, righted the buck next to River, and then patted it on the back. "Have a seat. You look a little pale."

River eyed the plastic statue skeptically, then carefully sat at an awkward angle to avoid poking her eye with its remaining antler.

"Clay, this is River Hemsworth. She's having a bit of car trouble." Grace looked up from her paperwork and pointed toward the crumpled Mercedes. "River, this is Clay. She'll take care of you as soon as we get all your information." She checked her watch. "Where the heck is my deputy?"

"Clay can take care of her car," Trip said, squatting in front of River. She made a show of looking at her watch as she wrapped her fingers around River's wrist to check her pulse. She was a big dog and could hunt in a crowd. "I'll be happy to transport River to her destination—just in case she has a delayed reaction to this terrible accident and needs medical attention." She grasped River's chin. "Look into my eyes for a moment so I can check your pupils." Trip smiled warmly when River obediently turned sapphire eyes her way. "Your heart rate is a bit elevated," she said, keeping her voice soft.

The line had never failed her before, but River was obviously big-city. Her accent, her clothes, the way she carried herself, screamed it. She'd probably heard that line and much better, because she withdrew her wrist from Trip's grip. "I'm fine. Really. But I appreciate your help, Dr. Beaumont."

Clay snorted, and Grace barked a laugh.

"Trip here might have *played* doctor with more than a few women around town," Clay said. "But she's actually our local veterinarian."

River choked on her next sip of tea.

Great. So much for her concerned doctor routine. Trip narrowed her eyes at Grace, who was supposed to have her back. She knew who had first dibs. Grace just lifted a hand and shook her head. She'd never take sides between them.

"Thank you for your assistance, *Trip*," River said, her eyes glued to Clay again. "But I should go with Clay to make the necessary arrangements to have my car repaired."

Trip started to move on to plan C—insist on checking on her later that evening—then hesitated. She looked at River, then Clay. It was almost as if they were the only two people around. What the heck? Trip turned to Grace, but Grace shrugged in a silent "don't ask me" gesture. So, she wasn't imagining the—hell, she didn't even know what to call it—between Clay and River. Grace had noticed it, too.

"Were you trying to make a quick getaway when the Clip 'n Curl cut you off?" Clay drawled out her words, low and melodious, like someone who just woke from a deep sleep. Trip grimaced. She bagged enough women with her cocky charm, but when Clay started talking, women swarmed to her like bees to honey.

"Excuse me?" River seemed confused rather than amused by the question. Maybe Trip did still have a chance.

Clay tipped her head in the direction of the car. "That's Ellen Gardner's car."

Trip really looked at the car for the first time. Leave it to Clay to recognize the vintage Mercedes. She was all about cars.

"Ellen was my aunt," River said.

"My condolences." Clay's face reddened and her expression was contrite.

Trip cleared her throat. "I'm sorry for your loss." She felt like an ass. She should have recognized the car, too, but she was too intent on hitting on River. "Ellen was a fine woman."

"The best," Grace added.

"Thank you." River looked from Clay to Trip and back to Clay.

Trip was relieved when Grace saved them from the awkward silence.

"Hey, Trip, can I talk to you a second before you leave?" She inclined her head toward her patrol car.

❖

Jamie slowed the cruiser to a crawl when the tow truck veered right to bump over the curb and onto the lawn where a crowd gathered around an old Mercedes. But she wasn't looking at the accident scene. She was staring at the truck and horse trailer she'd ticketed less than thirty minutes ago. Trip was here. Jamie had known they'd come face-to-face eventually. She thought she'd be ready, but the churning in her stomach indicated otherwise. Would Trip even remember that they'd parted on bad terms? Jamie narrowed her eyes. Queen Beaumont hadn't even pulled over to the curb. Her truck and horse trailer sat squarely in the middle of the right lane, and you couldn't see around it without straddling the centerline and possibly causing another accident. Jamie pulled over to the curb and rummaged in the glove box for a fresh pen, then climbed out of the cruiser.

Petunia was on her hind legs, her tail wagging as she watched the crowd of people across the lawn. She ran to the driver's side of the back seat when Jamie got out of the car. "Stay, P."

The little dog whined, then released another explosion of flatulence when she ran back to resume watching the crowd through the opposite window. Jamie would have laughed at the you-always-make-me-stay glare from her canine partner, but she had a serious situation here. She might have to finally face Trip, but she wasn't going to chew the old bone between them in front of her boss and a crowd of town gossips.

Jaime scribbled the ticket. At this rate, she would need a new ticket book by the end of the week. She should get a commendation for filling the town coffers with all these traffic fines, not to mention the federal forfeiture funds they'd received as a result of Petunia's first few drug finds. The wiper slapped against the windshield when she released it to hold the ticket where Trip would clearly see it. She stuffed her ticket book into her back pocket and took a deep breath as she rounded the front of the truck. Show time.

"That wasn't subtle or anything," Trip said as she followed Grace. She was a little miffed that Grace seemed to be aiding and abetting Clay's campaign in the River competition. "What's up?"

"Karla left Dirty Harry at my house yesterday when she vamoosed with a redhead. I think he's having a meltdown. Any chance you could take a look at him for me?"

"Karla's obnoxious, profanity-spewing parrot? Grace, look me in the eyes and tell me that you are not thinking about keeping him."

"Probably not."

"Good. Dirty Harry hates you."

"I just need to make sure he's physically okay before I decide anything."

Trip wanted to roll her eyes. "So, you are thinking of keeping him. Grace, when are you going to stop taking care of everybody and everything and look after yourself? Karla mooched off you for three months. I say good riddance to that one. And the bird, too."

"Don't blame Karla. We mutually used each other."

"I'm just saying you deserve better. You're the Glitter Girl. Go find someone who will give you the love you deserve." Trip didn't understand why Grace was still single. She was the best of the three of them.

"Yeah, like they grow on trees around here." Grace pulled at her utility belt, her tell that she wasn't happy with Trip's advice. "I'm talking about Harry right now. He'd make a nice addition to your waiting room. He's very entertaining."

Trip backed away, her hands up. "No way. He's loud and has a filthy vocabulary. He'll scare my patients to death, unless one of them eats him the first day."

"I have to do something before he wrecks the rest of my place. Please?"

"No can do, my friend, but I'll check him over. Bring him by the clinic sometime. Right now, I'm on a rescue mission." She wiggled her eyebrows and strode back to Clay and River. She had to rescue River from Clay.

"River, if Clay can't sort everything out for you, I'm always—"

Clay elbowed Trip. "Didn't your afternoon office hours start ten minutes ago?"

Trip checked her watch. "Crap." She hadn't realized how long she'd dawdled in the yard of the Clip 'n Curl. "Yes, and I need to get these horses home and out of that hot trailer." Clay had clearly jumped Trip's claim while she'd been tending to Grace's problem, so she might as well leave River in her capable hands. There'd be other hot-looking tourists Trip could pursue. "River, have a nice stay in Pine Cone." Trip gave Clay a good-natured shove before offering a little salute to Grace, then heading for her truck.

"Catch you later, pal." Clay gave a casual wave, her eyes never leaving River.

Trip went directly to the rear of the horse trailer to peer inside. The two mares were still munching hay, but their hides were dark with sweat, and the mare on the left shifted impatiently, causing the trailer to sway slightly. She needed to get them unloaded at the clinic soon. She hopped into the truck and fired up the diesel engine when a flutter of paper caught her eye.

"What the hell?" She hit the window control and, as the glass slid down, reached around to snatch the new parking ticket from under the wiper blade. "Son of a bitch." She gritted her teeth and scanned the area, then checked her side mirrors. A second squad car was parked behind Grace's. Trip crawled over the truck's console, swearing when she banged her knee on the emergency brake lever. The cop was talking to Grace, facing away from Trip. With the Stetson hat that was part of the uniform pulled low, she wasn't sure whether the new deputy was male or female. But it didn't matter. Trip was ready to chew a hole in either gender. She was about to barrel over to where Grace and her ticket writer stood, but the trailer rocked again as the horses shifted restlessly. Damn. They'd been in that hot trailer too long already. Her dice had been rolling snake eyes all day anyway. She'd take care of the rogue rookie tomorrow.

"Glad you found it okay," Grace said.

"I wasn't far away," Jamie said, scanning the crowd for Trip.

Grace handed Jamie the clipboard, the report having a few items already filled in, then pointed to an attractive woman sitting on the back of a one-antlered lawn ornament and waved for Jamie to follow. Clay and the woman were staring at each other, oblivious to their approach until Grace cleared her throat.

"Ms. Hemsworth, this is Deputy Grant. She'll get your information for the report while Clay gets your car ready to tow."

"I'll need your driver's license and vehicle registration, please." Jamie turned toward the sound of a diesel engine firing up while the woman gathered the requested information. The vise gripping her insides loosened as she watched the truck and trailer pull away. She wasn't sure how they missed each other, but she was relieved the inevitable confrontation with her old college basketball teammate wasn't going to happen today.

Chapter Three

Trip drove slowly along the wide main drive of the sprawling farm carved out by her grandfather. He'd raised warmbloods for the steeplechase and eventing circuits, and planted a little tobacco on the back forty as insurance for when the economy went sour and the horse business—a luxury item—periodically slacked off. When he died, he willed the entire estate to Trip, the only one of his grandchildren who shared both his passion for horses and his commitment to land conservation. She planted the tobacco fields with peanuts and soybeans. The profit wasn't as high, but her conscience was lighter. And she converted the farm manager's cottage into a small animal clinic, kennel, and surgery. Behind the clinic, a hundred-stall, U-shaped stable was dedicated to equine patients and her own stock.

Trip pulled around the stables to unload the mares and was reaching for the latch securing the trailer's rear exit when Jerome, her farm manager, showed up to unlatch the opposite side and help lower the heavy ramp.

"How many today?"

"What makes you think I got any tickets today?"

"That scowl on your face." He grabbed a manure shovel when one of the mares lifted her tail and produced her opinion of the overlong stay in a hot trailer.

Trip slipped between the mares, murmuring softly to them. The scent of horse sweat and hay filled the trailer as she untied the irritated mare's lead and tugged gently to encourage her to back out. Well trained, the horse exited the trailer, then shook like a dog as soon as she was free of the confined space.

"Grab the other one and let's turn them out in number two." Trip hadn't just changed the stable when she took over the farm, she instituted strict business protocols. The paddocks had been referred to by an oak tree that grew in one, the stallion who once lived in another, or the dogleg shape of another. But Trip kept thorough records on each horse and each pasture and paddock, right down to which type of grass was planted in it and how often it was fertilized and mowed. For record-keeping purposes, each was assigned a number.

Jerome nodded.

"Two," Trip said as they walked the mares toward the three-acre paddock behind the stables.

"Heard you."

"No, two tickets."

Jerome grinned. "In one morning? Lord, it's a good thing you're a white girl. If you were black like me, you'd be so far under the jail by now, there'd be no finding you."

Trip glared at him. "That's not funny, Jerome. You know I don't think that's something to joke about."

Jerome's grandmother had been her grandfather's housekeeper-in-residence for years at "the big house" which was now Trip's residence. Although a younger relative managed the household now, Essie still lived in the rooms that had been her home for decades. Trip would have insisted, even if it hadn't been a stipulation of Grandpa's will, because Essie was like an old aunt to her. She'd grown up fishing and skipping stones with Jerome, Essie's grandson, and she trusted him like a brother, actually way more than she'd ever trust her biological brother. That's why Trip turned the farm part of the estate over to him while she ran her four-county veterinary practice.

He opened the gate and they slipped the halters from the mares' heads, releasing them to roll in the grass to relieve the itch of the sweat drying on their hides. "Lighten up. I thought you'd be in a good mood, nice and relaxed after a visit with Hot Mama Hathaway."

Trip laughed, despite her irritation. "Don't let anyone else hear you call her that." She swatted at him with the lead rope in her hand.

He neatly dodged, laughing with her. "She was particularly wild today." She rubbed her sore butt. "Next time, I'll make sure no riding crop is within reach when she's yelling 'faster, harder.'"

Jerome's eyebrows shot up. "No shit?"

"Yeah. Hasn't been my day." They walked back to the trailer and Trip grabbed the bagged lunch, now cold, from the seat of the truck. "Jolene caught me swiping a doughnut in the diner—that's where I got the first ticket because I parked in front of the hydrant to keep the trailer under the shade trees across the street—and some babe in a Mercedes nearly rear-ended my trailer on my way here. That's where I got the second ticket because I left the rig in the street while I checked on the other driver."

"She hit your trailer?"

"Nope. Swerved and ran right into the Clip 'n Curl."

"Dang. I'll bet that was something to see."

"Yeah. She sure was. Long dark hair, blue eyes. A real looker."

He laughed again. "I meant the car crashed into the beauty shop."

She grinned. "I know."

"You got a date tonight, then?"

Trip shook her head. "That's what I'm saying. My whole day's been off. I was working it, ya know, but this was no country girl. She had big city written all over her and was hard to impress."

Jerome stared at the ground, his lips quirked in a small smile. "Yeah, Tonya was the same way. She made me really work to get her to look my way." While Jerome loved living vicariously through Trip's exploits, he was totally devoted to his wife who he'd met while getting his degree in agricultural science and animal husbandry at the University of Georgia.

"Then Clay comes up to tow the car off, and this woman is suddenly captivated." Trip threw her hands up. "She wants nothing to do with a gallant doctor but practically drools when the tow truck driver with grease all over her hands arrives."

Jerome slapped his leg and laughed deep and long. "You guys kill me. If somebody else said something like that about Clay, you'd be all over them."

Trip ignored the truth of his words and made a show of folding her arms over her chest and huffing. "What's Clay got that I don't?"

"Maybe it's what you have that Clay doesn't...your scent-of-horse-sweat perfume."

"It's better than Clay's oil-and-gasoline odor."

He chuckled. "Then I reckon it's that sultry artist mystique. Sucks them in every time. I would have had a lot more dates in college if I'd been able to play a musical instrument or rap."

"You would have flunked out because you'd have hung out in bars and never gone to class."

Jerome was quiet, their teasing suddenly turned serious.

"Sorry, man. I really wasn't thinking about Jo-Jo or anybody specific when I said that." Jo-Jo was Jerome's younger cousin who was lost to the family, having disappeared several years before while playing a string of seedy clubs up north to feed his heroin addiction.

"I know, Trip. We've all got skeletons, right?"

"You know it." She smiled and slapped his shoulder to lighten the mood again. "And keep your shovel handy. There's going to be a new one to bury as soon as I catch up with that rookie cop who's putting all those parking tickets on my truck."

"Obviously, this rookie doesn't recognize Pine Cone royalty yet."

Trip drew her shoulders back and gave him a haughty look. "Obviously."

He snapped to attention with a click of his heels and swept his arm toward the clinic area of the stables. "I believe your newest servant awaits her lunch, Princess Beaumont. Permit me to clean and secure the royal trailer for you."

Trip lifted her chin, affecting a snobbish air. "Why thank you, Jerome. Your assistance is appreciated. Carry on." She chuckled at his hearty laugh that rang out as she headed for the back door to the clinic.

❖

The veterinary technician struggled to hold Churchill in a headlock while Dr. Dani Wingate bent over the squirming massive

English bulldog with her finger in his anus in an attempt to force his backed-up anal glands to drain. Trip watched from the doorway as the dog's claws scrabbled against the metal table and he dragged them both to the edge.

"Hold him still, Cindy," Dani said through clenched teeth. "I can't do this with him moving."

"I'm trying, Dr. Wingate. He's just too big. I don't know how Dr. Beaumont does this without help."

Trip decided to give Dani a hand. She ducked into her office across the hall from the treatment center, returning in time to see Churchill leap from the table, scattering medical supplies and taking both Cindy and Dani to the floor with him. Ouch. That had to hurt. "Is Churchill giving you guys a hard time?"

"Is it true that you handle this dog by yourself?" It sounded more like a challenge than a question, and Dani's grim expression told Trip she'd better do something fast or Dani was going to be headed back to the city as soon as she could pack her car.

"Actually, I always call out the troops to help." She revealed the orange tabby cat she'd been hiding behind her back and set him on the floor at her feet. The battle-scarred old tom bowed his back and growled when he saw the dog. Churchill, who was about to lift his leg on a box of cleaning supplies, froze then cowered. "Churchill's scared to death of Otis. Put him back on the table. He won't give you any trouble."

Dani and Cindy lifted the heavy dog onto the table where he remained still as a statue, his eyes never leaving Otis. Dani quickly performed the required procedure, then wrote a few notes on his chart. She looked up at Trip. "Looks like his infection is all cleared up."

Trip smiled. "Excellent." She scooped up the cat. "Another battle won, Otis." She hoped she'd also won Dani over a little. She'd been searching a long time for the right associate to hire, and Dani was the best fit for her unique client list. "Cindy can return Churchill to Mrs. Swenson. Come on back to my office. I picked up some lunch for us."

Dani's face reddened when her stomach growled loudly. "Thanks. I didn't have time for breakfast and I'm starving, but the waiting room is full of patients."

Trip shrugged. "The longer they wait, the more they can complain when they see their friends in the grocery aisle tomorrow. Besides, I'll bet if you walk out there right now, they'll all be on their cell phones gathering gossip about the woman who drove her Mercedes into the side of the local beauty shop this morning. You'll just interrupt them."

Dani chuckled and shook her head. "I am hungry."

Brenda, the receptionist, popped into the office. "Here you go, Doc. All reheated." She placed two plates on the desk between them. Each plate held an oversized bun stuffed with pulled pork dripping barbecue sauce and surrounded by finger-sized corn fritters. Trip added two Styrofoam containers of potato salad and extra-large cups of sweet tea.

"Eat up," Trip said. "It's the best barbecue in this half of the state. The only thing better is Friday's special—Bud's fried flounder sandwich."

They ate in silence for a while. Trip knew Dani had taken the job because she felt she had few immediate choices after being unexpectedly laid off at the zoo where she worked with exotic animals. She knew squeezing anal glands on a dog must feel like a huge step down from zoo work. But she hoped Dani would give Pine Cone a chance, because the tiny Southern town truly was a gem in the lush lowlands of southern Georgia. Maybe Trip needed to help her see that.

"I need to clear an afternoon soon to take you around to check on some of my special clients."

Dani hesitated. "What if there's an emergency—an animal hit by a car or something?"

Trip waved her hand dismissively. "Until I hired you, the clinic was always without a vet on the afternoons I had to make farm calls. Cindy's a licensed vet tech and she handles routine things like removing stitches, drawing blood for lab tests, ultrasound treatments for orthopedic injuries and administering vaccinations that I draw up for scheduled appointments in advance. She'll triage and call if anything serious comes in."

"Okay." Dani nodded, then her expression turned wary. "Special animals or special clients?"

Trip licked barbecue sauce from her fingers and stuffed her lunch trash back into the plastic takeout bag. She held out her hand for Dani's trash, too. "Got a mastitis case to check and a mare to ultrasound, so I'll throw this in the dumpster on my way out. Ants love Bud's barbecue sauce as much as I do." She paused in the doorway to look back at Dani. "Special? Both the animals and their owners. But don't worry. I'm not shoving my difficult customers on you, just my unusual ones."

❖

Trip parked in the wide dirt pullout. She was the first to arrive since neither Clay's vintage Ford pickup nor Grace's Corolla were here yet. She smiled. The Glitter Girl and Paintball to her Fast Break. That'd been their CB handles since high school, and they all still kept the radios in their vehicles—partly because of spotty cell coverage in the area, but mostly because the radios reminded them of more carefree times before adulthood saddled them with work and responsibilities.

She got out of the truck and narrowed her eyes to stare down the road both ways. There was nothing illegal about parking on the side of the road, was there? She wouldn't be surprised if that stinking new deputy was lurking down a side road, just to write her another ticket. Since no vehicles were in sight, she ambled down the path to the secret swimming spot on the Altamaha River where they had shared hurts and successes, opined about women, and puzzled out the path to world peace…or just drank and shared gossip…since their high school glory days.

The river's source was somewhere in the mountains of the Cherokee Nation, and by the time it reached the pine-forested plain of southeastern Georgia, it had become a wide, majestic river, flowing with gentle windings through a vast green patchwork of field and forest, nearly a hundred miles, until it completed its journey to the Atlantic. A variety of trees and bushes crowded the river's edge—wax myrtle, sweet bay magnolia, spicebush, and red bay. Their spot was a small patch of beach ringed by a slim strip of grass and equipped with a tire swing hung from an ancient oak that stretched out over a recess that cut deep into the riverbank. It was a perfect swimming hole because the Altamaha's current had lined it with sandy silt, rather than the slimy mud usually coating a river bottom.

Trip sat in the grass and pulled a beer and a pint of Fireball from her six-pack-sized cooler. She alternated sips between the two and stared at the ebb and flow of the river while she waited. She'd felt oddly restless lately. Business was better than good, but her wild rides with Virginia Hathaway and sleepovers with Shayla didn't hold much interest lately. Even a weekend in Savannah to prowl for a new hookup didn't appeal. Was her libido dying on her already? She was only in her mid-thirties. No. Her libido was fully operational at the Clip 'n Curl earlier that day. She sighed. It depressed her to think this was all life held for her. She wanted more, but she couldn't put her finger on what "more" meant.

"Those must be some deep thoughts, pal."

Trip shrugged and dug into her Playmate for a wine cooler. She opened the bottle before handing it to Grace.

"Thanks. I didn't bother with a cooler because I knew you guys would have extras." Grace had pulled her hair back and tamed it with a hair tie. She'd obviously taken time to stop by her place first to change out of her uniform into shorts and a scooped-neck T-shirt.

"Always for you, Grace."

"So, what was the big sigh about?"

"I dunno." Trip shrugged again and changed the subject. "Clay's coming, right?"

"Said she was."

They both turned toward the path at the sound of footsteps.

"You're late." Trip reclined on one elbow and took another swig of her beer, then followed it with a sip of Fireball. She liked the cold ale, then hot, sweet cinnamon combination.

"It's that damn Bo Mathis. He kept skulking around the garage and I couldn't lock up until he left." Clay took a bottle from her cooler, popped the cap, and then used the red-topped cooler for a seat.

"I thought your granddad let him go after he almost set the place on fire," Grace said.

Clay took off her boots and socks and left her seat on the cooler to walk past them. She rolled up the legs of her jeans and sat on the bank's grassy ledge to sink her feet where the river water continually spat cool, damp sand. Clay seemed as restless and moody as Trip felt.

"I talked to him again today about cutting Bo loose, but he's decided to give him a second chance," Clay said.

"Wouldn't this be more like his twelfth chance?" Trip snorted. It irritated her that Clay's grandfather didn't take her advice to get rid of the unreliable guy he hired to change tires and run errands for the shop. Clay practically ran the garage for him, transferring his handwritten receipts and orders into a business software compatible with insurance filing. The old man had been shocked when Clay showed him that he could simply file for an insurance adjustment rather than call up and argue with a clueless customer service agent when the damage was more than their adjuster estimated.

"Yeah, maybe. I sort of lost track," Clay said.

"Well, in other news, I heard from MJ that you drove River to check into the B and B. How'd that go?" Grace fished a wine cooler out of Clay's cooler this time and slipped off her sandals to join Clay.

"I dropped her off, along with her rolling luggage, and took her car to the shop."

"And?" Grace tweaked an eyebrow.

"And nothing."

What? Trip had passed on River, only to have Clay fumble the handoff? She stepped out of her pricey leather flip-flops and settled on the other side of Clay. "Okay, hold on a minute." She dug her toes into the sand and leaned forward with her elbows on her knees to scowl at Clay. Mary Jane, who Grace often called MJ, was the woman who managed the bed and breakfast for Grace after Grace's parents dumped it on her to become world travelers. MJ was information central and a reliable source. "You had the hottest woman to land in Pine Cone in the past five years in your truck and you just...dropped her off? No offer to show her around? No invitation for dinner out?"

"No, I—"

"Hottest woman in the past five years?" Grace cut Clay off. "Who'd I miss?"

"Remember the grad student that was working in Judge Freemont's office? What was her name…" Trip rarely forgot a hot prospect.

"Oh, yeah. She *was* pretty." Grace nodded in agreement and air-toasted Trip with her bottle. "Her name was Shannon. She was too young for you, by the way."

"Hey! That was five years ago. I was a lot younger then." Trip frowned and flipped sand in Grace's direction with her foot.

"Watch it," Clay warned her, shoving Trip's shoulder when she caught more of the sand than Grace did.

"Sorry for the interruption, Clay, please continue." Grace relaxed back onto her elbows again and sipped her wine cooler.

"There's nothing else to tell. I dropped her off, end of story." Trip and Grace stared at her for an awkwardly long, silent minute. "Why are you giving me that look?"

"What look?" Trip furrowed her brow and pointed at her own face. "This look? The one that says you're a *dumb ass*?"

"I can't deal with getting involved with anyone right now."

"That's right, you don't need any *serious* involvement." Trip was incredulous that Clay hadn't thought this through. "That's why River is the perfect girl for you. She's not local. She's only here for a few days…a week tops…*and* she's clearly into you."

"Into me?"

"Yes, which is why I wouldn't let Trip hit on her." Grace playfully reached around Clay and shoved Trip's shoulder. "And trust me when I say she was swinging away with that doctor routine."

"Hey, I'm only human. I have a weakness for damsels in distress, especially the pretty ones." Trip grinned and took a long pull of her beer. She loved this back-and-forth with her two best pals. And for the record, her doctor routine had a ninety-nine percent success rate—River being that one percent that didn't fall for it.

"Anyway, as we were saying, River was definitely checking you out. In an *I'd like to see you again* sort of way," Grace said, with Trip nodding her agreement.

"I just can't do it." Clay glared at Trip. "And if you'd ever gotten your heart stomped on like I did, you'd understand. You're always the one doing the leaving, so you don't ever have to find out what it feels like to be the one left behind."

"Ouch." Trip mimicked getting skewered in the chest with her fist. She'd told them about her college crush on Jamie, and that Jamie had left to join the army. She'd never told them that Jamie had stolen her heart, but hadn't wanted it. "Listen, I've had my disappointments, same as Grace, same as you, but I don't wallow in them the way you're doing." She almost flinched at the edge in her voice. After all these years, she was still angry at herself over the mistake she'd made with Jamie. She needed to get over it, and so did Clay. "You need to get out and start dating again."

"You act like it's been years since Veronica and I split up. It's only been a few months. I deserve to wallow a little."

Trip looked over at Grace. Clearly, they were going to have to perform an intervention with Clay.

"Oh no, don't go trying to set me up. I can read your minds, you know." Clay waved her hands at them in a back-off gesture.

"We wouldn't dare," Grace said, then reached behind Clay to clink her wine bottle against Trip's Fireball bottle.

Trip took a big swig of Fireball, then chased it with cold beer. Yep, setting up Clay would be just the thing to get her mind off herself and out of this funk she'd been in lately.

Chapter Four

Jamie had received a text from a "private number" early that morning, directing her to a local motel and nondescript Chevy pickup—color, year, window sticker of a stylized deer head to explain the hunting rifles in the rack behind the driver, and license plate number. She wasn't on shift until later that day, so she took her personal vehicle, which was an equally nondescript white Ford truck. After all, the text could be a prank to make her look silly. Maybe Trip had figured out who was writing all those parking tickets and was getting her back. She might have gotten Jamie's cell number from Grace by telling her that they were old college buddies.

Just as she neared the motel, the truck she sought pulled onto the highway in the same direction she was traveling, and Jamie followed. The two-lane highway was a main route from town to Interstate 95, so she wasn't worried that her truck following this fellow was anything other than normal traffic. And she wasn't surprised when he turned into the large truck stop that was a popular place to gas up before getting onto the interstate. The busy restaurant and store was also a good place to make a drug exchange.

She pulled into the truck stop but parked on the other end of the huge parking lot from where the suspect was headed. Cars and pickups darted between lumbering eighteen-wheelers as they sorted themselves to line up for their turn at the gasoline or diesel pumps. Jamie was glad they patrolled this truck stop daily. It'd be easy to pick out anything that wasn't the normal rhythm of truckers and tourists stopping for fuel, food, or restrooms.

The suspect's truck wasn't visible from Jamie's position, but she still went through the motions that would make her appear as someone just passing through. She got out of her truck and stretched as though she was stiff from driving a long time. Then she lifted Petunia out and clipped a leash on her collar. While the interstate flanked the truck stop on one side, the other side and behind the truck stop was an open field of weeds, so Jamie walked Petunia through the field in a meandering route, much to Petunia's delight. The field was awash in the tantalizing scents of mice, stray cats and dogs, and even raccoons—that came to feast on the trash and food tossed by the truck stop's customers.

Once they worked their way behind the building, Jamie spotted her suspect's vehicle. She took out a cigarette and lit it. She hated the taste and never actually inhaled, but let it dangle from her lips. Petunia gave her a long-suffering look and sneezed.

"Sorry, P. You and the cigarette are good cover for us while we watch our guy." She started to add that it wasn't as bad as Petunia's noxious odors, but she wouldn't tease her partner about a medical condition. Even if her partner was a dog.

Anyway, Petunia wasn't listening. She was joyfully rubbing her face in some raccoon scat, and Jamie groaned when Petunia flopped down to roll back and forth on the pile of poop.

"P, no. Now you'll have to get a bath before we report to work." She stopped grumbling when motion near the suspect's truck caught her eye. A black Mustang flipped around to back in the space next to the truck, then idled in the spot for a few minutes before the engine quieted and a woman climbed out. She looked young, maybe in her twenties, and wore ripped jeans and Western boots. Maybe the foreign drug cartels had figured out that attractive women had a better chance of talking their way past mostly male American law enforcement.

The male suspect rolled down his window as the woman sauntered over and smiled. She braced a hand against the truck's cab and bent toward the man. A casual observer would assume she was flirting with the driver, who opened his door after a few seconds and the two went into the truck stop restaurant.

Jamie tugged on Petunia's leash. "Let's get to work, P."

Hearing "work," the little dog hopped up from her romp in the poop and shook the fragrant remains from her wiry coat before looking expectantly at Jamie. Deputy Petunia was reporting for duty. Jamie dropped the leash as she pretended to put out her cigarette and light a fresh one. She flicked a hand signal toward the two suspect vehicles and spoke softly. "Go find."

Petunia shot off like a bullet and Jamie hesitated, then ran after her as though the dog had escaped. She slowed when Petunia reached the vehicles and began sniffing at the tires. The dog quickly dismissed the Mustang, but sniffed only one wheel before diving under the truck with a flurry of barking. Petunia's usual alert was simply to sit and stare at where the drugs were hidden. She only barked when the find was big. Jamie dropped to her knees and peered under the truck. Petunia twisted onto her back and scratched at a large, shallow metal box clamped to the truck's underside.

"Good girl, P. Stand down." Jamie pushed speed dial on her phone while Petunia scrambled out from under the truck.

"Sheriff's Office."

"This is Deputy Jamie Grant, Canine. I need immediate backup from any available law enforcement. Ten-twenty is Jack's Truck Stop, back corner of the parking lot, interstate side. Suspect vehicles are a black Ford Mustang parked next to a white Chevy Silverado that my canine indicates is carrying a significant cache of illegal substances. Occupants are currently inside the restaurant."

"Copy that, Deputy Grant."

During the ensuing pause, Jamie led Petunia back into the field and behind the building—still within view of the vehicles, but close to a dumpster that she could use for cover if needed.

"HP and two Pine Cone units responding," the dispatcher said.

"Please advise that I'm not in uniform, but armed and observing from the dumpster behind the building." Jamie was rattling off her mobile number for those responding when the female suspect appeared, walked straight to the truck, and climbed inside. "Female suspect is on the move."

The truck pulled out, disappearing between fueling tractor-trailers. Jamie dropped Petunia's leash and ran to keep the truck in sight.

"White late model Chevy Silverado, license plate Charlie, Alpha, Whiskey, two, zero, two, seven. Just turned onto the north ramp of I-Ninety-five."

In the pause that followed, Jamie's male suspect emerged, walking directly toward the Mustang.

"HP has your suspect in view."

"Ten-four. Second suspect is flying. Moving to intercept." Jamie moved her holstered gun from the small of her back to her side for easy access, pulled her badge wallet from her back pocket, and trotted toward the suspect with her phone still pressed to her ear.

"Your backup is pulling into the parking lot," the dispatcher said.

"Ten-four." Jamie ended the call, then flipped the wallet open to display her badge and held it out as she shouted at the man. "Police. Stop where you are."

He stopped and spun to face her with his hands out. His smile was smug. "I don't understand, Deputy. What have I done wrong?"

"You are suspected of conspiring to transport illegal drugs."

"I'm innocent." His smile widened as he held up the Mustang's key fob. "Search my car, if you like."

"We will...eventually...and the truck you drove here. Your contact who took it is being pulled over by state troopers right now."

The man's smile vanished and he turned to run for the Mustang. Jamie cursed, but she'd barely taken a step when Petunia blurred past her and latched onto the man's ankle, breaking his stride. Petunia yelped when he dislodged her with a kick to her ribs. The half-second advantage put Jamie close enough to launch herself forward and execute a tackle that would make the NFL proud. Two Pine Cone Police Department cruisers screamed into the parking lot and blocked in the Mustang before their drivers jumped out and approached with weapons drawn. They slowed and holstered their weapons when they saw Jamie was already cuffing the suspect.

Her tackling maneuver had knocked the wind out of him, but she checked Petunia before helping him into a sitting position as he gasped for air. She gently pressed on his upper abdomen. "Relax and take slow, deep breaths. One. Another. That's right."

"God damned mother-fucking pig," he growled as his stomach relaxed under her palm and his breaths grew deeper. Petunia, sitting directly in front of him, growled, and he attempted to kick her again. "That stinking stray bit me."

"Stand down, P. Guard." Jamie stood, her hands on her hips. "That stray is a certified drug and explosive detection officer, and you'll also be charged with assaulting a member of law enforcement if you kick her again. That's after she ignores your foot and goes for your throat this time."

"That ain't no police dog."

"Sure is, buddy." Thompson, the deputy Jamie would be relieving later, laughed as he joined them. "And if you don't shut up, we'll let Deputy Petunia ride with you on the way back to the station."

As if on cue, Petunia stood and blasted a long, audible fart as she wagged her tail. She liked Thompson.

"Christ almighty." The suspect coughed and tried to scoot away.

Anderson, a local boy just hired after getting his law enforcement certification from the community college, waved his hand in front of his face as he approached. "Man, that's rank."

Jamie's cell rang and she answered. "Jamie Grant."

"This is State Trooper Austin Ivers." Ivers's deeply Southern baritone filled her ear. "I've detained a young lady driving a white Chevy truck on Interstate Nine-five near exit four-nine. I'm requesting assistance from your drug detection canine to search the vehicle."

"Copy that," Jamie said. "The Pine Cone Police Department has custody of your driver's suspected accomplice. I'll—"

A loud crunch sounded behind them and Thompson swore. "Damn it to hell, Anderson. How many times have I told you to put the cruiser all the way in park, not neutral. I'm going to let you explain to Grace how this happened a second time."

Jamie twisted to see the source of Thompson's consternation. Red and clear glass was scattered on the pavement below where the taillight of Anderson's cruiser met the headlight of Thompson's cruiser.

Anderson's face screwed up in grimace. "Aw, man, I'm going to be on foot patrol in the hottest week of the summer."

"More like the entire month," Thompson said.

"Deputy Grant? Everything all right there?" Trooper Ivers asked.

Jamie shook her head but responded in the affirmative. "Sorry. We're good. My ETA is ten minutes. I'm in my personal vehicle, a white Ford One-fifty." She ended the call and picked up Petunia's leash. "Gotta go help out HP, guys. The suspect is all yours, but one of you should stay to keep an eye on the Mustang until it can be towed."

"I'll get dispatch to call Cahill for a tow," Thompson said. "Anderson can babysit and do the accident report while I haul this guy to jail."

"Ask Cahill to pick up a white Silverado, stopped by HP near exit forty-nine first. That's the vehicle carrying the drugs. The Mustang's probably clean, but Anderson should still stay with it to preserve the chain of evidence in case there is something in it."

"Will do." Thompson waved her off while Anderson hauled the suspect to his feet.

Jamie led Petunia back to her truck and toweled her off with an old rag. Bits of sand and fine gravel clung to spots of dark oil that soiled her wheat-colored hair where she rolled onto her back under the suspect's truck. "You're an awesome tracker, but you really need a bath now."

Petunia was a rare dog who loved a bath and yipped happily as she stood on her hind legs for Jamie to give her a boost into the truck.

Trip circled a three-block route for the fourth time. Still no open parking spaces. Damn it. She didn't have time for this with a full afternoon of appointments waiting. She'd just have to double-park to pick up her lunch and hope that ticket-writing rookie wasn't around. She turned up a side street next to the diner, spotted some open curb and whipped into the spot. Right next to the No Parking Anytime sign. Well, at least she wasn't double-parked on Main Street, and she wouldn't be long because she'd called ahead and reserved her favorite booth.

She hopped out of her truck and jogged around the corner. She scanned the street, her eyes stopping on the police car parked across the street from the diner. Just her luck. She relaxed mid-grind of her teeth. There was a long, wide scratch along the back fender. Grace's cruiser.

"Whoa." Movement in her peripheral vision barely registered in time for Trip to dodge the glass door of the diner swinging open.

Grace stepped out onto the sidewalk. "Hold up there, hoss. I nearly brained you with the door. Where's the fire?"

"Sorry. I was looking at your car. I thought it was my stalker until I noticed the scratch on the fender. When are you going to let Clay fix that?"

"I haven't had time. I had a new deputy I needed to drive around for orientation, then...well, other stuff happened. I'll probably get it over to the garage later this week. Anyway, what's this about a stalker?"

"Your new cop—"

"Deputy Grant?"

"I think he's stalking me."

"Stalking you?"

"More than twenty parking tickets in the past two weeks."

"You poor thing. Good news for me, though. I can finally order a new chair for my office with the fines you're going to pay."

Trip glared at her flippant tone. "It's not funny. It's police harassment."

"Why don't you try parking in a legal spot?"

"Grace."

"What do you want me to do about it? Tell Deputy Grant that she shouldn't enforce the law because you're my friend'?"

"You can explain that I'm usually on important business. I have emergencies and...did you say *she*?" Trip's agile mind switched in a different direction. So, River wasn't the only new girl in town. Maybe she and Clay could double fling...uh, date. "Does she play on our team? Is she hot?"

"Down, girl. I've been trying to get the town council to allot money for a drug-detection dog for the past ten years, but they're really expensive. I got a two-for-one deal with Grant. She owns a detection dog she trained personally, and I need for them to stay. I don't need Fast Break bird-dogging her."

"I was just going to suggest you bring her to the cookout this weekend. Once she finds out how charming I can be, maybe she'll stop slapping tickets on my truck every time she sees it." Trip raised an eyebrow. "And you haven't answered my questions."

"What questions?"

"Is she hot and does she play on our team?"

"Yes, in a sporty sort of way, and yes, I'm pretty sure she does."

"Awesome." Trip rubbed her hands together. "If you bring her to the cookout, I'll make sure my new vet comes. She's not my type, but she looks like yours." She wiggled her brows in a suggestive gesture. Grace was fun to tease. Trip was surprised, however, when Grace's green eyes flamed with interest.

"I'll see if Grant wants to come so she can meet some other people." Grace pointed a finger at Trip. "But *you* stay away from her."

Trip waved Grace's finger away and opened the door to the diner. "See you this weekend." Her lunch was waiting, but she paused and turned back to Grace. "Oh, and go see if your damned bird is ready to go home. I caught Brenda sharing her ham biscuit with him this morning. If those two bond, I'm going to let Essie roast him for dinner.

Grace smiled broadly and gave Trip a mock salute. "Headed there now."

Jamie whistled as she guided the patrol car toward downtown Pine Cone. An impressive thunderstorm the night before had tempered the heat and humidity, and the sun was shining down from a cloudless blue sky. The source of her buoyant mood, however, was the morning's success. Petunia didn't really know why they were happy, but she always reflected Jamie's moods. And after a shower for her and a bath for Petunia, they were ready to get back to work.

The reception desk was empty when they walked into the station, but Jamie could hear voices coming from down the hall. She followed the noise and walked in on Thompson entertaining a crowd of coworkers gathered in the break room. He was something of a storyteller, and if you believed his stunning account of the morning's events, she and Petunia were like Batman and Robin wrestling the drug mule to the ground and issuing orders to the state trooper. Everyone applauded and Petunia yipped when he finished with a flourish, but the gathering disbanded quickly when her barks were echoed by audible gaseous emissions.

Still, Jamie's chest swelled with pride. This morning was about more than a successful drug bust, even though that was why she and Petunia had come to Pine Cone. It was about earning the respect of their coworkers and making a valuable contribution to this community.

"Have you tried putting her on a gluten-free diet?" Anderson's suggestion was muffled by the handkerchief he held over his nose and mouth. "It helped my uncle. My aunt even moved back into their bedroom."

Jamie sighed. "I've tried every treatment known. Nothing seems to help."

"You should try Doc Beaumont," Thompson said. "She can figure out almost anything."

Jamie didn't want to talk about Trip Beaumont. "Is the cruiser gassed and ready?"

"You're not on until after lunch," Thompson said, frowning.

"You've got a mess of paperwork to fill out, explaining your busted headlight, right?" She offered up a smile she didn't feel. "Since I seem to be on a lucky streak today, I thought I'd grab some takeout and head over to Cahill's to see if they've searched that truck yet. I'll get an estimate on the headlight repair while I'm there."

Thompson's shoulders slumped. "I ought to make that rookie fill out his report and mine, too. I hate typing reports."

Jamie slapped him on the back. "I'm right there with you." She'd have her own reports to type up about the morning's arrest. But she'd do that later. She signaled Petunia to heel, then bent to give her a good ear scratch.

Yes, sir. She had a right to be proud. They were a formidable team. Like Batman and Robin.

"Come on, P. Let's clear out so folks can eat their lunches without gagging on your personal perfume."

CHAPTER FIVE

Every parking space on Main Street was filled, so Jamie rounded the block where the diner was located and, since her luck was running high today, a car pulled out of a large space on the side street next to the diner. Jamie figured she'd call in her order and ask for a callback when it was ready. She and Petunia could patrol Main Street while they waited.

Jamie surveyed the street while she fished her phone out of her pocket. Always know your surroundings. The habit had begun in the desert, but didn't stop when she returned to the States. She was about to scroll through her contacts for the diner's number, when her eyes settled on the F-450 dually parked under the No Parking Anytime sign. Well, well.

"Stay, P." Glad she'd remembered to get a fresh ticket book and a new ballpoint, Jamie grabbed both from the seat and clicked the pen repeatedly as she strolled over to Trip's truck. This had to be a record number of parking violations by one person. She opened the pad to a fresh ticket, then hesitated. Was it wrong to blame Trip after eighteen years? Until that drunken night, Trip had been her best friend.

The magnet school that she was bused across town to attend had landed her with a bunch of white kids who lived in real houses with yards, two parents, and a family dog. They were wakened by bacon sizzling or lawn mowers buzzing, not guns popping and sirens wailing. Trip grew up like those kids. Jamie was the girl who didn't fit in because she came from the projects downtown.

College was a new playing field, new players, with new teams forming. It stripped away the people who'd been dragging you down. It also stripped away the ones who'd propped you up. She remembered the first time she saw Trip.

Jamie stood with a small group of other female athletes she'd met in the two days she'd been on campus, and they eyed the striking blonde who stood by the older model, but well maintained, truck that was loaded with boxes. She was holding a map of the campus, turning it one way then another, and frowning.

"I say she's tennis," one girl said, her Brooklyn accent instantly revealing her hometown.

"Nope. She'd be wearing those little tennis skorts instead of cutoffs," a girl from Memphis said.

"I'm guessing volleyball. She's tall and thin enough. And blond. All those girls are tall and blond."

"Softball."

"Get out. You don't gotta be tall for that. You just have to have a ponytail."

The girl was biting her lip and looking hopefully their way, but Jamie's new friends just stared back. She suddenly saw herself standing on the playground in that upper middle class neighborhood while the other kids stared but didn't invite her to join them.

"Hey, where you goin'?"

Jamie ignored Brooklyn's challenge and crossed the parking lot to greet the stranger. When she approached, the girl smiled uncertainly. "Hey," Jamie said. "Need some help?"

"Uh, yeah, thanks. I just got here and was trying to find where the basketball team stays."

That had surprised Jamie. Maybe she was looking for somebody she knew. She pointed to the building behind them. "Looks like you found it. That's the dorm. Are you looking for somebody?"

The blonde tugged a paper from her back pocket and unfolded it. "I'm looking for room 620."

Jamie held her hand out. "Can I see that?" She took the paper and stared at it. "You're Tripoli Miranda Beaumont?"

"Trip. I play small forward."

Jamie looked up, then took the hand Trip offered. "Jamie Grant, point guard. Seems you're my roommate."

Trip's grin was wide. "No shit? That's great." Then her smile faltered. "I mean, I think it is. Unless you were hoping to room with somebody else."

Jamie turned and waved over the other girls, who were still watching them. "We'll help you carry your stuff up, then I'll show you where to check in over at the athletic office." The others trotted over. "This is Trip Beaumont, our new small forward. We're going to help her take her stuff up."

The girls watched as Trip lowered the tailgate after a few kicks to knock it loose. Then she begin pulling boxes to the rear.

"Where are we taking this stuff?" Brooklyn asked.

"She's assigned to room with me," Jamie said, then turned back to Trip. "Do you have a foot odor problem or sing in your sleep?"

Trip scratched her chin. "No foot odor, but I do sing a little blues before a history test."

Brooklyn clutched her sides in an overly dramatic display of laughter. "Is that accent for real?"

Trip selected another box from the truck, lifted it easily, and shoved it into Brooklyn's hands. Brooklyn staggered back a few steps as she struggled with the heavy load. "That's funny," Trip said, grinning. "I was going to ask you the same thing."

"Is Trip your real name?" Memphis asked. "Or a nickname because you trip people on the court?"

"Real name." She wasn't done with Brooklyn. "I hope you won't mind Rooster. He's in the truck. I wanted to bring my lucky rabbit, but Mama said no way they'd let me keep Rooster and Cottontail, so we ate him for my lucky farewell dinner. Daddy saved his paw, too, and made a charm I could rub for luck before each game. But no foot odor. No, sir. Not since Granny taught me to put a fresh clove of garlic in my tennis shoes each night when I take them off."

The girls all stopped and stared as Trip took the last box from the truck bed and turned to follow them in.

"She's kidding, you guys," Jamie said, motioning with her head for them to go on into the dorm. "You are kidding, right?"

Trip grinned. "Yeah. I'm kidding. We didn't eat Cottontail."

Jamie turned away and headed across the parking deck. Her new roomie had a sense of humor. She liked that.

"I'm saving him until Peter gets big enough for a matched pair to make bunny slippers."

If Jamie had known that day that everything was a joke to Trip, she would have never befriended her. Trip's flippant attitude toward life had ultimately been the knife that severed their friendship and stabbed Jamie in the back. She wrote the ticket with a flourish, tore it from the book, and pinned it to the windshield with a satisfying slap of the wiper. Trip was likely at the diner, so Jamie decided to alter her lunch plans. She needed something quicker anyway if she was going to Cahill's Garage to check on the impounded vehicles.

She hopped back into her cruiser, drove through Doug's Dogs—a local hotdog specialty joint—and ordered, then headed out to the highway and backed into her favorite spot for eating a quick lunch while catching speeders.

Trip ordered an omelet with a side of grits and a half pecan waffle. She loved that the diner served breakfast all day. She'd need the carbs as well as the protein to get through her busy afternoon of farm calls.

"Coming right up, hon," Jolene said.

The bell jangled brightly, and Trip looked up to see Clay push through the swinging door. Their eyes met, and Clay headed over to share her booth.

"Hey there, Clay." Clay seemed to be dragging a bit. Her expression lacked Clay's usual sultry nonchalance, and her stride was stiff, rather than her usual relaxed saunter.

"Hi."

"I'd say you look like you just lost your best friend, but I'm sittin' right here."

"I'll bring a menu over, hon." Jolene waved to Clay from behind the counter near the register.

"No rush." Clay smiled weakly at Jolene. Clay pushed her hat back and rested her elbows on the table.

Jolene approached with Trip's omelet and waffle balanced on one arm and a coffee carafe and mug in her other hand. "You want a coffee?" Clay nodded, and Jolene plunked down the mug and poured before handing the menu tucked under her arm to her. Then she slid Trip's meal onto the table. "Just wave at me when you're ready."

Trip didn't know why Clay was reading a menu. She always ordered the same thing. "I expected you to be a little tired, but a happy sort of tired."

"What are you talking about?" Clay looked up.

"I called the shop when you didn't answer your CB, and Eddie said you were out at Lynette's place. I know she's carrying a big torch for you." Trip plopped two pats of real butter on top of her grits to melt.

"Her battery was dead." Clay frowned.

"And the only thing you jump-started was her car? I'm starting to worry about you." Trip stuffed a big bite of waffle into her mouth and smiled as she chewed.

Before Clay could reply, the bell over the door jangled again. River paused when she stepped inside and spotted them. Well, well. This day was looking up for Clay.

Trip swallowed quickly as she stood and motioned for River to join them, ignoring Clay's frantic *No, no, no* signal.

"River, would you care to join us? Clay hasn't even ordered yet, so your timing is perfect." Trip made a gallant show, completely ignoring Clay's glare, and extended her arm to the empty half of the bench seat on her side of the table.

"Hello, Dr. Beaumont." River gave Clay a sideways glance. The expression on her face signaled uncertainty, and Clay made no move to make her feel welcome. "I wouldn't want to intrude."

"It's Trip, and please join us. I insist. Maybe you can help me cheer up my friend here."

Clay looked ready to bolt, so Trip moved her dishes across the table and slid in next to Clay, blocking her exit.

"Are you sure I'm not interrupting something?" River seemed to be picking up on Clay's unease.

"Not at all. Please, sit." Trip took the menu out of Clay's hand and handed it to River. "They serve breakfast all day, and the burgers are good."

"Thank you." River accepted the shiny trifold menu.

"If I'd known I was going to have company, I'd have waited to order." Trip figured she'd have to prime the pump with a little friendly chatter since Clay was doing her best imitation of an inert lump. "Y'all don't mind if I start without you, do you? This omelet won't be good if it gets cold."

"Don't wait for us." Clay's eyes flitted around the room, and she quietly tapped one finger against the tabletop. Yep, Clay was as skittish as a wild mustang in the presence of this woman, and Trip found that very amusing.

Jolene reappeared. "I see you picked up another guest. Y'all ready to order?"

Clay ordered her usual chicken fried steak, eggs, and hash brown potatoes, but River ordered a cheeseburger and fries. Trip would have figured her for a grilled chicken salad kind of girl. Apparently also surprised, Clay looked directly at River—more than a glance—for the first time since River had entered the diner.

"So, River, rumor has it that you're from the big city. What do you do in New York?" Trip asked.

Clay suddenly appeared to find the sugar canister more interesting than hearing River's response.

"I own an art gallery."

"Really?" Trip took a swig of her sweet tea. "Did you know that Clay's a painter?"

Clay tilted her head, but the brim of her cap didn't quite hide the dagger her eyes shot at Trip.

"What do you paint?" River asked.

"I don't paint anything," Clay said in a tone that ended that conversation but fueled Trip's determination that she and Grace indeed needed to mount an intervention. Something in her gut said this was an opportunity for Clay.

The food arrived, saving them all from an awkward pause, and even Clay joined her in watching as River daintily hoisted the huge burger and took a big bite.

Then Trip talked about the new renovations at her clinic and told a couple of funny incidents with her clients. But Clay certainly wasn't contributing much, so Trip decided it was time to just throw her in the river, so to speak, and hope she would swim. "Well, I better get going. Duty calls."

"Oh, so soon?" River glanced nervously at Clay.

Too bad. She was sure River had paddled among plenty of sharks in New York City. She'd do fine with Clay. Clay was good people through and through, and Trip wanted to bitch-slap the woman who'd taken the light from her eyes. "Yep, afraid so. I have to do ultrasounds on two of Virginia's Hanoverian mares." Trip dropped a twenty on the table and folded her napkin under the edge of her plate. "Virginia's meeting me there, and it's best not to keep her waiting."

She stepped out into the summer heat and waved farewell at River as she passed their booth on the other side of the diner's plate glass front, then chuckled at Clay's glare. The amusement died when she rounded the corner and saw the telltale flutter. Damn that Deputy Grant to hell. She stuffed the ticket into the glove box with all the others without looking at it. Grace wasn't going to be any help, so she probably needed to total them later and pay up before this Deputy Do-right decided to call Clay to tow her truck next time. Trip smiled. Clay would never do that. Then she frowned. Unless this deputy was really hot, like Grace had said.

❖

A huge oak tree provided shade and adequate concealment so speeders who blew past that first speed limit sign coming into town never saw Jamie until she flipped on her lights and pulled out in pursuit. Normally, she'd put out her wireless radar and give a break to the drivers who were in the process of decelerating, but she only planned to eat and count the cows in the pasture across the two-lane highway today.

Counting was what her military therapist taught her during rehab to cope with PTSD. Even after her physical wounds healed, part of her refused to leave the desert. Refused to accept that Sonar, her bomb-detection dog, and most of her patrol were dead. That part kept dragging her back to relive, and maybe try to change, what had happened. Nightmares at first, then daytime flashbacks too. The absence of Sonar, who'd been at her side for five years, was like a missing limb.

The Army refused to assign her a new dog until she was cleared for duty, but their doctors drugged her until she was little more than a zombie. Then a new doctor rotated in at Fort Bragg. He weaned her off the drugs so she could function again. Their counseling sessions were often long walks in quiet areas of the sprawling base with his golden retriever keeping pace between them. He taught her to count so she could cope without mind-numbing drugs. But in the end, he'd been honest. He couldn't recommend that she ever return to her old job detecting and disarming bombs. Instead, he strongly suggested she accept a medical discharge and use her dog training knowledge to build a career in the civilian world.

He knew some guys in the private sector that trained security dogs for high profile firms, but Jamie had opted for law enforcement when she realized her discharge contained nothing about her mental frailty, only her physical injuries. She liked the rank and order of the military, and law enforcement was the closest she could come to that. She needed the unchanging rhythm of routine and order. Like counting. Two always came after one, three always after two. No surprises. No exploding bombs. Petunia understood routine, and always huddled close when something still triggered an occasional flashback. She could never let another human see her that vulnerable. If anyone knew, they could revoke her gun license. How could she be a cop without a gun?

Before she dug into her lunch, she peeled back the lid from a small container of Petunia's special diet food and placed it on the seat. Petunia sniffed it but turned away and drank from her water in the cup holder instead.

"Come on, P. Aren't you hungry?"

Petunia looked at her with liquid eyes. Jamie was worried about her. She'd eaten very little in the past few days.

Jamie pushed aside her good sense and offered Petunia a very small piece of her hotdog, but Petunia barely sniffed it. Maybe Jaime should make an appointment. She didn't have to see Trip. Grace had mentioned there was a new vet who mostly kept the clinic hours while Trip made farm calls. An exam could indicate whether Jamie should seek out another specialist—maybe at the University of Georgia Veterinary School.

Chapter Six

"Dani, you here?" Trip felt bad that she'd pretty much just hung a clinic name tag on Dani and pushed her into the thick of things without much orientation. But this was a demanding time of the year for Trip. She'd artificially inseminated show mares across four counties after delivering their foals in the spring, and their owners wanted exams now to confirm whether they were pregnant or needed to be bred again. It wasn't that she didn't have confidence in Dani's abilities. She'd come highly recommended. But it wasn't good employee relations to leave her to swim on her own.

"In the back," Dani said.

Trip opened the door to the laboratory room where they did everything from nail clipping to anesthetizing for simple surgeries. Most animals were better behaved when separated from their owners. They still did hands-on exams and gave shots in the exam room while they chatted with the owners about any health issues. She flared her nostrils at the cloying—not an animal—smell that hit her like a wall. "Should've known. I can follow Michelle's scent through the whole building." She stepped back, fanning the air with her hands. "Jeez, Michelle, I told you about wearing a ton of that crap to work. We'll have lawsuits coming out our backsides for injuring the animals' olfactory senses. Go wash that mess off, right now."

Michelle huffed and rolled her eyes before strutting toward the restroom.

"Thank you for that," Dani said. "My eyes were starting to water. I felt bad for the animals."

"I like to run a relaxed but professional business. I told that girl when I hired her to leave that bait and her flirting at home. How's that going?"

Dani shrugged, unwilling to jeopardize Michelle's job because of her own discomfort.

"She obviously didn't listen to the first part of my warning, so I'm guessing she's been on the prowl and you just don't want to say." Trip patted Dani on the shoulder. "Never figured a northern girl for tact and diplomacy."

"She's pretty good with the clients, and I can handle myself around her. But that eau de awful perfume she bathes in has to go." The dog whose wound Dani had been checking sneezed in agreement before she lifted him off the table and put him back in his kennel.

Trip nodded toward the back door. She was more concerned about how Dani was doing than Michelle. "Let's take a walk and get some fresh air." She held the door for Dani, then led them toward the barn where the horses were stabled. "So, how are things going?"

"Fine."

Trip let the silence hang between them, hoping Dani would say more. But when Dani didn't, Trip prodded. "You're not much of a talker, are you?"

"If I have something to say."

"And you don't have anything to say other than fine? I hired you because of your extensive experience, and you came with impeccable references. I'm asking you for an evaluation. The large animal part of the practice is my main interest, but the small animal clinic is a moneymaker. Any changes you'd recommend for efficiency and better care in that area? Any equipment or supplies you feel we need that I don't already have? Do we have enough staff? I value your professional opinion."

"Oh…you mean work things."

Trip stopped halfway to the barn. "Look, Dani, I like you, but I don't get involved in my employees' lives, unless they ask for advice. And it's obvious you're not asking. So yes, as a vet, any suggestions?"

"It's a good clinic. You've got plenty of exam rooms in the main building and sufficient stalls in the barn. You could even expand if you wanted. Your equipment is top-of-the-line, and you're located conveniently to facilities in Savannah if you need a specialist. It's all good."

Trip smiled, nodded toward the barn, and started walking again. "Thanks. Do you have time to help me with a castration before you head out?"

"Sure."

❖

When the anesthesia buckled the knees of the six-month-old colt, Trip pushed him over as Dani shoved a ten-inch-thick pad against his feet from the other side to lay him on it. Their smoothly coordinated maneuver felt like they'd been working together for years. The rest of the surgery was quick and equally synchronized. The youngster slept soundly on his side, with Dani monitoring his vitals while Trip performed the routine operation in the barn's surgery stall. She'd lost track years ago of how many castrations she'd done over the years, but she never skimped or lost focus. Whether they were headed to the show ring, or just a family pet, she gave each patient her best.

Trip fed the medicine into his vein to wake him, and stepped back to wait for the moment they'd help him to his feet. She was aware of Dani watching her as much as the colt. It'd been the first time Dani had assisted her, and she was impressed with how seamlessly they worked together. Dani was obviously as experienced with large animals as she was with smaller ones. Yep. Dani was a keeper. She just needed to give her a reason to stay.

"So, are you going to come?"

Dani blinked as if Trip had pulled her from some deep thoughts. "Sorry?"

"My cookout. Tomorrow. It's an annual thing. Lesbians from two states will be there, along with some of the gay-friendly community."

"I'll probably go to Savannah. You know, for the clubs and women."

"Grace will be at the cookout." The comment floated like a pleasant aroma waiting to settle. "Jolene at the diner said you two had a nice chat the other day."

"We sat beside each other at the counter. It was the only seat in the place."

Trip raised her hands. "I'm just saying, she'll be there and she's good people. You couldn't do better if you're looking to make friends around here, and I hope you will. I'm only suggesting friendship because she's a close friend of mine, and I'm a little protective."

"Don't worry. I have no interest in Grace."

"Your loss, but that's probably a good decision. I'm sure you see this job as a step in your career, so you wouldn't be right for her. But come to the cookout. You'll know at least a few people—me, Grace, and Michelle. There'll be lots of women, and several of the clinic's best horse clients I'd like you to meet. Grace and I can introduce you around."

Dani shook her head. "Thanks for the offer though."

"My cookouts are a huge annual event. The Savannah crowd will all be here. At least think about it?"

Dani nodded and started toward the clinic. "I better get back to work."

CHAPTER SEVEN

Jamie's eyes went directly to Trip's veterinary truck as she cruised Pine Cone's downtown and the lunchtime traffic. Typical. When they'd been teammates on their college basketball team, she had to stay on her toes because Trip flowed around the court more than she followed plays. It frustrated the coach to hell and back. She flicked on her blue lights to double-park and stopped the patrol car, but just sat and stared at the truck. But, as point guard, she seemed to naturally plug into Trip's flow, and that'd made them the team stars. They'd been a showy duet of behind the back and no-look passes, net-swishing three-pointers, and fancy moves at the post that brought cheering fans to their feet. Her chest ached with the memory. Playing ball with Trip gave her a confidence that had carried her through life so far…through tours in Iraq and Afghanistan, through rehab after she was wounded, and through her decision to choose Petunia over the shelter program she'd hoped would be a new start for her. But those glory days had fallen apart at the beginning of their junior year. Trip had betrayed her in the worst way. Then the World Trade Center towers came down. Jamie left school to join the army. She later learned from another teammate that Trip had left the team at the end of that junior year to take an early acceptance to the University of Georgia Veterinary School, also abandoning their mutual dream of playing professional basketball.

Petunia whined, her front paws on Jamie's seat back, and licked Jamie's ear. "It's okay, P. We've got a new start here in Pine

Cone—you and me. I just have to face up to living in the same town with her."

The memory of Trip's betrayal pushed away the good memories of their former friendship, and Jamie scowled as she got out of the car. How many tickets was she going to have to write to get this woman to park legally? She scribbled the ticket quickly, but instead of initialing it at the bottom, she wrote out DEPUTY J. GRANT.

It was time. Grace had relayed Trip's invitation to the cookout tomorrow and she'd decided to go. Wondering if she was going to round a corner and bump into Trip at any moment was exhausting. Going to the cookout would allow her to be in control of the circumstances, give her the element of surprise. Unless Grace had already told Trip she'd moved to Pine Cone. But she'd said Trip insisted she "bring that new deputy." So, maybe she hadn't figured it out. The ticket signature would be a huge hint...or maybe a warning.

Bud had Trip's lunch bagged and waiting. She didn't even get a chance to swipe a doughnut, so Jolene wrapped up two and added them to her bag without asking, then rang up the entire contents.

Trip did have to exchange a few pleasantries with clients who were lunching, asking after one woman's Siamese, a man's Labrador, and another man's Chihuahua. Still, she was in and out of the diner in under ten minutes.

So how was she staring at another ticket fluttering from her truck's wiper?

This deputy had to be stalking her. She knew she should admonish herself for being ready to pin this deputy's ears back when she thought it was a man trying to bully her. But Grace's revelation that the new deputy was a woman had changed everything. Maybe Trip had been thinking about this all wrong. Maybe this new deputy was just trying to get her attention.

She set her lunch in the truck and freed the white slip of paper. Hmm. Deputy J. Grant. The back of Trip's neck prickled. Something familiar danced around the edges of her mind, just out of reach. She shook her head when a face came into focus. Grant was a common name. The J. Grant from her past was probably occupying an office in the Pentagon after multiple tours in Afghanistan. The world was too big for them to finally cross paths again in this small South Georgia town. If only she could go back in time and correct that one monumental mistake, the biggest regret of her life.

She stared at the ticket again. She'd never again felt connected to a woman like she had with the J. Grant she'd known in college. They were so young, and Trip was so infatuated. But Jamie had her eyes on someone else, and in a weak moment, Trip had given in to a stupid idea she'd hoped would make Jamie see her as more than a buddy.

Her appetite stolen by the overwhelming memory, Trip dug the pile of parking tickets out of the glove compartment and smoothed them out on the seat before starting the truck. It would wreck her schedule, but she was going straight to the courthouse to pay all of the fines and vowed to only park in a legal space here after. More than eighteen years later, she still couldn't get that past J. Grant out of her head, but she could get this Deputy J. Grant off her back.

Chapter Eight

The Beaumont Summer Cookout was an all-day event that drew lesbians from Savannah, Georgia Southern University, Fort Stewart, and up from Florida. Some of Trip's veterinarian lesbian pals flew in from even farther distances, and she'd negotiated with the local Holiday Inn Express to give her guests a special convention rate and provide a shuttle to her property for any who would be imbibing. Even a small campground was set up for nature lovers in a newly harvested hay field.

Women had begun arriving as early as ten that morning to sun around the pool with fruity cocktails and Bloody Marys and graze the catered brunch table while a mix of nostalgic and new tunes played at a moderate volume to allow comfortable conversation. By two o'clock, the crowd swelled to more than a hundred, and groups made use of the volleyball net, the cornhole games, and a small Frisbee golf course, while others called for someone to crank up beach tunes for shag dancing.

Trip was careful, though. As the cars rolled in, everybody's identification was checked by an experienced bar bouncer, who recited brief rules—absolutely no recreational drugs, drivers had to pass a breathalyzer test to leave the property, no dyke drama that dampened the festive mood, and no touching or giving alcohol to anyone wearing an orange tank or T-shirt with "Beaumont Summer Extravaganza" printed on the chest. While she didn't go so far as to search their coolers, all those who were over eighteen but under the legal drinking minimum were given colorful bracelets that told bartenders to deny service and identified them to a small crew of women she trusted and paid to keep the younger crowd sober and safe. The handful of high schoolers were directed to the house where they had to swap their own shirts for the orange ones. Most didn't mind because Trip let them keep the shirts and she'd seen them pop up around town occasionally, a sort of bragging rights that they'd been to the coolest party around. She refused to deny these youngsters the chance to be around a diverse group of successful role models, but she always sent them home when night approached, before the adults got too drunk and frisky, and skinny-dippers filled the pool.

She was chatting with one of the young orange shirts who wanted to be a mechanic, when Jerome waved to her from the open front door. "You should talk to my buddy, Clay," she said to the teen. "She'll be here later."

The baby butch's mouth dropped open. "Clay Cahill? She's here?"

"She will be. Watch for her. She's always happy to talk about cars and engines."

"Cool. Thanks." The girl was already pushing through the back door.

Trip chuckled and headed for Jerome. "Mick will be putting meat on the grill in the next thirty minutes."

He waved her off. "I just came to get Granny. I'm still having to listen to Mama's rants about what Granny packs in her pipe sometimes since she hung out with some of your crowd after dark last year."

"Tell your churchgoing mama to lighten up. A little weed is probably good for Essie's rheumatism."

He laughed and nodded. "Yeah, and she's put on some much-needed weight. Granny isn't happy about me dragging her away to Mama's house today, but I'm following orders."

Trip clapped him on his shoulder. "Come back later and grab some ribs and potato salad for your family."

"I'll do that. Thanks."

Jerome started toward Essie's rooms, but stopped to see what Trip was staring at through the front windows.

"Looks like your new associate can't peel her eyes off Michelle's ass," Jerome said too low for anyone but Trip to hear. "You didn't warn her about hitting on that?"

"I'm pretty confident Dani has zero interest there, but you can't blame her for appreciating Michelle's assets. Both of us would be looking, too, if we were walking behind that show of hip-swinging."

"Hey, Doc," Michelle said as they climbed the six wide stairs to the porch.

"Hey, Michelle." Trip patted Dani on the back. "Glad you made it. I was beginning to wonder if you were going to blow me off."

Michelle squealed and ran to hug someone across the room. Dani, Trip, and Jerome shared a mutual smirk at her antics.

"Girl, you would have been better off coming stag than bring her for a date," Jerome said.

"Not my date. We just walked over together after finishing up at the clinic," Dani said.

"Good to hear. I didn't want to bust your chops for dating the underage help right out of the gate." Trip couldn't resist teasing her.

"Underage? But she looks—"

"She's not really underage. She just acts like it," Jerome said. "Next time you need a date, I'll talk to my cousin. She's pretty hot and I think she'd be into you." He waved as he walked away. "She's probably here somewhere. Get Trip or Grace to introduce you. I've got to deal with Granny."

Trip spotted one of her horse clients clearing the entry checkpoint. "Get a drink and some food and wander around a bit. I've got to make the rounds to check on things, but I'll look for you in a bit to introduce you to some clients who have already arrived." One greeting led to a conversation with another group, a check on the grill crew, then a stop by one of the alcohol stations to score one of her favorite craft beers before scanning the backyard crowd.

Oh, good. Grace was talking to Dani. She wanted her friends to like Dani and, hopefully, help Dani make friends that might anchor her in Pine Cone. Trip frowned. Why were they standing so close? And who exactly was doing the crowding? Trip couldn't really tell. Dani put her hand on Grace's arm, but Grace abruptly walked away.

Dani stared after Grace, and Trip moved to intercept and interrogate. Where was Clay? She needed backup.

"Grace, wait," Trip said, keeping her saunter casual as she sidled up to her. She didn't want Dani, who was still staring at Grace, to think Trip was getting into her personal business. Even though she was about to do exactly that.

Grace was flushed and her eyes a bit wild when she glanced at Trip. "Why, Grace Booker, you look about to swoon." Trip resisted the urge to look back at Dani to see if she wore the same strange expression.

"No. Well, maybe." Grace sighed. "Yes. Yes, I am."

Trip stared at her.

"I know she might not stick around, but I can't help it," Grace said.

"Then I'm sorry."

Grace turned to her. "Sorry for what?"

Trip shrugged. "I kinda told her that you'd make a good friend, but she should keep her hands off you since she might not stick around for long."

Grace gave Trip a disgusted look. "Don't you think you should talk to me before you screen my potential girlfriends?" Grace waved her hands in front of her. "On second thought, don't answer that. I know my track record isn't great."

Trip followed Grace to the house. "Wait now. There's no reason to get down on yourself. We can fix this if you really want. But you need to summon the charming and charismatic Grace, not act like an ice queen. Even I felt the chill way over here when you walked away from her."

"I tried that. My usual charming and charismatic self sent her running for the hills, so I've just toned it down a notch. You don't chase a spooked horse, do you, Trip?"

"Depends on the horse, but I wouldn't think you'd have to chase that one long. Her eyes are still glued to your back." Trip glanced over her shoulder and chuckled. "Correction. Glued to your backside."

Grace kept walking. "But when I'm around, she's standoffish and weird."

Trip cupped Grace's elbow and guided her toward a group of women. "Maybe you need a teaser to reel her in."

"For God's sake, stop talking in animal terms and speak plainly."

Trip held on tight when Grace tried to pull out of her grasp. She'd just spotted the perfect person. "Jay is the best teaser in the county. She flirts with everybody, looks like she's the biggest whore dog around, but is basically harmless."

"What *are* you talking about, Trip Beaumont?"

They stopped just out of earshot of Jay. "There's two kinds of teasers, but I won't bore you with technical stuff. We use teaser horses to both test for readiness and stimulate the interest of a potential breeder."

"Seriously, Trip? You're comparing me to a breeding mare?"

"You're missing the point, Gracie. Trust me, you'll have Dani eating out of your hand if she thinks Jay's sniffing around you. Just go with it. Talk with Jay for a bit and let this play out. I know what I'm doing."

Grace shook her head and turned her back to Jay when Trip tried to nudge her in that direction. "I don't like games, Trip."

"You're just being sociable." Trip caught Jay's eye and reached behind Grace to covertly wave Jay over.

"Hey, Grace."

Grace jumped when Jay spoke from right behind her, then stepped around to face her. "Hi, Jay. How are you doing?"

"I've been trying to get a minute alone with you since I got here. Walk with me?"

"See you later." Trip stepped back. Her work was done here.

Women filled the front, side, and back yards, eating, talking, swimming, sunning, and joining in the various games, and Trip was sure it was a record turnout. Clay was still missing, but Trip didn't worry. Clay was probably circling, deciding which woman she might cut from the herd for some personal attention.

And Trip, well, she felt way too sober. It was time to have some fun. She grabbed a beer chaser and strolled over to sample the table of Jell-O shots, slippery and buttery nipples, and her favorite apple cinnamon shots made from Fireball and Royal Crown Apple whiskies. She rolled a buttery nipple over her tongue to savor the sweetness, took a sip of beer to cleanse her palate, and upended an apple cinnamon shot. It burned down her throat, and she sucked in a deep breath to prolong it. She downed another and closed her eyes as the heat spread through her body. She'd prowl for a little human heat later, but she was feeling lazy right now.

She yanked her T-shirt over her head to expose the skimpy bikini top that matched her board shorts. More skin to soak up the sun she craved. She gathered two more beers in one hand and managed to palm three shots in the other, then headed for the pool.

Even though she'd rented twenty in addition to the dozen permanent poolside loungers, every chair was filled. No matter. She had offers from at least six women to join them, but straddled the lounger of a longtime friend she knew was safely attached to a partner and slid in to sit behind her.

"Hey, Patty." Trip set her beers, then shots on the concrete and relaxed against the raised back of the lounger. "Where's Aisa?"

Patty pointed to the side yard where the volleyball net was set up. "They begged her to fill an opening on one of the teams."

Trip looked toward the group just in time to see Aisa spike the ball into the opposing team's court. She laughed. "Yeah, I'm sure they had to twist her arm." Aisa Eriksson had been a top player at the University of Florida, before graduating to dedicate herself to teaching—a calling she felt stronger than a career in sports. Trip downed a shot and sipped her beer.

"She's having fun," Patty said, blowing a kiss to Aisa when she turned their way and waved. She patted Trip's knee. "I'm going in the pool to cool off. Swing your legs up here and keep those knees together." She stood and waggled her finger at Trip. "I don't want to come back and find that you've spread your legs and let some floozy take my seat."

Trip grinned and downed the second shot while those in the chairs around her hooted at Patty's admonishment. Then she obediently stretched out her legs, opened the second beer, and scooped up the third shot. She closed her eyes behind her sunglasses and let the sun and alcohol warm her. Life was good. One thought led to another as she drowsed over the memory of last year's cookout when she and Aisa had waged battle over the same volleyball net. She'd held her own until Aisa unleashed and took her to school. She'd invited Patty and Aisa back the next weekend, and she'd unlocked the barn to teach Aisa a few lessons on the basketball court. Afterward, Jerome and one of his cousins challenged them in a rousing two-on-two game. That was fun. The guys won, but she and Aisa had given them a good fight. Aisa was a natural athlete in any sport, but playing with her wasn't like playing in college…with Jamie. They'd clicked from the beginning, seamlessly anticipating no-look passes, always knowing where the other was on the court. It was as if their brains had a psychic connection.

A splash of cold doused her bare stomach and Trip jerked. She peered up at Aisa, who was tilting her beer to also add a splash of cold to Trip's crotch. "I'm gonna kick your ass, Eriksson." She sat up and her brain swam in a muddled haze of alcohol and her brief nap.

"You're slowing down, pal. Even Grace is getting more action today than you are."

Trip straightened. "What? Where is she? Do we need to rescue her?"

But Aisa's attention was suddenly focused on Patty playing in the pool. "Later, maybe."

Trip blinked at the empty spot where Aisa had been standing. "What the hell?" She struggled out of the chair, but swayed when she stood. She needed to clear her head.

Trip slid her sunglasses into the side pocket of her board shorts and dove into the deep end of the pool. The refreshing water glided against her skin, and she wished for a second that everyone would be gone when she surfaced. Today felt…off, but she had no idea why. She opened her eyes instinctively as she approached the wall at the shallow end and put her hand out to stop her forward motion, planting it between two legs dangling in the water, and popped up to the surface. She shook her head, spraying water like a dog to the shrieks of several women who also were dangling their legs into the cool water, then wiped the water from her eyes to offer a friendly grin at whoever she'd nearly plowed into.

She blinked. Her jaw dropped. Then for a tiny second—or maybe it was an eternity—her lungs forgot to draw breath and her heart froze a few beats.

"Hello, Trip." Jamie Grant's face was expressionless, but her hazel eyes were bright when they met and held hers. "Still the life of the party, I see."

"Jamie." Trip whispered the name. Was she still dreaming? Her mind jumped from thought to thought so fast she couldn't complete a single one, much less form a coherent sentence.

"Hey, Jamie Grant. You're the next challenger on the cornhole sign-up." Someone shouted from across the yard, and Jamie's eyes flicked over Trip's shoulder.

"Be right there." Jamie smoothly levered to her feet and stared down at Trip. "Gotta go."

Trip watched her walk away from the pool. Jamie Grant. In the flesh. And even more attractive all grown up. Her tennis-style shorts hugged her slim hips and muscled thighs, and the Lycra V-neck appeared molded to her still perfect torso and shoulders. *Say something. SAY something.* But Jamie was too far away now.

"How do you know Jamie? She said she just moved to town," one of the other women asked.

The question brought Trip back to earth. She cleared her throat, but her eyes stayed on Jamie. If she looked away, Jamie might disappear. "From another time, another life."

Her cryptic answer drew a teasing chorus of "oh" and "ah," but Trip ignored them and got out of the water. What to do? Should she follow Jamie and talk to her? She needed to sober up so she could think. Trip took a towel from one of the stacks set out for guests and dried herself. She hadn't thought she was hungry, but she realized as she neared the grill where Mick was dishing up juicy cheeseburgers that she hadn't eaten all day. She washed down her burger with three bottles of water and wolfed a bowl of peach cobbler and ice cream without taking her eyes from Jamie across the yard.

She didn't want to talk to Jamie in a crowd. There were too many eyes and ears interested to see who drew Trip's attention today—a repeat hookup or somebody new? Hell, there was usually a betting pool on both her and Clay. Grace always held the money because she was the most trusted person at the party.

No. She wanted, needed to talk with Jamie alone. Surely, Jamie didn't still hold a grudge. They were college students, for God's sake, eighteen years ago. Trip smiled when Jamie slid the second of her corn bags cleanly into the hole and the friends of the woman she was challenging groaned.

After graduating veterinary school, Trip had done a surgical residency at a big private veterinary practice in Atlanta. She'd looked up Jamie's mother, who no longer lived in the dangerous projects downtown. Jamie was in Afghanistan, Mrs. Grant told Trip, and she worried for her because her job was to locate and disarm bombs. When had she left the service? And, most importantly, how did she end up in Trip's small town? Had Jamie deliberately tracked her down and come to Pine Cone because Trip was here? Hope speared through her, but wavered just as quickly. Jamie's reaction to Trip's stupidly mute greeting had been indifferent. Maybe a bit chilly. Still, Jamie had driven past the iron gates proclaiming Beaumont Farms, so she had to know she would likely bump into Trip.

Another collective groan from the cornhole game, but this time combined with cheers from Jamie's newly formed fan club. Trip watched Jamie shake the hand of the loser, then hand over all but one of her corn bags. She arched the last pouch overhand like shooting a basketball and bowed to the group when it dropped neatly into the hole. Trip shook her head and grinned. It wasn't required as a point guard, but Jamie had been a sharpshooter on the college court and obviously hadn't lost her touch. But now she was abdicating her throne as cornhole champion, and heading for the house.

Trip rose to follow, but her progress was slowed by having to weave her way through the partiers. "Excuse me. Sorry. Whoa, watch it." She stopped to catch and steady an inebriated woman who had stepped backward into her path while talking to friends, then realized the path was now clear. She ran for the door.

One woman snored from where she was propped in the corner of the sofa, and a handful of others were waiting their turn at the bathroom down the hall. Jamie was apparently comparing the length of the bathroom line to the line of cars, visible through the huge front windows, waiting to clear the breathalyzer checkpoint to leave. She glanced over as Trip started toward her.

"I'll hit one of the Porta Johns outside." She moved to step around Trip.

Trip touched Jamie's arm to stop her. "Wait." She could have directed Jamie to the half-bath off her home office, but she'd just seen Dani leading Grace that way. So she untied the police tape Grace had strung to keep amorous women from going upstairs to make use of the bedrooms. "Hang a left at the top, first door on your right."

Jamie hesitated, then nodded. "Thanks."

Trip watched Jamie take the stairs two at a time, then retied the yellow police tape behind her and followed more slowly.

Jamie cursed her full bladder. She should have just left, or gone to the portable toilets. But it was too late to change her mind now without looking foolish. She was surprised when the door she opened was a bedroom. A bedroom someone obviously lived in. Clothing hung from one corner of the four-poster bed frame. Two pairs of running shoes were in a haphazard heap next to a wing-backed chair in the corner. The dresser top held the usual tray of watches, keys and coins, and a jewelry box. Several veterinary and horse magazines were piled on the bedside table. She started to back out and try other doors, but spotted a partially open door on the other side of the long dresser. A bathroom.

When she emerged, Trip was propped against the end of the bed, waiting. Trip stood and they stared at each other. She'd put her T-shirt back on, but it didn't keep Jamie's traitorous brain from recalling Trip's long, smooth abdomen when she popped out of the water inches from Jamie's hands. At least Trip wasn't still as ripped as she was in college. Jamie gritted her teeth at the memory of Suzanne raving over Trip's muscles. If she had to admit it, Jamie liked Trip's slightly softer woman's body…still athletic, but not skinny.

"It's good to see you, Jamie," Trip said quietly. "It's been a long time."

"Thanks for the use of your bathroom." She gestured toward the hallway. "And thanks for telling Grace to invite me, but I need to go home to let my dog out." She'd barely taken a step toward the door when Trip's hand on her arm stopped her.

"Can we have dinner…or a beer sometime? Catch up with each other?"

Jamie was surprised by the conflicting mix of emotions that surged through her. She wanted to slug Trip for stealing her first girlfriend. At the same time, she wanted to hug the closest friend she'd ever had, the woman Jamie hadn't allowed herself to crush on because Trip Beaumont always had a line of coeds angling to date her. She'd thought she was ready to face Trip, but maybe not. "Look. I came to Pine Cone because Grace made the right offer for me and my canine partner. I'm not looking to relive the past."

"Are we ever going to talk about what happened?"

"Let the past stay in the past." Jamie pulled away from Trip's grasp, making it to the doorway before Trip spoke again.

"What if I don't want to, James?"

Jamie stopped, and her throat tightened. "You don't get to call me that anymore, Beaumont. That nickname came from a friend who betrayed me."

Trip persisted. "What if I want a chance to set things straight?"

Jamie whirled and paced back to Trip. "Maybe your mama raised you to think you can do whatever you want, but there are rules decent people follow." She poked Trip in the chest to emphasize her words. "Rules even for small town royalty like you."

Trip caught Jamie's hand and held it against her chest. "Tell me your rules, Jamie. I'll follow every one if you'll give me a chance. We…we were good friends before."

Jamie jerked her hand back. "You can start by parking in legal spaces. I'm running out of ticket books." She stalked out the door before the sensation of Trip's heart throbbing against the back of her hand weakened her resolve to keep Trip Beaumont at a distance.

CHAPTER NINE

Sunday morning had dawned bright and clear, and Jamie smiled when she saw the three men sitting on the porch of the old depot. She was a bit later than usual, because she was careful to alter her patrol route each day so any criminals never knew what time of day she might appear on their side of town.

She'd been restless and unsettled after seeing Trip, so she asked MJ's permission to use the B and B kitchen and baked two peach cobblers the night before. She left one for MJ. The second cobbler was nestled in her trunk next to a cooler that contained a half-gallon of vanilla ice cream. Cooking was something she took up while rehabbing. Her goal was to improve her diet and fitness level as she recovered from the shrapnel that killed her canine and nearly tore off her leg. This cobbler recipe wasn't exactly healthy but one her physical therapist, who was from South Carolina, shared with her.

Petunia barked a greeting and hopped around the back seat, eager to go greet the men. Jamie released her from the car, but ordered her to heel, and Petunia complied after a tiny, impatient dance. Jamie wasn't about to let her get sloppy while she was on duty.

She called out to the men. "Hi, guys. I brought you a surprise." She took the cobbler from the passenger seat and placed it on the warm hood of the cruiser. "I've got ice cream, too," she said as they cautiously approached.

"Hoo-wee." Pete jogged the rest of the way to be first in line. "Look what the po-po done brought, boys."

Jamie scooped a huge helping of cobbler topped with ice cream into a plastic bowl and stabbed a plastic spoon into the top before handing it to Pete. He dug in, overfilling his mouth and humming his approval.

Toby wiped his hands on a dingy handkerchief while he watched Jamie fill a second bowl. "It's very good of you to think of us, miss," he said, taking the bowl and closing his eyes as his lips moved in a brief prayer before he dug into his treat.

"I suppose you got stuck working on Sunday because you're the new deputy," Toby said.

"Nah. The other guys all like to go to church with their families and were rotating the Sunday duty. But I'm not much for organized religion, so I offered to fill the shift permanently. Sundays are generally quiet, a good way to start my work week."

Adder hung back, but his eyes flicked from the other men to the third bowl Jamie was filling.

"Come on, Adder," Jamie said softly. "I know you like peaches. There's no trip wire."

He came closer, and even though he avoided looking at Jamie, she could see his dilated pupils, huge and black. Petunia quietly left Jamie's side and sniffed his pants as he took his first bite. She sat and looked up at him. "Not sharing this with you, pup. You'll have to beg from the other guys." His words were low and gruff.

"Actually, she's not begging." Jamie kept her voice soft. "She's alerting me that you're carrying either drugs or a weapon."

Adder froze, so Jamie spoke quickly before he could bolt.

"I'm not going to arrest you for having a small stash." She waited a heartbeat until he looked up, shame written across his tanned features. "But if I catch you selling or transporting for dealers, I will."

His lip curled in a slight, grim smile. "Maybe I am."

"If you are, you're not carrying much today. Petunia knows." Jamie took a bite from her own bowl of cobbler. "She'd be barking her head off instead of gazing up at you." She stared off into the distance, aware that Toby and Pete were watching them. "And if she was, my gun would be in my hand and you'd be in cuffs. Is that what you want, Adder?"

He stared into his bowl, then closed his eyes as he spoke. "I want the desert to get out of my head." His face twisted into a tight grimace. "I want the screams of my buddies being blown to pieces to stop so I can sleep at night."

Toby was at his side in a second, one hand ready to catch Adder's bowl if he dropped it and the other rubbing comforting circles on his back. "It's okay, son. We all have our demons to fight. Victory is not always winning the battle, but rising every time you fall. Give yourself time. You'll find a way to beat this."

Adder nodded, and although he didn't look up, he resumed eating.

Jamie stared at Toby. Who was this homeless man quoting Napoleon Bonaparte? Pete shifted anxiously from foot to foot; he'd gobbled up a second bowl of cobbler when Toby shoved it at him so he could go to Adder. Still, Pete's eyes darted from them to the half pan of cobbler sitting on the trunk. She needed to get back on patrol, but she pulled a business card from her wallet and scribbled her personal cell number on the back and held it out to Adder. "I still hear them, too," she said. "Call me if you need to talk, or just want someone to sit with for a while."

He hesitantly took the card, but still avoided her gaze.

"Pete! You were supposed to hold that for me, not eat it." Toby's scold held no anger, just admonishment as though he was reprimanding a child.

Pete giggled and bounced on his toes. "You didn't say that, so I figured you didn't want it." He reminded Jamie of that old television character, Ernest T. Bass, who definitely had some mental issues.

She turned back to the cruiser and handed the cobbler pan to Toby. "How about you guys finish this off for me?" She patted her stomach. "I spend way too much time sitting in that patrol car, and I don't want to ruin my girlish figure."

"We don't want that neither," Pete said, his eyes locked on the goodies. "No, sir. It's our duty to keep you from it."

Toby bowed slightly. "We thank you, Deputy Grant. It's very kind of you."

"Jamie. I'm just Jamie to you guys." She handed Pete the half-full carton of ice cream and opened the door for Petunia to jump in.

"You should eat that up pretty quick before it melts. I'll be seeing you around. Church lets out services in a bit, and I need to go direct traffic so the Baptists and the Methodists don't run over each other to get a table at the Cracker Barrel."

❖

Trip swallowed the last bite of buttered toast and downed another dose of aspirin with her third bottle of water. It'd been a decade since she'd drank enough to induce a hangover. Coming face-to-face with Jamie had thrown her. Even though she'd known Grace's new deputy was female and J. Grant, never in her wildest dreams did she really think it could be Jamie. Her Jamie. No, not hers. Because she'd screwed things up with the one woman she desperately wanted.

Jamie had grown from a smokin' hot coed to an even more attractive woman. All of it—her infatuation, the undeniable connection, and the ache of her unrequited interest—flooded back tenfold. Jamie obviously didn't feel the same.

After Jamie left, Trip plastered a smile on her face and dutifully circulated among her guests until the grills shut down, dusk fell, and the crowd thinned. That's when she retreated to the front porch with a glass of ice and a bottle of her favorite blended whiskey. She wasn't sure when the party ended, but the sky was beginning to lighten when Jerome, headed to the barn to feed horses before Sunday morning church services, shook her awake. She'd spent the night in a straight-back rocking chair, and her thirty-six-year-old body complained plenty when she stood to stagger inside.

She took a long, hot shower, downed some aspirin and two bottles of water before climbing into her much softer bed for six hours of sobering sleep. Her headache was better now, but her heart was still sore from the emotional impact of finding Jamie back in her life. Or was she? She'd disappeared from Trip's life before with no notice, no note of explanation. But Pine Cone was even smaller than its geographical borders when it came to tripping over the same people week after week. And Jamie wasn't just passing through like Dani probably would.

Trip sucked in a deep breath and blew it out. Her brain wasn't up to sorting this out right now. The clinic was closed on Sunday, and though a kennel helper would have fed animals and cleaned pens, she needed to check on the patients with wounds or hospitalized with serious illnesses. She trudged across the drive to the clinic, only to realize Dani's car was parked by the back entrance. Still, she went inside and pulled on a lab coat over her normal Sunday attire—loose basketball shorts and her favorite faded vet school T-shirt. She found Dani in the treatment room, inserting a new IV in the leg of an Irish setter who'd pulled his previous one out during the night.

"Hey, haven't you read your contract? You're not scheduled to come in on Sundays. That's my job because you cover Saturdays while I go to horse shows."

Dani glanced up and smiled as she finished taping the IV securely to the setter's leg, then ruffled the dog's ears affectionately and softly scolded him. "Now leave that one alone or I'll be fitting you with a cone of shame next time." The dog wagged his tail, oblivious to her threat.

"I don't think your scolding penetrated that thick Irish setter skull," Trip said. She liked the way Dani handled her patients, and how they responded to her.

Dani shrugged. "You know what they say in vet school…"

"Some dogs have brains and others have red coats," they quoted together.

"This is his last bag of fluids, anyway," Dani said, hefting him from the table and walking him back to his cage. "He's feeling a lot better. I'll be calling his owner to come pick him up tomorrow. I doubt we'll have to worry about them being careless with antifreeze again once I show them their bill."

"Their teenager was the careless one, but it won't happen again. Not only did he come close to losing his best friend, he'll be working off most of that bill slinging hay bales for Jerome. Trust me, that's hard work he won't soon forget."

While Dani gently checked the IVs and administered medicine to a pair of Yorkie pups suffering from parvo, Trip pulled a terrier mix from a smaller pen and checked his multiple stitched wounds earned in a fight with a dog five times his size. "This guy looks like something out of a horror movie, but he should be good to go home tomorrow, too."

"You were right about the cookout, by the way."

"How so?"

"I met a lot of great people and even picked up a new client for us."

"Do tell."

"Yeah, a terrier mix with a gastric problem. It was a shelter pup, so its medical history is sketchy. It's a chronic issue, and several visits to specialists have helped the owner manage it somewhat. But she's worried because the pup seems to be having some abdominal pain and has lost interest in food."

"Could be intestinal cancer," Trip offered, closing the terrier back in his pen. "Who's the owner?"

"Jamie Grant. It'd be a shame if it is cancer. The terrier came from a program that turns the most unwanted shelter dogs into service animals. Jamie works for the sheriff's office and trained this dog herself to sniff out drugs and explosives."

Trip had stopped listening the second Dani said Jamie's name. Her brain whirled with this new information.

"Trip? Are you all right?"

"Yeah. I'm fine. My brain just sidetracked to something else for a minute. It's still a little foggy. What were you saying?"

"I've already been through the cat room, so we're done."

"Oh, right. Remind me why you're here on a Sunday?"

Dani ducked her head. "Well, I saw you, uh, napping in the chair on the front porch and had an idea you might not be up for dealing with clogged drainage tubes and double diarrhea from the Yorkie twins."

Embarrassment heated Trip's neck and ears. "Yeah. Not usually my style. At least, not since I graduated vet school a decade ago." She rubbed her temples. "And it'll be two decades, if ever, before I'll do it again. But thanks for having my back."

"No problem," Dani said.

Trip started to leave, but stopped in the doorway. "Did Jamie make an appointment for her dog?"

"Tomorrow. Nine o'clock. Before they start their shift."

"My morning is flexible tomorrow. I'll handle that one if you don't mind. Jamie and I were teammates on the basketball team where I did my undergrad. I'd like to handle this one personally."

"Sure, no problem. Jamie didn't mention you guys were friends. I sure hope it isn't cancer so you don't have to give her bad news."

"Thanks. See you tomorrow morning, then."

❖

Jamie pulled into the small parking lot next to the windowless brick building. When she'd interviewed for the Pine Cone job, she'd been impressed that the sheriff was an advocate of community policing. And she was pretty sure she nailed the interview when she asked if they had a local Boys and Girls Club because she'd been a volunteer when she was a college student.

As expected, the club was located in a blighted neighborhood where teens idled on street corners and parks were little more than rusted swing sets and cracked concrete basketball courts. She slowed as she approached the front entrance with Petunia at her heel. A dejected group of kids, five boys and two girls she guessed to be between seven and twelve years old, sat on the sidewalk with their backs against the dirty brick of the building. The kids stood and shifted away as she walked to them, their wary eyes taking in her uniform.

"What's up, guys?" Jamie asked.

"Ain't no crime to sit on the sidewalk," a scowling boy said as he stepped to the front of the group. "We ain't bothering nobody."

Jamie put her hands up, palms out. "Whoa. P and I aren't here to hassle anybody."

Taking her cue, Petunia balanced on her haunches and held both front paws in the air, mirroring Jamie's gesture. The smallest girl giggled, and several other faces lit up with smiles, but all remained behind their spokesman.

"I'll bet it's a lot cooler inside," Jamie said, pointing to the door.

"It's locked," a different boy said. "Miss M ain't here today."

"She's real sick," the older girl said. "Some days, she doesn't come."

Grace had told Jamie that Millicent Williams, the nonprofit's director, was struggling to keep the center open.

"So, nobody else opens up when Miss M is sick?"

"The Preacher Tom comes on Tuesday and Thursday, but nobody else," another boy said.

"What's your dog's name?" the small girl asked.

"This is Canine Officer Petunia," Jamie said, signaling P, who touched her paw to her brow in a cute salute. The little girl giggled again.

"That ain't no police dog," the group's leader said.

"She sure is," Jamie said. "She's specially trained to sniff out explosives and illegal drugs."

The boy frowned but didn't respond. Sweat trickled down his temple, and he wiped it away with a shrug of his shoulder.

Jamie scanned the area. On the other side of the center's squat building was a single basketball court partially surrounded by rusting chain-link fence. The goals were dented metal and the hoops netless. Trash and weeds cluttered a vacant lot across the street where a lone, scraggly oak stood. Next to it, a store with ancient gas pumps had thick bars on the windows. The neglect was even worse than the inner-city project where she'd grown up. Was there no place for these children to play?

"So what do you guys usually do when you hang out?" she asked.

"Duh." The leader of the group pointed to the locked door of the center. "We go in there."

"Miss M has video games, and we paint and draw and she gives us cookies," one of the younger boys said, bouncing on his feet.

Jamie scratched her head. "Hmm. Well, I don't have a key to get inside today. But I might have an idea. P, stay." She jogged across the street to the store. The store was nicer on the inside than it was on the outside. A wall of glass-front refrigeration units was mostly filled with beer, but several others held bottled water, sodas, and a few grocery essentials. She grabbed seven sodas. Near the register, a warmer that looked more like an old movie popcorn cooker held foil-wrapped hotdogs, and a freezer was filled with various ice cream treats. Jamie scooped up seven Klondike bars. She put the sodas and ice cream on the counter. The old man at the register began to ring up her items. "And I'll take seven of those dogs."

The old man bagged the ice cream bars and sodas and recited her total. While she dug out her wallet, he slid seven of the foil-covered hotdogs into another bag, along with a handful of ketchup and mustard packets. He looked across the street to the kids, who were all watching the store. "You're not the first one, you know. Others with good intentions have come down here and fed them or helped them for a day or even a few weeks," he said. "But it's not really a kindness, because you do-gooders eventually don't come back and those kids are reminded again and again that they aren't worth anyone sticking around." He held out her change.

Jamie took the money and gathered up her bags, then leveled her gaze at him. "I might not look like it now in this uniform, but I was one of them once," she said softly. "And I'm here to stay."

She crossed back to the kids and began handing out the treats. "Eat your ice cream first before it melts," she said. "P and I will be back in about fifteen or twenty minutes, so don't go anywhere." She pointed to the group's leader. "You're in charge. Make sure everybody puts their trash in the bags."

The food was gone and the trash bagged when she returned. They eyed the wide broom she held in one hand and the cloth shopping bag she held in the other.

"Since we can't get inside to paint and draw, we'll do it out here," she said. Jamie put the bag down and dug out one of the boxes of fat colored chalks. "As soon as I sweep it clean, the sidewalk will be our canvas."

Young brows wrinkled with this revelation.

"We'll get in trouble for writing on the sidewalk," one child said.

"My brother got arrested because he painted on the outside of the school," a boy said.

Jamie nodded. "You can get in trouble for spraying paint on a private or government building without permission, because it costs lots of money to have it cleaned off. And you'll get in even more trouble if you paint bad words." She took up the broom that she kept in her trunk for sweeping glass off a street after an accident and began to clean the sidewalk in front of the center with it. "But this sidewalk belongs to the public, and that includes you. Besides, we're going to use chalk. It'll wash off the next time it rains."

One boy pulled at his lip, considering this.

"Trust me," she said. "I'm a police officer. I know what's right and what's wrong."

That pronouncement was enough to send the kids diving to claim their favorite color from the boxes of chalk. But as soon as the words left her mouth, she realized she could only say that about the law. Right and wrong wasn't always crystal clear in life. And she wasn't sure she trusted herself to recognize the difference.

Trip twisted the key in the padlock and pushed the barn doors open. The new easy-glide doors she'd installed on the century-old building were a big improvement. Actually, except for the massive axe-hewn corner posts and overhead weight-bearing beams, little of the original structure remained. Years of housing a variety of animals and weathering a multitude of storms had been hard on it, inside and out. Her grandfather had converted the old barn into a basketball gymnasium when Trip was a lanky kid and it became obvious that she'd inherited Grandpa's talent for the game. He'd completely stripped the dilapidated structure, then rebuilt it on the original bones.

She'd abandoned her dreams of playing as a pro when her personal world, and the bigger world, seemed to fall apart the beginning of her junior college year. Even so, this court where her grandfather had patiently coached and challenged her was still her sanctuary.

She flipped the series of switches next to the door, and the polished boards of the court gleamed under overhead lights. White nets hung from bright orange hoops attached to fiberglass backboards. The floor was better than the court at the new high school. The only things missing were a scoreboard, the cheering crowd, the referees' whistles, and the sound of the horn that signaled for play to begin or resume. The bounce, bounce, bounce of the balls echoed in the cavernous building as she tested several from a rack along the wall. Jerome was the only other person she allowed to use her gym, so he made sure the balls were kept properly inflated and the floor maintained.

She began with dribbling exercises. Up and down, up and down the court. Left hand, right hand, between the legs, behind the back, full run, half run, weaving run, change lead, stutter step. Up and down again and again.

Sweat ran down her temples, between her breasts, down her legs. She began to shoot, starting at the left wing and working her way around to the right wing. Beyond the arc, top of the key, layup, reverse layup, old-fashioned hook, turnaround jumper, and rolling around an imaginary guard to jump high and dunk it over the rim. Yes, she could jump high enough to dunk. Actually, several women on her college team could, but didn't because it was simply a showy move and high risk for the fine bones of women's hands and wrists.

"I see you're feeling better."

Trip clutched her chest when her heart nearly jumped out. She'd been so focused on the bounce of the ball and the swish of the net, she hadn't noticed Jerome standing at the other end of the court in basketball shorts and his worn Michael Jordan's. "Christ almighty. You nearly scared the life out of me." She glared as he walked farther into the court. "Is there a reason you're sneaking around scaring innocent women?" She fired a hard pass right at his gut.

He grinned as he caught the pass. "Okay. I'll concede the woman thing, but I'd buy swamp land in Florida before I'd believe you innocent of anything." He fired the ball back at her. "Do you want to talk about what's got you drinking yourself into a stupor last night, then pounding the court today?"

She caught the pass. "No. I want to play ball." She rocketed the ball to him and backed up to defend the goal.

"First to score thirty," he said. "If I win, you spill."

"And if I win, you have to get your wife to put together two of her incredible lasagnas for my freezer."

He groaned. "You drive a hard bargain. But since I'm going to beat you anyway, I accept." He dribbled right, then left, then pulled up and swished a long three-pointer into the net.

Trip retrieved the ball, dribbled out to half-court, stutter-stepped, then rolled left to take advantage of Jerome's clumsy footwork. He stumbled off-balance, and she streaked to the basket to lay the ball neatly in the net.

The next twenty minutes were filled with trash talk, the swish of the net, squeak of shoes on the polished floor, and showy displays of speed and agility. In the end, a simple pull-up jumper put Trip's scorecard at thirty-one.

"I think you cheated."

Trip laughed as the ball bounced a few times, then rolled to an eventual stop. They collapsed and sprawled on the floor where they stood mid-court. Trip stared up at the ceiling while her breathing slowed.

"You want to talk about it?"

She lifted an arm and began stretching her overworked muscles, while Jerome did the same. "Don't have to. I won."

"You know you want to." Jerome tapped his big foot against hers, and his words held a hint of tease.

Trip sat up and leaned low over her legs to stretch her hamstrings. Jerome mirrored her movements. "Jamie Grant is in Pine Cone."

Jerome wrinkled his brow. "Who's Jamie Grant?" Realization dawned. "The girl from college? The one that went in the army after nine-eleven?"

"Yeah."

"Man." Jerome knew more than anyone. She'd been a wreck when she came home for the holidays after Jamie left school. She'd cried on his shoulder, and he ran interference for her when her mother—and her grandfather—wanted to know what the hell was wrong with her. "That was a long time ago. You still tore up over her?"

Trip stopped her stretching and stared at the floor. "I didn't think so, but when I ran into her…yeah. I guess I am."

They were both quiet for a few minutes. "I guess that she hasn't gotten ugly or married some guy and spit out five kids."

Trip smiled and shook her head. "Hotter than ever. The women at the cookout were drooling. Grace says she's single and married to her job."

"Where does Grace fit into this?"

"Jamie's one of the new cops she hired."

Jerome's mouth dropped open. "Not the one who's been putting tickets on your windshield every time you stop at an intersection."

Trip nodded. "The very one."

"Damn." He wiped his face on the tail of his T-shirt, then chuckled. "I don't know any man or woman who can get in bigger predicaments." He sprang to his feet, his smile big. "But you always manage to roll off that screen and score anyway." He demonstrated with a twirl and pretend jump shot in the direction of the goal. "Swish."

"This is different, J." She looked up at him. "This one really matters. Even if she doesn't want anything to do with me, I need to set things straight."

He offered his hand and she let him pull her to her feet. "Then make a game plan before you hit the court."

"I had a plan in college, and you know how well that worked out," Trip said. She stared out the door where the big barn doors were still open. "I'm going to try something different and just be myself. If she finds me still lacking, well, then it wasn't meant to be."

Chapter Ten

G litter Girl to Fast Break and Paintball, do you copy?"
Trip smiled at Grace's voice and scribbled faster to finish
the billing statement she was filling out. This guy was going to pay
a hefty emergency fee for calling her out on a late Sunday afternoon
just because he wanted to go fishing with his pals tomorrow morning
instead of waiting for her to come out then. She was about to stick it to
him, when she reconsidered. He could have gone fishing and waited
until Tuesday to call, leaving his horse to suffer two more days. She
relented and marked down her usual fee. She knew he wasn't one of
the county's super wealthy and had been looking forward to this rare
outing. Her client peered past where she sat in the truck to the CB
radio snugged under the truck's dash.

"Didn't know anyone still used those things," he said.

Trip totaled the bill on her cell phone's calculator app. "They
still come in handy occasionally. Cell service can be sketchy in some
remote areas."

Several clicks sounded from the speaker, then "Come in, guys."
Grace was getting impatient.

Trip handed over the bill, and the client handed over his credit
card. She used her phone to swipe the card and finish their transaction.

"Paintball here." Trip turned down the volume on Clay's
response.

"Here you go," she said, handing back the credit card. "Soak that
hoof twice a day for the next five days, but don't stop the antibiotic

until it's all gone. It should be fine, but call me if you think I need to look at it again."

"Sure thing, Doc."

Trip upped the CB volume again as she drove back onto the highway.

"Where are you?" Grace asked.

"On a pickup near the county line, about thirty minutes outside town," Clay said. "Are you okay?"

Trip grabbed her mic and cut in. "Fast Break, I copy. What's up?"

"Any chance you guys could meet me at Mosquito Alley for a powwow?"

"Paintball ETA about five thirty," Clay said.

"Fast Break same."

"Thanks, guys. This could take a while. I'll bring food. You bring drinks. Glitter Girl out."

Trip chewed her lip. She was so preoccupied with the sudden appearance of Jamie, that she'd forgotten other things were afoot. This was a good idea to check in. Or was it? She wasn't sure she wanted to confess about Jamie, not even with her two very best friends. Having a chance, well, trying to *get* a second chance with Jamie felt very fragile. Like the tiniest misstep could turn it all wrong again. So, maybe she'd just see what was up with Grace and keep the Jamie thing quiet for now. Yeah. Quiet. Oh, but find out if Clay was making any progress with River.

Trip carried her flip-flops and towel in one hand and Playmate cooler in the other as she padded barefoot down the sandy path between the highway and their special spot by the Altamaha. Clay was already sitting by the river's edge, propped against a cooler and sipping a beer. Nostalgic flashes of the three of them splashing in the river, drinking their first alcohol here, and sharing secrets instantly peeled away the adult in Trip. She dropped the cooler and barreled down the path, yelling a battle cry and flinging her towel and shoes at

Clay as she shot past. A thick, knotted rope dangled from a huge oak limb that stretched out over the water, and Trip launched smoothly from the small beach to grab the rope and swing out as far as possible before dropping into the water.

She came up sputtering just as Clay cannonballed into the water next to her. They laughed, splashed each other, and wrestled to dunk each other until they both were gasping for air and coughing swallowed river water. Damn, this felt good. They grinned at each other and chorused "Dude" in a mutual greeting.

"So, what's up?" Trip swam closer to shore in a lazy paddle until she found footing on the sandy bottom.

"Don't know." Clay followed until they stopped in chest-deep water. "Grace called this meeting."

"Hey, where are you guys?"

"Speaking of Grace." Trip turned and cupped her hands to yell back. "Cooling off. Bring your mosquito spray."

"I could use a hand with the *food*," Grace called back.

Again, they spoke as one. "Food." Their base brains ran on the same wavelength, even though Trip's higher thinking was all science and Clay's was deeply artistic.

Trip sprang toward the bank. "Last one—" Her words turned to a gurgle as Clay pushed her face-first into the water to gain advantage and spring ahead.

"Dibs on the drumsticks," Clay shouted as she sprinted up the path.

Trip scrambled to catch up. "You always were a leg woman."

"Did somebody mention food?" Clay, her shorts and tank top dripping, grabbed Grace in a big wet hug. "Where's your swimsuit, woman?"

Before Grace could answer, Trip hugged her from the back, effectively soaking her from both sides. "The water is just right."

"Who needs to swim when I have you guys?"

In an unspoken and time-honored ritual, Clay grabbed Grace's cooler while Trip carried the picnic basket. Grace could kick butt with the best of them, but her flair was a bit more feminine and always triggered Clay's and Trip's innate butch chivalry.

At the water's edge, Trip set the basket down and signaled Clay with a conspiratorial smile.

Grace was having none of it. "Don't even think about it, Trip Beaumont. If you throw me in that water, neither of you will get anything to eat."

Trip shrugged, nudged Grace closer to the water, and then darted around her side and jumped in, splashing just enough to cool Grace's legs. Trip pointed at Clay, who held her ground next to the food. "Chicken."

"Exactly," Clay said, pointing to the picnic basket.

"You're just afraid Grace will get out the handcuffs. No, wait. From what Shayla says, you like that kind of thing."

"You made that up." Clay helped Grace spread the picnic blanket, then plowed into the river to resume their earlier water war. After a few minutes, the clink of beer bottles brought them up short.

"Cold one?" Grace didn't have to ask twice.

"Okay, hand over my money." Trip held out her hand to Clay.

"What did you two bet on this time?" Grace asked.

Clay riffled through her dry clothes until she found her wallet and handed a ten-dollar bill to Trip. "How long you'd wait to talk. I said thirty minutes, and Trip guessed fifteen. So, what's up, Gracie?"

Trip searched for somewhere to tuck the bill. Her dry clothes were up the hill, in her truck. Finally, she tucked it into her wet sports bra. It would dry later.

"Aren't you hungry? I brought all your favorites. Chicken wings, ribs, cracklings, and potato salad."

Trip cocked her head at Grace's oddly evasive tone. "Now you're stalling. We know where the food is. What's going on with you and how can we help?"

Grace took a deep breath. "Dani Wingate."

Trip looked at Clay, who hesitated before fishing another ten from her wallet and handing it over.

"Seriously, guys?" Grace frowned at them.

"I'm a sucker for a sure bet," Trip said. "Besides, Jolene at the diner is telling everybody the two of you've already slept together."

"*What?*" Grace glared at her. "I hope you set her right."

Trip shook her head. "She could know something I don't."

"She *is* your type," Clay said, taking another swig of beer.

"And what exactly is my type?"

Clay looked at Trip for help.

"I'll let you hatch that egg, pal. You laid it." Trip bit into a chicken wing to indicate she wasn't going to attempt an answer.

Clay shrugged. "You know, like…us." She wagged a finger between herself and Trip. "Handsome, butch, sporty…did I mention handsome?"

Trip swallowed her mouthful of food. Okay. Maybe she'd help Clay a little. "In other words, if we weren't like sisters, we'd probably be trying to date you."

"There's a significant difference between you guys and Dani. She doesn't even want to be around me."

"What makes you think that?" Trip asked.

"She barely speaks to me unless she has to, tenses if I try to touch her, and goes to Savannah at least twice a week, probably to hook up."

Trip frowned. "You mean when I send her to the airport to ship or pick up semen?" She tossed her chicken bone into the woods for natural recycling. This was breeding season, and frozen semen was big business in the horse world. She'd been sending Dani to Savannah to keep her from feeling isolated in Pine Cone. Trip glanced at Clay, but Clay was studying Grace who stared out at the river as she sipped her wine. Trip, too, turned her gaze on Grace. Holy crap. Was Grace—?

Grace seemed to flinch under their gaze. "No, no, no. I'm not falling for her. Really."

"Then why can't you look at us?" Trip asked.

"And why is your left eyebrow doing that little quirky arch like it does when you're not being entirely honest." Clay waved a rib in front of her face like a magic wand. "You looked pretty cozy in the alley the other day."

"Yeah. Wait. What alley?" Whoa. Clay had been palming an ace.

"She said nothing was going on, but it looked pretty cozy to me," Clay said.

"You're imagining things," Grace said.

"I don't think so," Trip said. She'd get the details on this alley thing from Clay later. "Did I imagine seeing Dani drag you into my office yesterday?"

Grace was insistent. "I'm not falling for her, and I probably won't. It's like she's afraid of connecting, I mean *really* connecting."

Trip shifted uneasily. She was sure this was a career issue for Dani, not a Grace issue. If she and Clay helped Grace nail Dani, this could go two ways. Grace could be the anchor to keep Dani in Pine Cone. On the other hand, Dani might leave anyway and break Grace's heart. Trip stood and walked around Clay to sit on the other side of Grace. The two knights now flanked the princess they were sworn to protect. "What do *you* want, Grace?" Trip waited while Grace scanned the river for an answer.

"I can't stop thinking about her," she said at last.

Clay nodded, her eyes dreamy and fixed on the flow of the water, as though the river had also spoken the same answer to her.

Trip should admit the same. Jamie had been on her mind constantly since the cookout. But the confession stuck in her throat. She'd look like a fool if she let her friends know she wanted to risk letting Jamie break her heart again. She shoveled a spoonful of potato salad into her mouth to stop from blurting out something stupid. Yeah, she was being a coward, but this wasn't about her.

Trip put down her plate and slapped her knees. Nothing chanced, nothing gained. "Okay. You've got a pulse and you're hot. You have to slow down and take your time to get a skittish horse to cross the creek. We both know you're the Glitter Girl, and for once, I agree with your choice. Your problem is that you always break out of the gate early and set the pace too fast."

"*What?*" Grace grabbed a drumstick and tried to fling it at Trip.

Clay, always a great wingman, snagged it from her hand and endorsed Trip's advice. "Nothing wrong with wanting forever, Gracie, but it's not a good idea to advertise the fact on the first few dates."

"So far you guys aren't being very helpful. I need useful advice not a list of what I'm doing wrong. You know her, Trip, what's the best approach?"

"Yeah, Fast Break, tell us more," Clay said, opening a couple more beers and passing one to Trip. "I'd like to get something besides a full stomach and a swim for my twenty dollars."

"Very funny." Trip washed down her potato salad and turned to Grace. "If you yank on the lead rope to force a horse to follow, he's either going to balk or his flight instinct will kick in and he'll drag you off your feet. So instead, you guide the horse to go where you want by teaching them to give to pressure. It's how a stallion moves a herd, or a boss mare leads it. Before you know it, she'll be following you around like a puppy."

"I thought we were talking about dating, not riding lessons." Clay shook her head. "Seriously, dude, how did you ever get a woman, much less bed half of Pine Cone with advice like that?"

"Dating, training horses, a lot of the same techniques apply. That's why I'm so good at both." Trip blew on her fingernails and brushed them against her shoulder.

"Okay, I get it, maybe," Grace said. "But you know I've got no game."

"Absolutely none." Trip had to agree. Grace was no player. Whether she admitted it or not, Grace went on every date unconsciously hoping this woman would be the one.

Clay draped her arm around Grace's shoulder. "The important thing is to just be yourself, Gracie. You're a people person who enjoys chatting and sharing time, and that's all it takes. Just let Dani see the real you. Let her know you're interested. She'll either come around or she won't. And if she doesn't, she's not worth your time anyway."

"Exactly," Trip said. Dani could be good for Grace. She was a good vet and the compassion Trip saw when Dani interacted with clients and their animals spoke volumes about her. Yep. Trip liked her.

"She practically bolted from the cottage the other night, like her butt was on fire."

"Your cottage?" Trip asked. Now Grace had been withholding information.

Clay rolled her hand, encouraging Grace to come clean.

She shook her head. "It wasn't like that. She's trying to figure out why Harry hates me, so I asked her to come by and check out my place. We had a couple of drinks, and…"

"What were you wearing?" Trip caught and held Grace's gaze.

"Perv," Clay said, nudging Trip with her foot before looking again at Grace. "Tell me it wasn't your Daisy Dukes."

Grace nodded.

Trip couldn't stop her howl of laughter. "You're killing me, Gracie."

Clay touched her beer bottle to Trip's. "Dani's a goner, but doesn't know it yet."

"And we almost kissed…or I almost kissed her. I'm not exactly sure who moved first. It just sort of happened, but it didn't. I felt like I'd accosted a teenager on her first date. All I saw were elbows and dust shooting up from her shoes all the way back to the house." Grace paused, her face flushing red. "Then she kissed me at the cookout." She gave Trip a shy glance. "I think she was jealous after she saw Jay crying on my shoulder."

"Yes." Trip pumped her fist in the air. "Then what'd you do?"

"Well, her kiss was a bit awkward. Sort of like 'There. I did it.'" Grace ducked her head and grinned. "Then I showed her how to really kiss."

Clay hooted, and Trip reached behind Grace to bump fists with Clay.

"Sounds to me like she's coming around," Trip said.

Grace frowned. "I don't know what to do next."

"Cook for her," Clay added, her stomach never far from any conversation.

"Screw her brains out at the first available opportunity," Trip said. "She can get good food at a dozen restaurants, but great sex—"

"You guys are worthless, totally worthless." Grace pulled up two handfuls of grass and tossed them simultaneously. "Let's talk about something else." She eyed Clay. "Like maybe Clay scoring with the gorgeous River Hemsworth?"

"Wait, what?" Trip looked at her.

"Nothing," Clay said.

"Come to think of it, why did you leave yesterday in such a hurry? You didn't even say good-bye. And you left River poolside looking kind of upset." Trip's attention was fully focused on Clay now.

"I don't want to talk about me. We're here for Grace, remember?"

"Too late," Grace chimed in.

"So? What happened yesterday?" Trip wanted to know that at least one of them was doing more than treading water.

"We had a misunderstanding," Clay said.

Trip gritted her teeth. Dragging information out of Clay was as hard as starting an IV on an iguana. "And?"

"We spent last night sorting it out." Clay's cheeks flushed red.

"All night?" The pitch of Grace's voice notched up.

"And this morning." Clay's smile was slow and dreamy.

"I knew it." Grace smiled too, the worry finally gone from her face. "I knew she was into you. That very first day under the maple tree, sitting on that stupid fake plastic deer. If you'd been ice cream, she'd have poured herself all over you like hot fudge."

"Yeah, well, it just took me a little longer to figure it out."

"Maybe you'll finally cheer up. I miss my pal, Clay." Trip playfully punched Clay's shoulder. Still, she knew this thing between Clay and River wasn't a done deal. The toothpick Clay chewed and rolled from one side of her mouth to the other told Trip that she was still worried. Would Clay return to New York with River? They picked at the grass, scratched a few mosquito bites, and peeled damp bottle labels, but nobody was ready to talk about that elephant sitting on the riverbank with them.

Clay rubbed her hands over her face. "Okay, okay...enough about me. We're here to help Grace, remember?"

"Talking with you two always helps." Grace smiled. "More chicken? And don't forget the potato salad."

Clay and Trip reached for second helpings of both, then settled back to eat. They ate in silence until Clay tossed her empty plate into a garbage bag and offered it to Trip.

Grace wrapped an arm around Clay and kissed her on the cheek, then looked at Trip. "And what about you, Fast Break?" Grace smoothly moved the spotlight away from Clay, who relaxed and lay back on her elbows. "Who's the next unsuspecting woman to fall victim to the Trip Beaumont charm?"

"Nobody, really." Trip shook her head. She'd been sure earlier that she wasn't ready to talk about Jamie, her biggest regret in life. Even eighteen years and lots of women since hadn't lessened the shame or changed the feeling there would always be a tear in her soul. But how did she explain it? She finally shrugged. "It's…complicated."

"Oh, do tell." Grace rubbed her hands together.

Trip peeled at the label on her beer bottle. Maybe this wasn't a good idea after all, but she'd already put it out there. "She's someone from my past, and she's not the forgiving type."

"Somebody you were in a relationship with and you cheated on her?" Grace stared at Trip and sipped her wine cooler. Her smile was slow as she swallowed. "No. You're too honorable to make a promise, then cheat." Grace tapped the bottle against her chin, her gaze wandering over the evening light playing in the swirls of the river. Her eyes snapped back to Trip. "Did you sleep with this person's girlfriend?"

Trip stared at her feet. "When they were together." She held back the most incriminating detail. Revealing that would be an invasion of Jamie's privacy.

Clay sat up. "Oh shit, dude, really?"

Grace's eyebrows shot up. "The girl from college?"

Trip studied her feet, digging her toes in the sand.

Clay frowned. "Did you run into her in Savannah?"

Trip shook her head. "Here. She's in Pine Cone."

Grace looked at Clay. "Who did we miss? The only new women in town are…let's see…Dani and River." Grace began to sputter as realization dawned across her face. "Jamie? My Jamie?"

No. My Jamie. Trip nodded to confirm it.

Clay shook her head. "I'm confused. Isn't she the one who's been sticking parking tickets on your truck like wallpaper?"

Trip smiled grimly. "She's always been Jamie Do-right."

"She's just doing her job, Trip. I've asked her to use more discretion, but she's military—by the book."

"I'd be happy to pay every single ticket if she'd just talk to me."

"We're a sorry bunch," Grace said.

Trip sighed. "Pathetic."

They were all silent for a few long moments, staring out at the river while they contemplated their woman issues. Then Grace threw her head back and laughed.

"You guys can sit down here and sulk if you want." She turned both her thumbs toward herself. "Glitter Girl is going after her woman." Grace pointed at them again. "And as soon as y'all are done with your little pity party, go home and put on your big girl pants, then go courting too."

Chapter Eleven

Trip looked up when Dani tapped on the open door to her office.

"They're in exam room three," Dani said.

"Thanks," Trip said, putting her pen down and rising from her chair. She'd been staring at breeding charts without digesting any of the information for the past thirty minutes. She wiped her sweaty hands on her jeans and stopped herself from combing her fingers through her short hair. She'd carefully styled it into a messy look and didn't want to un-mess it. She tried to seem casual, but Dani was a veterinarian. Since their patients couldn't talk, vets were trained to observe, and Trip was overly aware of Dani watching her. When she brushed past, Dani's hand on Trip's arm made her pause. Before she could speak, Dani reached around Trip and neatly slipped the white lab coat from the hook by the door.

"I'm told that a white coat with doctor on the name tag always impresses," Dani said, handing the coat to Trip.

Trip wanted to smile but could only manage a nod and a weak "thanks." Yep. Dani was a keeper.

Michelle stepped out of exam room three, pulled the door closed, then gasped for breath. "Oh my God," she said, her voice carrying down the hallway. "I should've put that one in a room with a window you could open."

Trip saw red. She'd had just about enough of Michelle's immaturity.

Dani jumped in. "Michelle, can you give me a hand with the Hollister beagle in the back?"

Trip stopped her. "Actually, Dani, I'd like you to see the Grant dog with me. Two heads will be better than one." Trip glared at Michelle. "I want you to wait in my office. We're going to have a little chat about your continued lack of professional decorum."

Michelle opened her mouth to say something, but checked herself and went directly to Trip's office. Dani wisely refrained from comment.

Trip sucked in a deep breath and opened the door to exam room three, Dani trailing silently behind her.

"Hey, Jamie."

Jamie looked up, her eyes questioning when they slid from Trip to Dani. A wheat-colored, wire-haired terrier mix sat on the exam table, watching them with wary eyes and pressing herself against Jamie's chest. "I thought we were seeing Dani this morning."

"Dani and I talked about what you told her Saturday and agreed that two brains would be better than one to try to figure out your pup's problem." Trip spoke in a soothing tone for Petunia's benefit, but hoped she could put Jamie at ease, too. "Will you introduce us?"

Jamie seemed to consider refusing Trip's input, but finally stroked the terrier's head and nodded. "This is Petunia." Jamie's face twisted in a grimace. "I just call her P. I'm thinking that some joker at the shelter named her that because of her gastric problems."

"Hello, P." Trip held out her hand for Petunia to sniff while Dani made notes in Petunia's chart. "Hey, girl. I understand you've got a bit of a bellyache." Petunia's lips curled into a silent snarl.

Jamie cleared her throat. "It'd probably help if you ditched the white coat. She was rescued from a research lab, and they probably wore lab coats."

"Sorry. You didn't tell me that," Dani said, shucking her coat and taking Trip's as well. "I'll toss these in my office."

"While you're doing that, will you send Michelle out back to help Jerome for the rest of the morning?" Trip kept her voice nonchalant so she didn't upset Petunia, but she was fuming inside. "Then call Jerome and let him know she needs to strip some stalls for him." Shoveling out the bottom layers of urine-soaked wood chips was the worst job in a stable.

Dani grinned. "Sure thing, Trip."

But Jamie frowned. "You don't have to do that for me. I'm used to people saying crap about P's gastric problem."

Trip looked up sharply. "Not in my clinic. Not about my sick clients." *Not about your dog.* She took a deep breath to settle her emotions and extended her hand to Petunia again. She got another lip curl.

"Stand down." Jamie's tone was so stern that Trip dropped her hand and stepped back, blinking in surprise. For the first time, Jamie's mouth twitched with the hint of a smile. "I was speaking to P, not you."

Trip felt her face heat. "I knew that." Damn. Why did she feel like she was back in college? She cleared her throat. "Look. I swear this isn't some kind of trick, but I need for her to relax with me so I can palpate her abdomen. If she's tense, I won't be able to tell as easily if I hit a sore spot."

"You want to sedate her?"

"No. That would also mask any pain reaction." Trip shifted and cleared her throat again. "I want you to hug me."

Jamie stared at her. "You want me to hug you." It wasn't a question.

"If she sees that you like me, then she hopefully will too." Trip slid her hands in the pockets of her jeans and out again, then shrugged. Jamie made her nervous. "Maybe you could pretend for a few minutes?"

Jamie looked down at Petunia, absently scratching behind her ears. "P, stay," she said softly. She rounded the table to where Trip stood, but hesitated when their eyes locked.

The moment she felt Jamie's stiff arms slide around her shoulders, Trip closed her eyes and tugged her close for a long heartfelt hug. Jamie smelled of soap. "You can't fool animals, Jamie. Relax, for Petunia's sake." Trip whispered into Jamie's ear. "I really do want to help."

Jamie's arms relaxed a bit, then a bit more, but Trip lamented the armored vest Jamie wore under her uniform shirt. Could Jamie feel her heart pounding? Could she feel Trip's arms around her? Ever hopeful, she gave Jamie a last squeeze when she heard Dani slip quietly into the room. Jamie's face was flushed when she stepped back, and Trip offered a soft smile. "Now, let's see if Petunia is buying it."

Petunia's dark eyes went from Jamie's face to Trip's, and she sniffed at Trip's scent on Jamie. Trip tucked the diaphragm end of her stethoscope inside her shirt to warm it against her breast and held out her hand to Petunia again. Petunia snuffled Trip's hand, then stood on the table to thoroughly examine Jamie's scent on her. Trip scratched behind Petunia's ears like Jamie had done, then knelt next to the table to put herself at eye level with the terrier, but not so close as to be in Petunia's personal space.

"So, P." Trip worked her scratching fingers around Petunia's neck to her chest, then her back. "Your mom and I go way back to when we were both baby dykes strutting around the college campus like we thought we were special. Actually, Jamie is sort of special."

Petunia thumped her tail against the metal table as if agreeing with what Trip had said, then her back foot when Trip scratched a particularly itchy spot along her spine.

"She upped my game on the basketball court so much, we both were being scouted to play pro." She kept up the running monologue while her scratching turned to a massage and she slowly stood. "But things happened and she ran off to join the army. I didn't even get to talk to her before she left, and I was really scared when I found out she was doing tours in Iraq." Trip finally chanced a look at Jamie, who was watching her with an unreadable expression.

Petunia sighed and rolled onto her back, releasing a long expel of flatulence as she relaxed into Trip's gentle massage of her belly. Trip continued, keeping her voice low and even, and Dani scribbled notes as Trip dictated. "Possible neuter scar along the belly crease, but since she came from a research lab, it could be from a different, more extensive surgery. Significant bloating, but flatulence odor is indicative of incomplete digestion rather than fetid bowel. Tenderness apparent in the upper quadrant upon palpation and a thickening of tissue which could indicate a number of things—intense inflammation, blockage, scarring from previous surgeries, intestinal cysts or tumors."

Trip pulled her stethoscope from her shirt, keeping up the massage with her other hand. "Jamie, can you stroke her lightly while

I do some listening?" Jamie trailed her fingers lightly along Petunia's chest while Trip listened to her bowel sounds, then along her belly while Trip listened to her heart and lungs. "Heart and lungs sound good, but her gut is definitely painful and producing a lot of gas." She held the stethoscope out to Dani and stepped to the side. "How about you take a listen—just in case you hear something I didn't."

Dani put her notes aside and rubbed her hands together to make sure they were sufficiently warm. Petunia's only reaction when Dani's hand replaced Trip's was to let out a long snore. She was a picture of relaxation. They waited in silence for Dani's verdict.

"Heart and lungs good," Dani confirmed. "And I concur on the tenderness." Petunia's hind foot twitched when Dani probed her upper belly.

Trip gently rolled Petunia onto her side when she began to sneeze from lying on her back. The terrier stood and shook herself, then looked to Jamie.

"So," Jamie said.

"I understand that Petunia has a history of bowel problems, but let's talk specifically about why you brought her in today," Trip said.

"She's been reluctant to eat lately. I've been feeding her prescription food that a specialist in New York prescribed, but she's either tired of it or doesn't feel like eating at all."

"Well, if her intestines are tender or she's feeling too bloated, that could discourage her appetite," Trip said. "Dani, let's draw some blood and get a panel on her."

"I brought stool and urine samples," Jamie said, pointing to a pair of plastic containers by the exam room's sink.

"That's great," Dani said, gathering what she needed from the cabinets over the sink counter.

"I know the drill. I've taken her to several vets, trying to fix this for her." Jamie's voice broke on her last words, and the muscle in her jaw worked while she watched Dani's quick, efficient technique.

Trip was no stranger to owners becoming emotional over their animals, but Jamie's distress choked her throat, too. She took up the chart Dani had started and asked some questions to steady herself and distract Jamie. "So, can you give me some background on Petunia? You rescued her from a research lab?"

Jamie shook her head. "I got her from a kill shelter. They said she'd originally come from a research lab. The people who left her there said their son had adopted P from the SPCA after the lab gave in to public pressure to stop animal testing. Then he dumped her on them when he decided to travel overseas after graduating college."

"If we could track down the type of research they were doing, it might give us some clues about her problem," Dani said as she finished drawing the blood.

"The shelter asked, but the couple didn't know and their son was hiking overseas and unreachable. I asked if I could talk to the people who turned her in, but the shelter said they'd give the people my request, but the people never called."

"What was the name of the shelter?" Trip asked. "I'd like to talk to the vet they use to see if they can give me any better history on her."

Surprise showed in Jamie's eyes, then a glimmer of hope. "Nobody, none of the vets we've seen, ever asked me that before."

Dani patted Jamie's shoulder. "I promise that Trip and I will leave no stone unturned. Trust us."

Jamie looked down at Petunia, her throat working. When she looked up, her eyes searched Trip's, not Dani's, and the swirl of uncertainty in them cut Trip like a scalpel.

Dani held up the specimens. "I'm going to get these off to the lab."

"Thanks," Trip said. She turned back to Jamie when the door clicked shut behind Dani. "I'll do everything in my power to help P, Jamie. But you have to let me do everything I feel is necessary. I want to fly her up to Athens for an MRI at the veterinary school and consult with one of my old professors."

Jamie hesitated, and Trip wondered if it was the expense that worried her.

"I have a friend with a plane, and he owes me several favors. I'll call him and the vet school to see what I can coordinate." She shoved Petunia's medical file across the table and held out her pen. "If you'll write your cell number down, I'll call and let you know when so you can check with Grace about covering your shift."

"I can go with her?"

Trip chuckled. "I think it would be best, considering her dislike for lab coats. There'll be a lot of them at the vet school."

Finally, a slow smile spread across Jamie's face. She was a handsome woman, but when she smiled, she was so beautiful Trip's heart skipped a beat...or two. "Does that mean I'm going to have to hug a lot more veterinarians?"

Trip shook her head. She wanted all Jamie's hugs reserved for her. "I'll let them know ahead of time to ditch the lab coats."

Jamie scribbled down her number. "How soon should I expect to hear from you?"

"Write down the name of the shelter and the dates of when Petunia was there, as well as you can remember." Trip tapped the file to indicate where. "By the end of the week," she said in answer to Jamie's question. "Sooner if I can arrange it."

Jamie scribbled down the information, then lifted Petunia to the floor. The scruffy little dog sat obediently at Jamie's heel. "Okay." She reached for her wallet as she turned to go.

Trip called after her. "Oh, and don't worry about the bill. Since she works for the sheriff's department, they'll cover her medical costs."

"But she doesn't belong to the county. P belongs to me. I'll pay her bills."

Trip nodded but smiled. "Grace said between my parking fines and the federal kickback they get from your drug busts, the county is flush with money."

Jamie shook her head, but Saturday's anger was gone from her eyes and a quick grin revealed the dimples Trip remembered from college. "Then I'll be sure and leave more tickets on your truck. I wouldn't want the county to run short of funds."

"Police profiling, I tell you." Trip smiled back at Jamie but pointed at the door. "Out. Back to patrol. I'll call you."

Jamie gave her a dismissing wave and stepped into the hall. Petunia followed, but paused in the doorway. She tensed and grunted, then sighed audibly after squeezing out a loud burst of flatulence, and then trotted to catch up with Jamie.

"Thanks for that, pup." Trip sniffed cautiously. Her best guess was poorly digested food and a hint of blood. She wouldn't let herself contemplate the possibility of cancer, because her heart was soaring. Jamie had smiled at her. A true smile, not forced or sarcastic. She strolled the opposite way down the hallway, glad that Michelle was shoveling crap in the stables rather than waiting in her office. Trip had phone calls and arrangements to make. And Jamie's smile to fill her daydreams.

The elation of Jamie's smile was dampened by a frustrating morning of phone calls. The only person she could catch in his office was Joe, her client with the plane. She bartered flying time in his plane in exchange for vetting his wife's hunter-jumpers. He was pretty open the rest of the week, but she needed to know when the vet school could fit Petunia in their clinic schedule. She left a message and her cell number for her former professor who mentored her. He had the clout to squeeze her in their MRI schedule. A call to the shelter where Jamie found Petunia produced the name of the vet clinic they used, but it was a big, busy practice and their doctors serviced the shelter on a rotating basis. The office manager said she'd research the dates to see if she could tell which doctor might have seen Petunia, but the constant ringing of phones and interruptions while she was trying to talk to the woman left Trip less than optimistic that she'd actually remember to do it.

Doubt began to eat at her. If multiple vets and a few specialists hadn't been able to help Petunia, why did she think that she could? She was an equine specialist and tended to refer any complicated small animal cases to a veterinary hospital in Savannah. Was she destined to screw up with Jamie again?

Jamie said none of the other vets had delved into Petunia's history. Maybe there were other possibilities they neglected to investigate. One step at a time. She stood and tucked her cell phone into the back pocket of her jeans. Right now, she had a few farm calls to make.

Trip stepped out to the front desk to let Brenda know she would be out doing calls the rest of the afternoon. But her receptionist wasn't behind the desk. She was standing in the waiting room, where only one client—Mrs. Townsend holding a cat carrier in her lap—was still waiting to see Dani. The room had been full by midmorning. Yep, Dani was a great hire. She'd reorganized the clinic and its staff for maximum efficiency. Trip had never been able to give the clinic her full attention because she was out on farm calls three or four afternoons a week.

"Hey, Brenda. I'm on my way out for the rest of the afternoon."

"Dr. Beaumont. Can you give me just a minute of your time before you take off?" Brenda was pure Southern country girl, but she was unfailingly professional. She never called Trip anything but Dr. Beaumont in front of clients, was a genius at juggling appointment requests, and kept meticulous records. She wouldn't give up her tobacco habit, but used a variety of tastefully scented waxes or aromatic oils in the ceramic warmer on her desk to cover the cigarette odor.

"Sure. What's the problem? Do we need to go in my office?" Trip offered Mrs. Townsend and her cat, Muffin, a nod and a smile to acknowledge them, but Mrs. Townsend looked to Brenda for a response.

"Thank you, but no. The problem is out here." Brenda pointed to the dusty oil painting of dogs sitting around a poker table, and Mrs. Townsend backed her up with a vigorous nod.

"I don't understand."

Brenda tucked her chin to look over her reading glasses at Trip. "We've painted the walls, trim, and ceiling in this room, and changed out those old hard church benches you liked so much for some comfortable, updated chairs."

Mrs. Townsend smoothed her hand over the pleather seat of the chair next to her. "They're so nice."

Brenda swept her hand downward to direct Trip's attention to the floor. "This vinyl plank flooring is as easy to clean up as it is beautiful."

"Beautiful," Mrs. Townsend said. A yowl from Muffin confirmed that she liked it, too.

"Your point?" Trip wasn't following. What did all this have to do with her dog art?

Both women turned pointed stares at Trip.

"That painting needs to go," Brenda said. "We need some real art to jazz up the walls. I'll be happy to hang dogs playing poker in your office so you can look at it as much as you want."

Trip had found this treasure at a very reputable flea market, but Brenda's expression brooked no argument. She looked to Mrs. Townsend for support.

"Needs to go," Mrs. Townsend said.

"Okay, you can move it to my office. But you'll have to find some reasonably priced art to replace it out here."

Brenda put a hand up. "Not a problem. I hear that Ellen Gardner's niece is selling everything in her gallery before she goes back to New York City."

"Good idea. I'll ask River if she can drop by to get a look at our wall space and color scheme, then she can pick out some pictures for us from the stock in the gallery."

Brenda patted Trip on the arm, then rounded the front counter at the sound of toenails scrabbling along the floor to take payment from the man being pulled toward the exit by a fat Labrador retriever. "Cindy will be out to take you and Muffin back as soon as she wipes down the exam room," she said to Mrs. Townsend.

"Thank you, dear," Mrs. Townsend said. "But there's no rush. We're quite comfortable in these new chairs."

Trip turned to go out the rear of the clinic, then stopped when a new idea bloomed in her head. She walked to the front of the counter and picked up the nameplate that stated "Receptionist," and tucked it behind the counter. "Order a new sign with your name on it and office manager underneath. Your promotion is effective immediately. We'll negotiate your raise tomorrow."

Brenda's eyebrows shot up. "Why, thank you, Dr. Beaumont. Frankly, I thought you might fire me for wanting to get rid of your dog picture."

"Nope. You're right. I'll get some fresh stuff to go out here." Trip smiled. "And, Brenda, your first task as office manager is to tell Michelle, when she returns from the stable, that I want the aquarium in the waiting room cleaned." She usually paid the local pet shop to come out and clean it, but she wanted Michelle to think long and hard before she maligned one of her patients when the owner or any other client could hear. "But tell her to do it after clinic hours."

Brenda raised a questioning eyebrow at the request.

"Then sometime tomorrow when you have time, could you review our professional standards with her? You can use my office."

Brenda's eyes narrowed as realization clicked in. "I'll be more than happy to do that, Dr. Beaumont."

Trip smiled. Brenda didn't care much for Michelle's flirting with clients and staff, and had made no secret she felt Michelle lacked any sense of decorum. Trip patted herself on the back. Michelle problem solved. Brenda would whip her into shape or badger her so much that Michelle would voluntarily seek other employment. Truthfully, Trip hoped Brenda could bring her in line, or else Michelle would have the same problem at her next job.

Trip was checking the supplies in her truck when Dani called to her from the clinic's back door.

"Hey. If you talk to Jamie, ask her if she can remember the other doctors who've examined Petunia. If we can get them to fax their files on her, reviewing them might turn up something."

"Excellent idea," Trip said. "I'll call her when I get in the truck." Damn, she should have thought of that. Instead, she was busy thinking about how good Jamie smelled. Well, at least she was smart enough to have Dani back her up on the case.

Trip started up the big diesel engine and headed down the drive to the highway. "Call Jamie," she commanded when the truck signaled it had synched with her phone.

Jamie answered on the second ring. "Jamie Grant."

"Hey, it's Trip."

"That was quick."

"I've got the plane on standby, but I'm waiting for callbacks from the shelter and the vet school. I was actually calling about something else."

"Okay." Jamie sounded wary.

"Do you have any records from the specialists who've examined Petunia?"

"Only billing receipts."

"Good enough. All I really need are their names, and the dates on the receipts would be helpful. We can call and request that they fax or email any records they have."

"Most of my stuff is in storage. I'm staying at the B and B until I find a house."

"Storage here?"

"That new one next to the truck stop."

"Can you meet me there around six? I should be done with farm calls by then."

"My shift ends at seven."

"How about seven thirty?"

"Okay. P and I will see you then."

Trip tapped a happy tune on the steering wheel. She was going to see Jamie again—twice in one day. She turned east toward Roy Horton's farm. His favorite mare dropped a new foal last night and, though the birth appeared to go fine, she needed to check mother and baby over to make sure there were no hidden problems.

She opened the iTunes app on her phone, selected her favorite playlist, and sang along with Jewel as the music flowed from the truck's speakers. She had the highway to herself, except for a motorcycle approaching from the opposite direction. As it drew closer, she realized it was Clay and they waved at each other as they passed.

Her thoughts turned to Clay and River. She was happy for her, but anxious that Clay might move back to New York and bust up their trio again. Maybe River had some of Clay's art for sale at the gallery. Wait. Clay had tried before to give Trip the paintings she had at her studio. Trip had a key to the place, and she was going to go right past there on the way to the Horton farm. She'd stop on the way back and pick them up. Then if Clay left, she would have something to remind her of Clay every time she went into the clinic. Trip could drop by the garage later to let Clay know she had them.

Chapter Twelve

C an I help you with something?"
Jamie was heading for the door to the garage's office,
but diverted when Clay called to her from the open bay. She'd seen
Clay at the Clip 'n Curl and at the cookout, but they'd never been
introduced. She offered her hand. "Jamie Grant. Sergeant Booker said
I should bring the car in for an oil change."

"Clay Cahill." She shook Jamie's hand.

Clay was pleasant enough, but seemed a bit edgy about
something, which always made Jamie suspicious. Petunia was doing
her pee-pee dance in the back seat, so Jamie scanned the area. Nothing
but concrete. The weeds on the edge of the pavement would have to
do. "Say, do you mind if I let my dog out for a minute? She needs to
use the weeds over there."

"Go ahead. There's nothing she can hurt around here, as long as
she doesn't go toward the road."

"She won't." Jamie pointed to the clump of weeds and signaled
"release."

Petunia ran to the weeds, gave them a sniff, then turned to give
them a long watering. Clay reached down and patted Petunia when
she bounded back to them. Petunia sat next to Clay's feet and wagged
her tail. She seemed to like Clay.

"Pull the car into the second bay and center it over that lift." Clay
knelt beside Petunia sinking her fingers into her wiry fur while Jamie
maneuvered the cruiser into the garage.

"I sent the guys to lunch after I got back, but one of them should be back any minute to change that oil. It won't take long," Clay said when Jamie emerged from the bay. "I'll go get the paperwork for you to sign."

Clay returned almost immediately with a steel clipboard. Jamie scanned the form and was signing at the bottom when Petunia began to bark from somewhere in the garage.

Jamie peered into the garage, but she couldn't see her. "P only barks if she's found something." She frowned. It was unusual for Petunia to wander off. The scent she had followed must have been strong.

"You mean like a mouse?" Clay took the paperwork back from Jamie.

Seriously? "No, usually something else." Was Clay that clueless or was she pretending she didn't know Petunia was a drug detection dog? Jamie headed inside to find Petunia, mindful of Clay following close behind.

Petunia was in a room with orderly shelves of car parts, tools, filters, hoses, and cans of oil. Clay switched on the overhead light and Petunia wagged her tail, then turned back to alert on an old metal toolbox that was tucked under a shelf and half hidden behind a large metal bucket.

"Does this toolbox belong to you?" Jamie asked.

"It's my grandfather's garage," Clay said. "All the tools, just about everything belongs to the business."

"Then I have your permission to open it?"

Clay seemed puzzled as she stared at the box. "Go ahead."

Jamie drew a pair of latex gloves from her pocket and donned them before moving the bucket and dragging the box out in the open. She used a flathead screwdriver from a nearby workbench to release the latch and open the lid. Once the lid was open, Petunia sat back and panted cheerfully. Inside the box were small clear bags of pills.

Clay leaned in for a closer look. "What the hell?"

"Prescription drugs." Jamie poked around the toolbox, moving some of the bags aside to look underneath. "Looks like codeine, fentanyl, oxycodone, and probably hydrocodone."

"Fucking hell."

"Good girl, P." Jamie gave her a good ear scratch, then peered up at Clay. Her anger seemed genuine. "All of these are highly addictive opioids."

"Well, they don't belong to me, or my grandpa, or Eddie…but I have a pretty good idea who put them there."

"Best not to assume anything until we dust this for prints." Jamie walked back to the squad car with Clay at her heels. "I'm going to call this in."

Jamie radioed Grace while Clay paced.

Trip swung into Cahill's Garage and stared. Jamie stared back from where she stood next to her patrol car and a grim-faced Clay. A million scenarios ran through Trip's brain as Clay approached. "What's going on?" Trip directed the question to Clay but couldn't take her eyes off Jamie.

"Jamie's dog found a toolbox full of prescription drugs in the storage room."

"No shit." No way it could be Clay's. Trip knew Clay was pretty straightlaced when it came to drugs.

"Yeah, no shit." Clay crossed her arms and glared at the large, dark opening of the bay door. "She's reporting it to Grace."

"Oh." Well, that would be good. Grace wouldn't go off half-cocked and arrest Clay or her grandfather. And to Jamie's credit, she hadn't handcuffed Clay.

"What's up with you and Jamie?" Clay peered at her suspiciously.

"Nothing…yet." Trip had already forgotten that she'd confessed her feelings for Jamie to Clay and Grace. Clay, however, wasn't apparently interested in any details. Trip watched her pace back and forth. "What's up with you? You're as tense as a rat in a room full of cats. Trip's joke drew a fierce glare rather than a chuckle.

"You mean besides finding a bunch of prescription drugs in the garage?" Clay opened her mouth as though to say more, but snapped her jaw shut when Bo's truck slowed and turned in. Clay took off toward him before the truck could come to a stop. "Hey, I need to talk to you."

Bo's eyes went from Clay to where Jamie stood, and he threw the truck in reverse. His truck roared back, barely missing one of the gas pumps, and then spun gravel as his giant off-road tires bounced back onto the paved road and peeled out.

"Asshole!" Clay turned back to Jamie. "I know those drugs belong to him."

"Who's he?" Jamie asked.

"Bo Mathis. He works here…barely."

Okay, there was way too much going on here. She didn't want to get in Jamie's way. "Listen, I just popped by to tell you I picked up the paintings."

"What did you say?" Clay turned slowly, her face an unreadable mix of emotions.

Trip shifted uneasily, squirming under the intensity of Clay's unexpected reaction. "The ones you told me a few weeks ago that I could hang in the clinic. I was out that way, so stopped by and got them."

"You…what?"

Weird. Clay was acting like Trip was speaking a different language.

"Brenda said she's tired of looking at my poker-playing dogs. I tried to call you, but I think your phone is off, or dead."

"I am such an asshole." Clay covered her face with her hands.

Whew. Trip had thought she'd done something wrong, considering the look on Clay's face. She gave Clay a friendly shoulder bump. "I knew that already. But seriously, buddy, what is going on with you?"

"I'll explain, but first I need to make a quick call."

Jamie and Petunia disappeared into one of the service bays, so Trip sauntered after them to get a drink, then sat on the chest-style antique soda dispenser. She was fascinated as she watched Jamie direct Petunia's search of the cabinets on the other side of the double bay. They were concluding their search when Grace pulled into the parking lot.

Grace got out of her squad car and strode purposefully over to Jamie. Trip loved watching Grace in focused "cop mode." When Jamie gestured to Clay, Grace's sharp gaze paused only a split second on Trip before going to Clay.

Clay, wild-eyed, whirled toward Grace, who was instantly at her side. Trip edged closer to them, but without getting in the way.

"What is it?" Grace asked.

"Bo, why are you answering River's phone?" Clay's fingers were white as she clutched the phone, but she held it out a little so Grace could listen. Trip easily identified Bo's high-pitched, nasal voice, but the only words she could hear clearly were Clay's curt responses.

"Bo, if you hurt one hair on her head I swear—"

Grace touched Clay's arm, shaking her head.

"Where? Where are you?" Clay's question was more of a demand.

More mumbled words from Bo.

"I'll bring your shit. It's not like I want it here at the garage anyway. But you better not hurt River. ...Bo—"

Clay lowered the phone and cursed at the apparent disconnection.

"Where is he?" Grace asked.

"He's got River. He wants me to bring the drugs and meet him at the old mill to trade for River." Clay stomped around. "Damn it all to hell." She stopped and looked at Grace. "I'm going."

"No, you're not." Grace was firm.

"He said for me to come by myself." Clay squared off in front of Grace. "He specifically told me not to bring you. So I'm going."

Grace wasn't buying it. "You're staying here with Jamie." She looked at Jamie. "Call dispatch and tell them we have an active hostage situation and drugs are involved. Who knows if Bo is under the influence of something right now."

Clay swept her fingers through her hair. "God, I'm such an idiot."

Trip felt for her. "Leave it with Grace, pal."

"But he'll see her and do something stupid. He said no cops."

"Clay, I've got this." Grace's voice was steady. "He's not going to hurt River." She strode toward her patrol car, but Clay followed.

"Aren't you going to wait for backup? Isn't that how this works?"

For a second, Trip thought she would have to grab Clay to keep her from jumping in the car with Grace.

"I can handle one redneck," Grace said, then whipped the cruiser around and onto the street.

Clay stared after the cruiser for a few seconds, then she held out her hand to Trip. "Give me your keys."

Trip shook her head and backed away from Clay. "No way. You can't just go charging in there." Even as she said the words, she glanced over at Jamie. How would she feel if Jamie was the one at risk? Would she be able to sit back and trust Jamie's safety to someone else, even a best friend?

"Give me your damn keys," Clay said. "I'm not gonna let Grace go in there by herself, and I'm not taking any chance of losing River. Not now, not ever."

Trip could see the desperation and determination in her eyes. Clay's outstretched hand hovered in the air between them. If she refused, Clay would probably hop on her motorcycle and kill herself trying to catch up to them.

"I'm driving," Trip said as she headed for her truck.

"Hey, where are you going?" Jamie half stood in the door of the squad car, the radio mic in her hand, but Trip waved her off. No time to explain.

When they reached Mill Road, Trip took a hard right. She could see a faint trail of dust about a quarter-mile ahead and stepped on the gas. They hadn't gone far before they saw Grace's cruiser stopped ahead, lights still flashing and the driver's door open. Trip stomped her brake pedal, and her double rear wheels kicked up a thick cloud of sand and dust that blew forward to envelop them. Clay jumped out before the truck came to a full halt.

"Clay, wait." Trip cursed, then offered up a prayer of thanks to any gods who might listen when a figure emerged from the dusty haze.

River, barefoot and soaked to the skin, was walking toward them. Clay ran forward and swept River up in her arms, lifting her feet off the ground.

Trip wanted to laugh in hysterical relief, her thoughts running in a stupid loop. *What if that were Jamie? What if that were Jamie in danger? Jamie targets big time drug dealers, not small fish like Bo. What if that were Jamie?* The thoughts roiled her stomach.

Even though it wasn't Jamie, Trip had to do something. She got the light blanket she kept in her truck and walked over to drape it over River's shoulders. River was shivering—shock, Trip knew, rather than cold.

"Thanks, pal," Clay said, tugging the blanket tightly around River to draw her close. She kissed River on the forehead and stroked her back.

Trip kept walking, partly to check on Grace, but mostly to give Clay and River some privacy as they clung together and said things that should only be between them. A kernel of loneliness swelled in Trip's chest with each step. Would she and Jamie ever mend fences enough so Trip could hold her like Clay held River? Trip had to try.

Jamie was standing guard while two people wearing dark vests with many pockets and FORENSICS lettered in yellow across the back took photos and collected evidence in the garage.

Trip didn't recognize them as local, but she didn't really care. She was focused on Jamie, who stood with one hand resting on the butt of her service weapon and the other on her utility belt. Heat rose up Trip's chest and neck, and her belly tightened. Damn, she was sexy in uniform.

"How's River?" Jamie asked.

"Fine. Justice prevails again." Trip smiled and squatted to give Petunia an ear scratch. "Grace has Bo in custody and is headed to jail." But Grace had probably already reported that on the radio. "The only casualty was Clay's truck. I just dropped her and River—unharmed except for maybe a few bruises—off at my place so they could borrow my Jeep."

Jamie glanced into the garage. "P and I went over the entire garage and found another stash, marijuana in a sealed metal barrel out back."

Trip stood again and shoved her hands into the pockets of her jeans. "Are you free for dinner tonight?"

Jamie stared at Trip. "Why would I want to have dinner with you?"

· Trip gentled her voice. "Because we once meant something to each other. Because we were very good friends before."

Jamie's lip twitched. "The key word here is 'were.'"

"Because we can talk about Petunia after we get those records from your storage and maybe you'll remember something that could give Dani and me a clue to the root of her problem."

"She still won't eat very much." Jamie tugged a folded paper from her back pocket. "I already went by and got the information you wanted. I'm going to be late getting off. I have to wait for the state crime lab people to finish, then take Mr. Cahill to the station so he can give a statement. Then I still have my afternoon patrol to make before I can fill out multiple reports concerning this drug bust. You can just text me when you have the trip to the vet school arranged."

"Meet me for lunch tomorrow, then."

"I don't think so," Jamie said, backing away when one of the crime techs called to her from inside the garage. "I have to go. We can talk about P while we're flying up to Athens."

Chapter Thirteen

A-hunting we will go, a-hunting we will go." Pete hopped from foot to foot in a weird combination of river dancing and clogging.

"What are you going to hunt?" Jamie wanted to know if they had guns, even though she couldn't confiscate them. There were no gun regulations to stop Pete from owning a gun just because he was mentally unstable. He'd have to prove himself a danger or threaten someone first. By then, it was usually too late for the victim.

"Cats," Pete said, grinning. "Big cats, little cats. Cats with balls and tomorrow's mothers. Not the ones with purple ears. Purple ear, steer clear."

"What he's failing to properly explain, Deputy, is that we get paid for humanely trapping feral cats and turning them in to be neutered and vaccinated. The ones with a purple star tattooed in their ear indicate they've already been trapped and processed."

"That's great, Toby." Jamie shaded her eyes from the sun as she watched Pete hop around. "So, someone has shown you how to trap without hurting them?"

"I know what you're thinking," he said. "Pete is admittedly a bit...well, my old grandmother would say tetched in the head. But he's amazing with the cats. He feeds two colonies of ferals, so they know him and the young ones will let him pet them. Others, we trap with cages."

"Someone helps you do this?"

"Yep. Jerome sets out the traps and we check and bait them every day, sometimes more often this time of year. Lots of new kittens are born each spring, and ready for neutering by now. I let the doc know when we have a handful to pick up. Then Jerome brings the kitties back after they're fixed and tattooed, and Pete and I release them back to the colony they came from. We get twenty dollars a cat."

"Sounds like a good deal."

"It is. Gives us some grocery money, and the doc gives us bags of food for them, too." The old man peered at Jamie. "I know that folks think homeless folk steal and beg to get food, but I'm not big on taking charity. Pete and I have odd jobs we do for a lot of different people around town. That's why you find us here at the old rail depot every morning. People know we'll be here if someone wants to hire us."

Jamie nodded, scanning the area while she listened. "Where's Adder today?"

Toby shook his head. "He's not doing so great. When the war gets too loud in his head, he runs a path along the river's edge. He's been running a lot and smoking a bit more than usual these past couple of days. He has rough patches. He'll be okay."

"You still have my number, right? In case you guys need help, or you see Adder getting too down?"

"Sure, sure. You'll be the first we call." Toby nodded, pulling a prepaid phone from his pocket and showing it to her. "We'll be fine."

"Okay, then." Jamie waved to Pete, who waved back. "See you guys around."

Trip jumped when the phone in her pocket vibrated to indicate an incoming call. Too bad the phone wouldn't vibrate long enough for her to hold it against her crotch. Jamie had filled her thoughts since she'd left Cahill's, and Trip's libido was primed for action. The call, however, wasn't from Jamie. The area code that popped up on her truck's Sync screen indicated an Athens area code. Trip tapped "accept" on the touch screen. "Hello."

"Dr. Beaumont, what a pleasant surprise to get your message."

"Professor Harrell, thanks for returning my call."

"I'm always happy to speak with one of my best students."

"I'm sure you've had many good students, but I can really use your assistance on a case."

"How can I help?"

Trip outlined Petunia's gastric problems and the meager progress she'd made in tracking down the research study in which Petunia had been a test subject.

"I can clear some time for you tomorrow, but I'm headed out of the country Friday and will be gone two weeks."

"We'll see you tomorrow then. I really appreciate this, Professor. This dog is a highly effective drug and explosives detection dog, and its owner is special to me."

"Then it's imperative that we do everything we can for the pup."

"I'll call when we touch down tomorrow morning to let you know we're on our way to the vet school. It should be around nine o'clock."

After the call disconnected, Trip fist-pumped. "YES!" She summoned her truck's voice controls with a "Hey, hot stuff."

"Say your command," the disembodied voice responded.

"Call Joe."

Joe answered on the second ring. "Hey, Trip. Do you have a departure day?"

"I know this is last minute, but I need to fly to Athens tomorrow. We'll probably be up there all day."

"Damn. I need to take Alice to a doctor's appointment at ten in the morning."

"Do you have other flights scheduled later in the day?"

"Uh, no. I cleared the day. Alice didn't want to tell anyone before tomorrow's ultrasound confirms everything is okay, but I'm about to bust with the news. We're pregnant."

"That's fantastic, Joe." Trip was truly happy for him. The couple had been trying for years, and Alice had already suffered through two early miscarriages.

"Yeah. I thought I'd surprise her afterward by taking her to Savannah for lunch and an afternoon of shopping for baby stuff."

"I'll make other arrangements. Alice deserves your full attention."

"Hold on." The faint clicking of a keyboard came over the truck's speakers. "Let me check one thing. ...Yes. Weather report says clear skies tomorrow. Why don't you just fly my plane?"

"Are you sure?"

"Absolutely. I know we haven't instrument certified you yet, but that shouldn't be an issue as long as you get back before dark. I'll leave the keys to the Cessna at the airport office for you."

"You're the best, Joe. Thanks, and good luck tomorrow. You hoping for a girl or a boy?"

"Just hoping for a healthy baby," he said.

Trip's next call was to Grace.

"Booker."

Trip laughed, her mood light with the prospect of spending the next day with Jamie. "You really should answer with your entire name because when you bark 'Booker,' it almost sounds like 'Booger.'"

Grace chuckled. "Only you would think something like that. You sound happy today."

"The fate of my exuberance is in your hands."

"Not literally, I hope. I think I've heard you use that line on Shayla before."

Trip loved Grace's sharp wit. "No. But I do have a favor to ask."

"How may I serve you?"

"It's hard to pass on a setup like that, but this is serious. Can you clear Jamie's schedule tomorrow?"

There was a second of hesitation. "You know I love you, pal, but I can't shuffle the work assignments just so you can woo one of my officers."

"This is concerning the health of one of your officers. I want her and Petunia to fly with me to Athens for a consult and MRI at the vet school."

"You should've led with that. I'll absolutely clear her schedule, even if I have to cover for her myself."

"Great. I'll call and give her the details."

"Tell her to swing by the department before six thirty. I'll give her a department credit card to take care of the expenses. The forfeiture funds we'll get from the feds for that big drug bust she and Petunia pulled off will more than cover Petunia's medical bills."

"Great. I'll do what I can to get you a break on the cost."

CHAPTER FOURTEEN

Jamie lifted Petunia down from the truck and looked up to see Trip emerge from an industrial metal building next to a three-story structure she figured was the control tower. Three County Airport was bigger than she'd expected. A few dozen small planes and several small jets lined up next to two huge hangers.

"Ready to fly?" Trip asked.

Jamie squinted behind her dark aviator sunglasses. She'd just changed to second shift and climbed in bed at one thirty only to rise four hours later. Her eyes rebelled at too little sleep and the bright, cloudless day. "Sure. Which plane is ours?"

"Joe had them taxi out his best plane for us. That sweet Cessna 400." Trip pointed at a sleek, low wing aircraft. "It should get us to the Athens airport in about an hour, including pre-flight and landing time." She hopped up onto the wing extending from the passenger side, opened the door, and folded over the front seat to give access to the rear two seats. "Hand Petunia to me while you hop up here."

Jamie shifted her hand to Petunia's hindquarters when she yelped at a hand under her stomach. "Sorry, girl." Jamie lifted her into Trip's waiting hands. "She's getting really tender in her abdomen." That tenderness had increased over the past few days, so Jamie was relieved that Trip had been able to arrange the excursion to the vet school so quickly.

"No problem." Trip expertly held Petunia against her side with one arm and extended her hand.

Jamie ignored it and leapt onto the wing and stuck her head in the plane to check it out. She'd ridden in some armored military vehicles that had even less space for passengers, and those vehicles certainly didn't have plush leather seats like this plane. A thick dog bed was in the seat behind the pilot's seat, with a harness attached to the seat belt. "This is great." She climbed in and held out her hands for Petunia.

"When Joe is transporting packages rather than passengers, he takes his dog with him. I told him we were on a veterinary mission, so he had the guys put Muddy's flying setup in for Petunia. They're about the same size so the harness should fit."

Petunia turned one circle after Jamie secured the harness and curled up in the bed, wagging her tail and expelling several tiny farts. Jamie started to settle into the seat next to her, but Trip waved her out of the plane. "What?"

Trip unfolded the front seat. "You sit here. You'll still be able to see each other."

Jamie peered at Trip. "Where are you going to sit?"

Trip pointed to the other front seat.

"That's the pilot's seat."

Trip pointed to her own chest. "Pilot."

"Seriously?" Jamie had no idea why that stupidly thrilled her.

"Yep. I've had my license for nearly ten years. Joe is a certified instructor and traded out veterinary services for lessons."

Jamie climbed into the plane and watched Trip walk around the plane and mark things down on a clipboard she'd pulled from the messenger bag slung over her shoulder, before joining them in the cockpit. Jamie was so mesmerized by Trip's methodical instrument check and conversation with the tower, that they were speeding down the runway before she had time to mentally prepare herself for the liftoff. It felt more like soaring than the disembodied elevator feeling of a large plane. Smooth. She liked it. What would it cost for her to take flying lessons?

"Okay. Keep your eyes peeled for other aircraft. We don't want to collide with anyone."

"What?" Jamie frantically scanned the horizon. What if she missed something?

"Just kidding."

Jamie stared out the window. "Always the jokester." She turned her head, in case she lost her hold on the smile that threatened. Fooling each other with little tricks had been a game they played constantly in college. It would be so easy to forget everything that had happened and fall back into the easy connection they'd had before. Before that night. Trip seemed to sense Jamie's mood shift. Silence stretched between them.

After a while, Trip spoke as softly as possible to be heard over the hum of the engine. "We'll figure this out, Jamie."

Jamie looked over at her. She wasn't sure she understood Trip's meaning.

"Petunia. We'll figure out what's wrong with her, and if it's medically possible, fix it."

Jamie nodded…because the possibility of losing Petunia choked off any words she would have said.

Trip slipped her fingers around Jamie's forearm and squeezed slightly. "I want us to figure out the rest, too."

Jamie didn't reply or nod this time. She turned her face away instead and stared out the window. Could she let go of the grudge she'd guarded all these years?

"Good afternoon. We have a special case this morning." Professor Harrell gestured to Trip, Jamie, and Petunia standing behind him. "Accompanying me today is Dr. Beaumont, one of my most outstanding former students who made a name for herself as a veterinary surgeon in Atlanta before returning to her roots and opening a mixed practice in South Georgia. With her is Deputy Jamie Grant and her detection dog, Petunia."

The control room of the magnetic resonance imaging machine was crowded with five senior students, the three of them, and Petunia. Still, Trip was filled with nostalgic memories of the time she spent absorbing everything Professor Harrell could teach her.

The professor lowered his chin to glare over his reading glasses at a late arrival who shuffled to the rear of the group. "Mr. Adcock, your emailed instructions were specific—no lab coats. Should I have sent a note to your mother instead?"

"Sorry, Dr. Harrell." The young man shed the offending coat, bunched it up, and tossed it into the hallway. Trip wanted to laugh. She'd forgotten how intimidating the faculty could be until you were at least third year.

Professor Harrell shook his head but continued. "Since this is Dr. Beaumont's case, I'll let her present the symptoms and test results to date." He stepped back so Trip could address the group.

"Our subject's background is sketchy. When Deputy Grant obtained her from a local kill shelter, she was told that Petunia had once been part of an unknown medical research project, then lived with a college student for a year or two before being turned into the shelter by the student's parents. The shelter was advised that she had a history of gastroenteritis that classified her as having special needs. The shelter staff also documented symptoms of alternating constipation and diarrhea, and extensive flatulence."

Petunia demonstrated said flatulence as though adding an exclamation point to Trip's recitation.

"Good grief," one male student muttered as the sharp odor of intestinal gas filled the room.

"Mr. Tillman, you are excused," Professor Harrell barked.

The student opened his mouth to protest, but the professor's glare silenced him. They waited as Tillman left.

"I apologize for the interruption, Dr. Beaumont. Please continue," he said. "Deputy Grant, if you and Petunia could come with me, we will need to administer a light anesthesia to keep her still for the MRI."

Trip gave Jamie's hand a squeeze when she hesitated. "Don't worry. He's the best. I'll join you guys in a minute or two."

Jamie nodded and followed the professor.

"Can anyone tell me what Tillman missed while he was being extremely unprofessional by complaining in front of the client?"

A tall, lanky student at the back tentatively raised his hand, then responded when Trip nodded at him.

"Without seeing a stool sample, I'd guess that I smell undigested food and a faint metallic odor that could be blood. I don't smell infection, like a rotted bowel."

Trip smiled. "What's your background, Mr.—"

"Upchurch, ma'am. I mean, Dr. Beaumont. I grew up working on my daddy's hog farm."

"Your observation was very good, Mr. Upchurch. When evaluating a patient, a good veterinarian uses all of his or her senses to collect information, not just lab work.

Trip recited the results of Petunia's lab tests, encouraged the students to quiz her about the patient's symptoms, prompted them on the questions they didn't ask, and discussed diagnostic tests that could narrow down the problem.

"Very good. Our preliminary findings are indicative of a mass or tumor somewhere in the digestive tract. Because her symptoms have escalated in recent weeks and she is a valuable working canine, we've opted to skip over some of the less expensive diagnostics and perform an MRI. This test could take more than an hour, so it's a good time for a quick bathroom break while we ready the patient."

Several of the students took her advice and headed for the hallway while Trip joined Jamie who was watching Professor Harrell and the MRI tech. Petunia was already asleep, snoring as the tech positioned her on the MRI's sliding bed.

Jamie's face was tight, her jaw working as she spoke through clenched teeth. "Why didn't you tell me that you suspected a tumor?"

The MRI tech shot Trip an apologetic look. "I always leave the intercom open when I'm in here so I'll hear if anyone walks into the control room."

Trip wrapped her arm around Jamie's shoulders and held tight when Jamie tried to shrug her off. "Because I knew you would instantly expect the worst. Every dog or cat owner does. I didn't tell you on the way here because I didn't want you to worry until we knew there was something to worry about. Besides, Petunia would sense if you were upset, and that would upset her."

"Let's keep an open mind, shall we, until we see the MRI results," Professor Harrell said calmly.

Several hours later, they were flying back to Pine Cone. Trip hadn't protested when Jamie kept the very groggy Petunia in her lap, rather than secure her in the back seat. When they boarded, Trip busied herself with the preflight checklist, but wasn't surprised when she set their cruise speed and looked over to see tears streaking down Jamie's cheeks. She wanted to cry in relief, too, when the MRI showed a tumor nearly blocking where the stomach empties into the small intestine, but the margins appeared clear. Petunia was immediately taken to a surgery suite where Trip assisted Dr. Harrell in performing laproscopic removal of the tumor.

"Hey, she's going to be okay. She'll be on a liquid diet for a few days, then soft foods for a while before she'll be able to digest much fiber. But once the surgery site heals, she'll be better than she ever was. I'm not sure why this wasn't detected before. Maybe the tumor hadn't grown large enough. Still, an MRI should have shown something."

Jamie turned her face away. "They all wanted to do other tests first that almost drained my savings, and the program she was in wanted to send her back to the shelter and pick another healthier dog. So we quit the program and got certified on our own. I had my army disability pay to live on, and I planned to save up enough after I got here to try another specialist."

"Well, you two just saw the best veterinarian in this state. I'm just glad he's headed out of the country tomorrow or I probably wouldn't have been able to talk him out of keeping her there overnight in case of any complications from the surgery."

"I didn't want to leave her there. She's been left behind too many times by people she trusted."

Understanding hit like a smack to Trip's forehead. Jamie never knew her father, was lost among the crowd of foster children her mother took in for extra income, dumped by her college girlfriend, then tossed out of the army after being injured, and shown the door by the "Shelter to Working Dog" program because she wouldn't give up Petunia. She wanted more than anything to pull Jamie into her arms and reassure her, but the confines of the plane and the fact that she was the pilot didn't allow it. Instead, she tried to reach out with words.

"I understand."

Jamie snorted. "How can you—a rich, privileged white girl?"

Trip tamped down the anger rising in her chest. "You're right that I haven't lived through what you and Petunia have experienced. But that only meant I didn't have the experience to shield my heart against the pain of having your best friend walk out of your life without a word...without even a good-bye."

"Grace and Clay are your best friends."

Trip chewed on that for several silent seconds, her anger draining away with the hurt she heard in Jamie's words. "Clay and Grace have been my very good friends since we were kids. But you were special, Jamie. Our connection was different."

Petunia whimpered in her sleep, and Jamie stroked her back to reassure her. "It's okay, P. I'm right here." She stared out the window but continued to stroke Petunia's wiry coat. "I don't want to talk about this now. We're upsetting her."

"Will we talk about it later?"

Jamie hesitated, then nodded. "Okay. We'll talk later. I owe you that after all you've done for us today."

"I wanted to help." Trip reached over to brush her fingertips along Petunia's back, like she wanted to trail them down Jamie's cheek. Instead, she offered Jamie a smile. "Besides it's been too long since I've had a chance to visit with Professor Harrell. He's excited about Joe flying him down next month to see my clinic and stay a few days to review a couple of my interesting cases. He loves teaching but enjoys getting outside the university occasionally."

"I hope Grace will give me a week off to take care of Petunia until she recovers."

Trip was relieved to feel the tension in the plane's cabin dial down. "Are you kidding? As much income as you two have added to the sheriff's budget? Grace says she's redecorating her office from the slush fund that's overflowing with my parking fines."

Jamie smiled for the first time since they'd touched down at the Athens airport. "You wouldn't get tickets if you would park properly."

"What? How else can I keep reminding you that I'm around?"

How indeed.

❖

Jamie followed Trip from the airport to the clinic. Petunia was awake and alert by the time they landed, but Trip said she wanted to check her heart and lungs for lingering effects from the anesthesia. They paused on the clinic lawn to let Petunia relieve herself, and Jamie was surprised when Toby and Pete emerged from the stables. They both looked a little strange, but Jamie couldn't put her finger on what was different.

Pete grinned, bouncing on the balls of his feet. "Hi, Jamie." Petunia walked slowly to them, and he squatted to pet her. "Hey, Petunia with a P, like Pete."

Toby shrugged. "He kept calling her Daisy, so I suggested that to help him remember." He held out his hand to Trip, then Jamie. "Dr. Beaumont, Deputy Grant. Good to see you."

"Hey, Toby. Got some kitties for me?" Trip asked.

"We sure do," Pete said. "Yippee-yo-ki-yay. Herded them up like cat-boys."

"Cowboys." Toby smiled indulgently as he corrected him. "Miss Brenda has summoned Jerome. He's taking care of some things in town and should be here soon."

"Cat-boys. We herded cats." Pete chortled at his joke.

"I'll bet that was a sight," Trip said, grinning at Pete. "How many this week?"

"Eight. Three males, five females," Toby said.

"We're going to buy some peaches," Pete said. "Maybe Jamie can cook us up some peach cobbler."

Trip turned to Jamie, her expression questioning.

Jamie couldn't help but smile at Pete. "You bet, Pete. But I already bought peaches yesterday. And apples. Which would you like?"

Pete screwed up his face. "Apples this time." He nodded. "Yep. Apples."

"You've got it."

"Is everything okay with Miss P?" Toby asked.

"We flew up to Athens to consult with one of my former professors about Petunia's stomach problems."

Pete stopped bouncing, but shifted from foot to foot, wringing his hands. "Is she sick? She can't be sick. I fart, too, when I get a bellyache, but that means I ate too many beans."

Jamie wanted to wring her hands, too. She didn't share Trip's confidence that everything would be okay. Petunia undergoing surgery had made her very nervous. "Her problem is a little more complicated."

"But we're fixing her up good as new." Trip pointed to the porch of her residence on the other side of the main drive. "I believe you're being summoned."

A tiny old black woman waved at them.

"Pie. Is it time for pie?" Pete stopped his hand wringing and focused on the woman like a setter pointing out a covey of quail.

"You better go." Trip smiled. "She might be retired as my housekeeper, but she's still boss of the manor."

"Indeed," Toby said. "We argue every time over whether she should launder our clothes or let me take care of the task." His smile was wry. "At least she conceded to let us make use of the stable facilities before we sit at her table."

Jamie realized for the first time what seemed different about them. Both were clean, hair trimmed and freshly shaven. Their clothes were clean and Toby's were crisply pressed.

"Y'all are welcome any time," Trip said. "You know that. Whether it's just for a shower and shave, or a night indoors." She winked at Toby. "Essie looks forward to fussing over you two, and Essie gets what Essie wants."

"You are most kind." Toby turned to Pete. "Come, Peter. We must not keep Miss Essie waiting."

Trip clapped her hand on Pete's shoulder. "Go on. I'll tell Jerome where you are."

Jamie watched them hurry toward the house, then signaled Petunia to heel and they followed Trip into the clinic. She waited quietly while Trip pressed her stethoscope to the dog's chest and belly.

"All sounds good," Trip finally said. She slung the stethoscope around her neck and shoved her hands in her pockets. "Look, Petunia should be on IV fluids for at least the next twenty-four hours so we can dose her with antibiotics, and some pain meds without having to put anything in her stomach. My office has a private bathroom, a door that lets out to a private side yard for P's restroom needs, and a pretty comfortable sofa bed. Brenda will close up the clinic in another hour, then Cindy and I will be out in the barn spaying and neutering cats. We have a surgery room out there for the ferals because we don't want to bring them and whatever they might have been exposed to into the clinic around our other clients. So why don't you and P stay here tonight. I'll check her again after we finish the surgeries."

"Thanks, Trip. For everything." She hesitated, then stepped into Trip's hug when she held her arms out in invitation. Trip was solid and warm. Jamie rested her head on Trip's shoulder. She was so tired of carrying it all on her own shoulders. College was a long time ago. Maybe she should let it go and give Trip a second chance. At least for now…until Petunia was well again.

Jamie brushed her lips against Trip's cheek, then immediately stepped back. Why had she done that? She cleared her throat. "So, you're the one who pays Pete and Toby to catch the feral cats?"

"Yep. I've tried to get them to work here full-time. There's a small apartment in the stables that they use occasionally. Jerome could easily keep Pete busy, and I've tried for years to hire Toby to help Essie in the house. He used to be a butler up north until the lady he worked for died."

"They prefer to be homeless?"

"They're not really homeless, just restless. Pete has a hard time being indoors, and Toby won't abandon him. Toby actually has an old truck that Clay keeps running so he and Pete can haul old tires to the dump for Cahill's Garage. And when the weather's bad, they stay in an old one-room cabin on the back of my grandfather's property. It doesn't have running water or electricity, though, so they come here to shower. Several women in town will launder their clothes in exchange for small chores." Trip smiled. "I think Toby's a little sweet on Essie. He's always dropping by with wild blackberries he's picked or pecans. Sometimes, he and Pete will snare a couple of rabbits for her to stew or bring a string of catfish for her to fry. She cooks for them, and they keep her up-to-date on gossip. They know everything that's going on in town. Homeless people are invisible to most folks, so they'll say anything in front of them. Other folks, well, they just figure two homeless guys won't be taken seriously if they do repeat anything they hear."

"So they're not actually homeless. It sounds like they have more work than they can handle and a roof over their heads when they want."

Trip shrugged. "Folks look at them and see two homeless men. They don't bother finding out who they really are."

Shame washed over Jamie as she stared at the floor. She'd done the same thing. Trip had taken time to know them. Every new thing she was learning about Trip made Jamie wonder if she'd been the one who was in the wrong eighteen years ago. "I guess I can stop worrying about them then."

"Jamie," Trip said softly.

When Jamie raised her eyes, Trip's gaze held hers.

"They might not need food and shelter, but they can use real friends—people who know and understand them. Don't stop being their friend."

"I won't. I promise."

❖

Trip's blue eyes were bright beacons in the dim light, staring up at Jamie. Suzanne's blond head was moving down Trip's long body, over ripped abs and between her legs, but Trip didn't seem to notice.

She reached up, her hands hot on Jamie's neck, her strong arms drawing Jamie down, her soft lips caressing Jamie's, a hot tongue questing and tasting. Then Suzanne was gone and Trip was hovering over Jamie. She whispered Jamie's name as their breasts pressed together. Long fingers were sliding into Jamie, over Jamie's taut clit, and finally inside. She straddled and slicked Jamie's thigh with molten silk, thrusting in sync with Jamie's hips. They fit and moved together as smoothly as on court, instinctively reading the other's intent. They knew what the other wanted, what the other needed, as they moved toward the goal together. There, there, yes, now.

Jamie jerked awake, panting through the aftershocks of the orgasm that grabbed at her belly. Holy crap. She had orgasmed from a dream? She reached between her legs and found herself soaked and still pulsing. She had never dreamed about that night. She'd thought about it plenty. But her conscious memory of what happened was different. Had Suzanne been right?

"I wanted her to want me, but she only wanted you." Suzanne pulled the drawer out and emptied the contents onto the growing pile *of Jamie's clothes and other belongings.*

"That's crazy. I told you I didn't want to do it, but you insisted. Trip has a line of girlfriends. She's only my friend...was my friend. I love you."

"Are you that blind or just stupid?" Suzanne glared. *"Maybe you are, but I'm not. She wants you. We've had fun, but we were never in love. Get your things and go back to your dorm. She can have you."*

Jamie's pillow was moving like someone was walking on it, so she opened one eye to catch the culprit. Petunia was pacing back and forth around her head. When she saw Jamie's opened eye, she licked Jamie's face and whined. Red digital numbers on Trip's desk clock read four thirty. She swung her legs over the side, then jerked back. Trip was wrapped in a blanket, sleeping next to the sofa on an air mattress. How had she come in with that mattress without waking Jamie and Petunia? She smiled at the sock dangling half off Trip's foot, and her slightly parted lips with a small, dark drool spot on the pillow below them.

Jamie wanted to laugh. Some things never change. When they'd roomed together in college, Trip seemed in a perpetual state of half dress. She might get into her sleep shirt, but fall asleep with her jeans still on...or get her jeans off and fall asleep in only her briefs with her sleep shirt in her hand. Jamie's chest flushed and heat flared along her neck to warm her cheeks and ears. That memory was a little too vivid.

Trip stirred, her long arms and muscular legs sprouting from the blanket and settling at such odd various angles that they draped over the edges of the single air mattress in every direction. Jamie's hands itched to touch the bared skin, but as she stared, Trip's figure turned into the broken body of a soldier whose arms and legs had been snapped and reshaped by a roadside bomb. The dangling sock became a dangling foot. The loose fist became a hand without fingers. Soft bare legs turned to red blistered skin exposed because the soldier's camo pants had been burned away. The spot of drool was blood, dripping from the mouth and nose. Another lost soldier. Another of her patrol dead.

Jamie wanted to cry. But the reality was that something, someone, had changed since they were coeds. Jamie had changed. She was too damaged to be a reliable friend, much less anything more serious, to anyone else. She scooted to the end of the sofa and swung her legs over to stand, then carefully lifted Petunia to the floor and unhooked her IV bag to make her mobile.

"Okay, P. Let's go for an early walk." She definitely needed to clear her head.

CHAPTER FIFTEEN

That was the last one," Brenda said, flopping down on the old leather sofa in Trip's office.

"Excellent," Trip said, digging in her file cabinet for a new pad of billing receipts. "I'm sending Cindy home since she was here very late neutering cats with me. Michelle will stay, but if Dani and I aren't back at closing time, she can go on home. I'll take care of the night medicines."

"That girl is a pain sometimes," Brenda drawled out. "But she's smart enough."

"She just needs to mature," Trip said. "And I want to reassure her that I still have confidence in her technical skills after I had to slap her down for being unprofessional on Monday."

"You're a good person, Dr. Beaumont." Brenda got up, opened a door on Trip's credenza, and handed her the pad of forms she'd been searching for.

"Thank you, Brenda."

Dani appeared in the doorway. "Ready to go when you are."

"I'm ready. Have you seen Michelle?"

"Essie called and said she had a blackberry cobbler right out of the oven, so Michelle walked over to get it," Dani said.

Trip shook her finger at Brenda. "Don't y'all eat all my cobbler."

"Maybe I'll call the Daughters of the Confederacy ladies to come over, and we'll eat every last spoonful."

Trip narrowed her eyes for what she hoped was an intimidating glare. Brenda knew how much she hated the DAR and the fact that her mother was a member. "I'll tell your husband that you've been stepping out with the new pharmacist."

Brenda hooted. "I could run off with the mayor and Howard wouldn't even notice now that he's taught the dog to get him a beer out of the fridge. My suitcase would probably be on the porch if he could get that fat old dog to walk all the way to the diner to fetch his supper."

Trip grinned. "You know that's not true. Howard's sun rises and sets with you."

"That's just because I cook his breakfast and his supper."

"Maybe you're right."

Brenda pointed her finger at Trip for emphasis. "I'm always right. I don't know why you're frettin' anyway. You know Essie's baked another cobbler just for you and a third one for Jerome's family."

"What about me?" Dani asked.

It was the back-and-forth they always had when Essie felt well enough to bake, and she was happy that Dani was jumping in. That meant she was feeling more at home. So maybe she could put a toe on that scale of happiness and tilt things a bit in Grace's favor. "You can have half of mine, Dr. Wingate." She flung an arm over Dani's shoulders and made a show of stage whispering into Dani's ear. "Essie always makes mine bigger than the rest."

Trip laughed when Brenda sputtered in search of a sarcastic reply and headed down the hall with Dani in tow. "Call us if anything walks in that Michelle can't handle. And don't fuss if Michelle's a while getting back. Essie enjoys her company."

Trip whistled as she headed down the road to their first client. She'd woken that morning in high spirits. Petunia's tumor appeared almost certainly benign. They couldn't be sure there wouldn't be a recurrence, but she felt very positive about the outcome. And then there was Jamie. If Trip closed her eyes, she could still feel Jamie's body pressed against hers, Jamie's head resting on her shoulder. Trip's belly tightened with the memory. Yep. The South Georgia summer was thawing the ice between her and Jamie.

Clay had pretty much disappeared the way lesbians do when they dive into a serious relationship, and Trip's prospects—given enough time—were looking up. And she didn't want Grace to be left out. Her morning calendar had been cleared in case they were delayed getting back from Athens, so she had Brenda shuffle their afternoon appointments to morning or other days and pitched in to help Dani clear the pileup in the waiting room. This afternoon, Trip intended to show Dani that her practice wasn't all horses, farm animals, dogs, and cats.

Dani eyed her from the passenger seat. "You're certainly in a great mood. Is that because of Petunia's diagnosis?"

"Some of it. But it's also a beautiful summer day...too beautiful to be stuck inside the clinic." Trip grinned at her. "And today is the day you get to see why I picked you over a dozen other capable applicants." Trip turned off the highway onto a long drive with a black iron sign arched over the entrance that said Green Acres.

A dozen bison populated the pasture on one side of the drive, and a mixed herd of miniature cows and horses on the other.

"Is this a petting zoo or something?" Dani asked.

"Tom and Betty King are the clients. They're partnered with the Livestock Conservancy and raise old breeds of chickens, rabbits, and other livestock that are designated as heritage stock. The bison are just a fancy of Tom's. The miniature horses and cows are Betty's indulgence." Trip drove past the log-style house and parked beside a large traditional red barn. That barn was flanked by four long barrack-style barns with signs that identified the residents of each—rabbits, chickens, cattle, horses.

"This is a big operation," Dani said, scanning the complex.

"Yep. They operate traveling petting zoos for county fairs and some zoos. Right now, there's also a brisk market for the heritage breeds. The free-range and organic farmers like the idea of raising the same chickens their great-great-grandparents did. And they supply zoos all over the country and beyond with some of the more exotic breeds. Today, we're here to see a rabbit."

A woman in a dirty T-shirt, baggy khakis, and knee-high rubber boots emerged from the rabbit barn and was walking toward them. Trip waved and they both got out of the truck.

"Hey, Trip."

"Hey, Betty. You and Tom doing okay?"

"Doing fine." The woman wiped her hand on her pants and held it out to Dani. "I'm Betty King."

Dani shook her hand. "Dani Wingate."

"Dani's my new associate veterinarian," Trip said. "I hired her because of her experience with exotic animals. She worked with a zoo up north."

"Well, we won't hold being a Yankee against her if she knows her stuff."

"I appreciate that," Trip said, smiling at Dani. "So, who's our patient today?"

"It's Thumper. I've got him in the red barn. You'll need sutures. His ear is shredded."

"Big Wig get him?"

"Yep. The youngster is near full grown now and made the mistake of challenging the old man over a doe. The North Carolina zoo wants him and a doe, so we'll keep Thumper and his chosen doe separate from the others until Thumper's healed and we can ship them out together."

The doors in front and back of the big red barn were open, and fans hummed over the pens. It was obviously set up for a petting zoo, but most of the pens were empty.

"We figured this would be the best place for him to recover since school is out and we don't have any groups scheduled for tours until August," Betty said. She led them to a pen in the back corner where a Flemish Giant rabbit was sprawled on fresh straw and nibbling on a large carrot.

"Wow. That's a big boy," Dani said, not hesitating to enter the pen. Giant rabbits were known for their gentle nature. She approached slowly, then ran a hand along Thumper's luxurious pelt.

Betty beamed. "Big Wig sires them large. He's near four feet long. Thumper is three feet six inches and still growing."

"How about you handle this, Dani. Betty can give you a hand while I go say hello to Tom."

"He's in the horse barn, waiting. He wants you to look at Ranger's eye. It's better but still a bit runny."

They left the King farm and dropped in on a client whose pet potbellied pig had gotten into a squabble with the neighbor's dog. Dani cleaned Annabelle's puncture wounds, instructed Mrs. Ludwell how to care for the wounds, and prescribed a course of antibiotics.

"I am so grateful, dear," Mrs. Ludwell said, digging through her voluminous purse and counting out the two-hundred-twenty-seven-dollar fee painfully slowly. "Annabelle doesn't usually take to strangers, but she likes you." She placed the last dollar in Dani's hand and patted her on the arm. "You wait just one more minute."

Mrs. Ludwell disappeared into the kitchen and returned seconds later with a cloth grocery bag half filled with peaches. "My sister visited last week from South Carolina and brought two bushels of these for me. I didn't have the heart to tell her that I quit putting up peach preserves and peach butter several years back."

"Thank you. But I'm still staying at the bed and breakfast. Maybe I can give them to Essie or MJ to cook something. I could never eat all of these."

"Oh, well, if you're staying there, just give them to Grace. That girl makes a peach cobbler that will make you slap your mama."

Trip almost burst out in hysterical laughter at Dani's expression as she stared at Mrs. Ludwell. "I'll second that," she said instead. "Grace's cobbler has actually snatched the blue ribbon from Essie a few times at the three-county fair."

Dani took the peaches but frowned. "These are from South Carolina? I thought Georgia was the Peach State."

"In name only. South Carolina peaches are the sweetest." Mrs. Ludwell put her hands on her hips and shook her head. "I don't know why South Carolina calls itself the Palmetto State. You can't eat a palmetto, and most folks have never seen a palmetto."

Trip nodded to confirm this, but Mrs. Ludwell barely drew a breath before forging onward.

"Could you come back next week and check to make sure Anabelle's healing okay? I don't know what I'd do if she became really ill. Anabelle's been such a comfort since Sherman passed away. I loved my husband, but he complained every time I asked him to come with me on my evening walk. Anabelle loves to walk. My grandson helped me order a pink harness and leash on the internet, and she gets so excited when I take it out of the closet." She bent to stroke the stiff hair on Annabelle's back and looked up at them with a shy smile. "I think it makes her feel pretty."

Fifteen minutes later, they'd finally managed to extricate themselves from the talkative old lady and Dani turned to Trip.

"Why would I want to slap my mama?"

Next up was a beautiful ten-foot albino Burmese python with mouth rot, and then they were headed to a local reptile farm to treat the infected claw of a six-foot alligator when Trip's truck indicated an incoming call from Jamie. She tapped the screen to accept the call.

"Hey, Jamie. Petunia okay?"

"She's at home, taking a sick day to rest. I didn't want her out in the heat. MJ's keeping an eye on her. She's handling soft scrambled or poached eggs really well, and lapping up the special prescription broth you ordered for her with the antibiotic in it. MJ said to ask you about some lactose-free ice cream, too."

"Good. Make sure she's drinking a lot of water, too. I'd like to look at the ingredients on the label before you give her any of that ice cream though."

"Okay. But I'm calling about something else."

Trip hesitated. Was this a personal call? "Okay. Dani's in the truck with me and you're on speakerphone."

"Good. I'm out on the highway at, uh…Big Earl's Exotic Emporium." Jamie sounded like she was reading the name from a sign. "We have an animal situation I hope you can help with."

Trip slowed the truck and did a three-point turn in the highway. "Is this an emergency?"

"I think so. Big Earl's orangutan, Kiki, has escaped her enclosure and managed to lock herself in a tourist's car. The car is parked in the shade, and the window is open about an inch, but I'm afraid the interior will heat up quick."

Trip stomped on the accelerator. "We're headed your way. ETA less than five minutes."

"Jamie, it's Dani. Get a towel or rag and dip it in cold water, ice water if there's any around, and pass it through the partially open window. Apes are smart and Kiki will use it to cool herself."

"Will do. See you in a few."

Trip grabbed the CB radio mic. "Fast Break to Paintball. Got your ears on?"

"This is Paintball. What's up?"

"Where are you?"

"At my place."

"Put your clothes on, grab your locksmith tools, and meet me at Big Earl's pronto. Kiki has locked herself in some tourist's car."

"Paintball out and on the way."

Dani raised an eyebrow and Trip shrugged. "The CB handles are something we dreamed up in high school and they just stuck."

Before Dani could comment, Trip whipped into Big Earl's parking lot. A small crowd was gathered next to a luxury SUV, its alarm horn blaring every other second. Jamie stood off to the side, positioned between a middle-aged Chevy Chase doppelgänger and Big Earl, who'd had a short career as an NFL lineman. The two men were yelling at each other over the racket of the car alarm.

Trip sauntered over to Jamie while Dani went to examine the situation at the SUV.

"Trip. Thanks for getting here so quick." Jamie was an island of calm in the chaos.

Earl stopped mid-insult and regarded her. "Dr. Beaumont."

"Hey, Earl. Great shirt," she said, shifting her sunglasses to the top of her head.

Sunlight glinted off his gold tooth as his mouth stretched into a slow, wide smile. He spread his arms like a choir director to properly display the raucous pattern of huge pink flamingos on his Hawaiian shirt. "It's a gift from Sweet Thang."

"How long has Kiki been in the car?"

He frowned. "Too long. Somebody cut the wire on the outdoor part of her playpen, and I didn't notice it when we came in this morning. She found it and slipped out."

The playpen Earl referred to was an eight-by-eight area sectioned off with heavy glass interior walls in a back corner of his store. An extra-large pet door cut into the back wall led to a half-acre outdoor play area enclosed by fortified two-by-two mesh on the sides and top.

The SUV owner, his face red and expression angry, stepped around Jamie and shoved Earl to the side to get into Trip's personal space. "I hope you brought a dart gun. That's a dangerous animal. It attacked my daughter, and I barely escaped when it jumped into my car, but this deputy refuses to shoot it."

Jamie was a blur of motion, positioning herself so that one outstretched arm blocked Earl's intent to shove the guy back and the other arm imposed a barrier between him and Trip. "Mr. Utley, please step back."

Big Earl surged forward, ignoring Jamie's elbow jabbing in his chest. "Nobody is shooting my Kiki, you stupid city son of a bitch. She just wanted to go for a ride. She likes riding in my truck."

"That monkey assaulted my daughter," Utley yelled at Big Earl.

"Kiki is not a monkey. She's an orangutan, which is an ape, and she was just trying to share the seat with your kid." Big Earl matched and one-upped Utley's volume.

"The MONKEY went after me, too." Utley sprayed spit with his last word.

Earl wiped spit from his face and roared. "Kiki has never hurt anyone. You just nearly wet your pants to get away, leaving your kid to fend for herself, and she fell down trying to get out of the car because you were yelling like an idiot."

His shouted words were punctuated by the continued blaring of the horn.

"QUIET." Jamie's loud order silenced both of them. She continued in her normal volume. "We are trying to remedy this situation so that nobody, not even the ape, is injured. Correct, Dr. Beaumont?"

Trip smiled. "Absolutely." She turned to Utley. "If we did shoot Kiki, you'd have one big mess in your vehicle, Mr. Utley. Besides all the blood, most animals and people release their bowels and bladder when they die. Even if you had the car's interior professionally cleaned—" She shook her head and wrinkled her nose.

Jamie nodded, reading Trip's play and backing her up. "You'd probably have to strip out the carpet and seats to get the complete inside reupholstered."

Utley glared at Big Earl. "You are going to pay for it if I do."

Big Earl snarled, and Jamie had to throw all of her weight against him to stop his advance. "Don't make me cuff you."

"Nobody is going to shoot Kiki." Trip put a hand on Utley's arm. "There are many other solutions, but right now I'm primarily concerned about her being in that hot car with the windows up."

"Who owns that Toyota over there?" Dani, who had been peering in at Kiki, asked. She waved over the woman who raised her hand. Trip couldn't hear the rest over the irritating horn, but the woman responded to something Dani said by digging in her purse and handing over her car fob. Dani dangled it next to the window where Kiki sat, wearing a wet bath cloth on her head.

"That's my associate," Trip said. "She has zoo experience, and I'm guessing that includes working with apes. Let's give her a chance." She headed to the locked vehicle with Jamie and the men following.

Kiki pursed her lips and made little squeaking noises, but her eyes locked on the fob Dani dangled outside the window.

"She's blowing kisses," one bystander said.

"No," Dani said, still waving the fob as if she was trying to hypnotize Kiki. "Orangutans do that when they're stressed or agitated."

"Aw, baby," Big Earl crooned. "Daddy's going to get you out of there."

"For God's sake," Utley said.

"Stand back, Earl, and let Dani work," Trip said. "You'll just distract Kiki."

Cahill's tow truck turned in, lumbered to a halt in the small, gravel parking lot, and Clay hopped out. "What's up?"

"Kiki's locked herself in that car and we're trying to get her out," Trip said. "Can you slip the lock on that door?"

Clay rubbed her chin and shrugged. "That model is too new to open with a Slim Jim. I'd have to drill out the key mechanism and replace it later. It's a pretty expensive way to go."

Utley growled. "This crappy little place is going to buy me a new car."

Big Earl lunged for the man, but Jamie was quicker, slapping a handcuff onto Earl's hand and using momentum to twist his arm and grab his other hand. His hands were cuffed behind his back before Trip could blink twice.

"Da-um," Clay said under her breath. "That's kind of hot, and she's kind of a badass."

"Back off," Trip said, equally quiet. She didn't want to spook Jamie when she was finally getting close again.

Clay nonchalantly sidled closer without taking her eyes from Jamie and the men, and repeated the phrase Grace often used to tease Trip. "Snagged and tagged?"

Trip gave her head an almost imperceptible shake. "On the hunt, but claiming rights."

"No worries. She's all yours, pal. I've found the one for me."

Trip bumped her shoulder against Clay's. "Good for you, buddy."

"Do you have some grapes?" Dani asked Big Earl.

"She ate the last of them yesterday," he said. "And I haven't been to the grocery yet."

"Mom, I've got grapes in my lunchbox," a girl among the bystanders said, tugging on her mother's arm.

"That's right. They're in the car. Go get them," the woman said.

Kiki touched the glass next to where Dani held the fob, but Dani immediately concealed the fob in her hand and pointed instead to the fob on the seat next to Kiki.

Kiki pursed her lips again and pointed to Dani's hand. Dani pointed to the fob on the seat. Kiki finally followed Dani's line of vision and looked down at the fob next to her, then picked it up. Dani pressed her fob against the glass and Kiki did the same with her fob. Dani set the fob on top of her head and Kiki did the same, beginning to mimic Dani's motions. Dani held the fob up and pretended to press the alarm button. Kiki actually pressed the button on her fob and everyone, including Kiki, seemed to relax in the silence that followed.

"Everybody get back," Jamie said, directing the growing crowd to step back about fifteen feet.

The girl returned with the grapes, and Dani beckoned her over. "What's your name, kiddo?"

"Amy." The girl was bold and confident. Trip judged her to be around eleven years old and a bit of a tomboy.

"Okay, Amy. I want you to stand by me and show the grapes to Kiki, then eat one. Smack your lips like it's really good, but don't smile at her. She'll think you're being aggressive by baring your teeth."

"Okay." Amy lifted the cluster of white grapes to the window then plucked one and popped it into her mouth. She had Kiki's full attention.

"Now eat another and smack your lips. And when I reach to take one, too, don't let me."

Amy did as she was told, pulling the grapes out of reach and shaking her head when Dani attempted to get one for herself.

"Good girl." Dani held up the fob in her hand and pointed to it. "In the wild, orangutans have been observed offering trades for items they want from another orangutan." She pointed to the grapes. "Now I want you to offer the grapes to me in exchange for this fob."

Amy did and they swapped grapes for fob while Kiki watched. Dani popped a grape in her mouth and smacked her lips. Then she held the grapes near the two-inch opening at the top of the window and pointed to the fob that Kiki held. The ape didn't hesitate. She pushed the fob through the opening and Dani squeezed the remaining grapes through into Kiki's waiting fingers.

"Jamie, can you uncuff Earl? I'm going to unlock the door and I want him to calmly help her out of the vehicle."

"Sure thing." Jamie released Big Earl, and he rubbed the small indentions in his wrists. "Sorry, Earl, but I had to do something to deescalate things."

"It's okay," he mumbled. "I get a little worked up sometimes, and I'm a little protective of Kiki. She's such a sweetheart and won't eat for days if she gets upset."

Trip took the opportunity to sidle up next to Jamie. "She doesn't look very upset to me."

Kiki was turning the steering wheel back and forth with her hind feet while she daintily picked one grape at a time from the cluster to eat them.

Dani unlocked the SUV with the fob, and Big Earl opened the door.

"Kiki, come to Daddy. Let's go inside and get an orange."

The orangutan held out her hand for Big Earl to take and climbed out of the car. The crowd cheered and Kiki blew them a raspberry, then waddled inside, still gripping Earl's hand.

"I'm going to get my stethoscope and check her out to make sure she didn't get too overheated," Dani said. "Unless you want to."

Trip waved her on. "All yours."

Jamie turned to Mr. Utley. "Your car looks none the worse for wear, sir. But if you want to press charges, I'll have to check with my sergeant to see what charges could be brought."

"Dad, can we go now? You said we'd make it to the beach tonight. I told you that I didn't want to stop here." A teen girl emphasized her whine of displeasure with that age group's signature huff, roll of the eyes, and small stamp of her foot.

An older teen wearing shorts and a T-shirt that proclaimed "Exotic Emporium" came out of the store and gave Utley a package of sanitizing wipes. "Big Earl said to give this to you to wipe down the inside of your car. He couldn't come out himself because Kiki won't let him out of her sight now that all the excitement has died down, but he asks that you accept his sincere apology for Kiki and sent this souvenir for your daughter." She handed over a taxidermized baby alligator, then returned to the store without waiting for a response.

Trip whistled. "Man, I've been trying to get him to give me one of those for years."

Utley looked it over closely with obvious interest, then held it out to his daughter.

She threw her hands up and backed away. "Eww. I don't want that dead animal."

"Wow. That's so cool," Amy, the grape girl, said.

"Here, young lady. I'd rather someone have it who will appreciate it." Utley put the stuffed creature in Amy's hands. "Consider it my thanks for you helping to get that ape out of our car."

"Thanks, mister. Thanks a lot." Amy ran to her mother, holding her prize up. "Look, Mom. Look at what he gave me."

Mom waved at Mr. Utley and mouthed a thank you. He sighed, much like his daughter had, and turned back to Jamie. "No harm done, Deputy. And I really don't want to have to come back to testify in court, so we'll just be on our way."

"Thank you, sir. If it makes you feel better, I'm going to have a chat with Earl about checking that outdoor pen every day before he lets Kiki into it."

Trip stood next to Jamie, waiting for her chance, as they watched the Utleys wipe down the seats, then climb in and pull out onto the highway. Trip punched Jamie lightly on the arm. "That was some slick move you pulled to handcuff Earl. I'll have to call you to help out next time I have to pull one of Jawbone's teeth."

Jamie gave her a sideway glance. "I'm afraid to even ask who Jawbone might be."

Trip slung her arm over Jamie's shoulders. "That's Earl's twelve-foot alligator he keeps in the pond out back. Earl rescued him after finding him in a big ditch. He was near dead from starvation because he had a jawbone of some kind stuck in his teeth so he couldn't close his mouth."

Jamie eased out from under Trip's arm. "Gator wrestling isn't in my job description."

"Before today, you probably didn't think wrangling orangutans was part of your job either." Trip attempted to imitate Kiki blowing a raspberry.

"You're spitting all over me." Jamie finally laughed as she pushed Trip away. "Okay. You got me there."

Trip loved Jamie's laugh and, damn, she was beautiful when she smiled. "Have dinner with me tonight?"

Jamie looked down at her feet. "Trip—"

But Trip wasn't going to let her slip away easily. "There is a popular brewery that's opened up down by the river. They have outdoor seating that catches the breeze coming off the water, and dogs are welcome so you can bring P. They also have really great burgers, fried green tomatoes, sweet potato chips, or all-you-can-peel-and-eat boiled shrimp. You don't even have to eat if you don't want to. Just have a beer or a glass of tea so we can talk." Her words had come out in a rush, but she paused now and softened her voice. "Come on, Jamie. Just give me a chance." Trip held her breath while Jamie stared down the highway for a long minute, then injected a teasing tone to lighten the serious moment. "If you refuse, I might do something drastic."

Jamie shot her a skeptical look. "Like what exactly?"

"I'll...I'll return to a life of crime...just park anywhere at any time of day. I'll be so devastated that I might just stop in the middle of Main Street and wander off with my big old truck blocking everybody."

Jamie shook her head. "I don't guess we can let that happen."

Trip's heart soared. "Awesome. Pick you up at six thirty?"

"Make it seven so I have time to change out of my uniform."

Dani had returned and was putting some instruments back in the veterinary truck. Trip decided she should leave before Jamie had a chance to change her mind. She started toward the truck walking backward so Jamie could see her grin. "See you and Petunia at seven then."

Jamie watched Trip's veterinary truck lumber down the street toward her. Trip had called a few moments ago to say she had an emergency, but it sounded like a quick stitch and bandage, and the location was on the way to their dinner destination. Jamie loathed to admit it, but she was a little excited about the chance to see Trip in her work environment. Sure, she'd seen Trip earlier at Big Earl's, but Trip had let Dani run the show. She'd seen her work with Petunia and instruct students at the vet school, but this was Trip's regular work in Pine Cone.

The passenger window slid down as the truck rolled to a stop.

"Hey, hop in," Trip said. "The bucket seats are pretty big, so Petunia can sit with you or she can sit in the back…whatever you prefer."

"Her feet are wet because MJ just watered the grass. If you have an old towel or something, I'll put her in the back on it."

Petunia, tail wagging, hopped onto the truck's narrow running board and in the front floorboard. Jamie reached to stop her next jump into the passenger seat. "Hey, you shouldn't be jumping yet. Stay down there."

"Jamie." Eyes as blue as the Caribbean sparkled with amusement. "This is my work truck. I've had a pygmy goat and a pig ride in that seat, and a miniature pony and giant rabbit ride in the back seat. A small dog with wet feet isn't going to hurt my upholstery."

"Okay." She gathered up Petunia, then climbed into the truck. Trip was right. The seat was comfortable enough for both of them. Jamie scratched behind Petunia's ears as Trip turned the truck toward the highway.

"So, how was the rest of your day?" Trip asked.

Jamie stared out at the road ahead and the houses slipping by—at anything but Trip in leg-hugging jeans and a dark green polo shirt that stretched tight over her tanned biceps and broad but still slender shoulders. "Routine."

"I guess Pine Cone is a bit boring after the places you've been and the things you've seen."

Jamie was surprised at the trace of sadness, the hint of vulnerability in Trip's words. "Are you kidding? Pine Cone might seem like a sleepy little town on the surface, but there is so much going on under its cute tourist town veneer. I've made the biggest drug bust of my career, assisted in a kidnapping case, rescued an orangutan, and found worthwhile volunteer work at the Boys and Girls Club. Oh, I shouldn't leave out that I already hold the Pine Cone record for writing parking tickets, thanks to you."

Trip laughed, her posture and grip on the steering wheel relaxing. "Glad I could help in some way."

Jamie warmed and her tension eased. It was so easy to slip back into the easy camaraderie they'd established in college. It had been as if they'd known each other in another life and their souls instantly recognized each other. They fit together like pancakes and syrup, like biscuits and gravy, like cornbread and butter. But could she trust Trip? And why would anyone want a relationship with someone with a sometime tenuous grip on their sanity? That was the fly in the soup.

An awkward silence filled the truck until Trip cleared her throat.

"Uh, I have to ask a special favor, but I don't want you to take it the wrong way."

Jamie took a deep breath. Here it was already. The fly swimming in the soup.

"What is it?"

"This is one of my biggest clients. Vetting her show horses is probably thirty percent or more of my large animal receipts."

"What's the catch?"

"She's married, but only when her husband is within eyesight, if you get my drift."

"That's a problem for you?" Jamie didn't try to rein in her sarcasm.

Trip scowled, her eyes fixed on the road. "I'm a veterinarian, not a call girl. She doesn't seem to understand that."

Whoa. Jamie had definitely poked a sensitive area. She softened her tone. "Okay. What's the favor?"

Trip turned down a long drive, then shifted in her seat and cleared her throat. "Um, well, just follow my lead. If Virginia behaves, it might be nothing. If she gets too friendly, I might need for you to, um, pretend us having dinner tonight is a, well, um, a date."

Jamie had never seen Trip so...so unsure of herself. Her stumbling speech and flushed face was kind of cute. "Date?"

Trip shrugged, stopping the truck in front of a very impressive barn. "She gets very handsy. I almost stuck myself with a needle last time she decided to grab my butt when I had my hands full."

It was Jamie's turn to laugh as Trip's frown turned into a disgusted pout. "Okay. I'll play along."

❖

Trip wasn't surprised when Virginia Hathaway emerged in a form-hugging latex tank top and skintight riding breeches to crosstie the raven black stallion at the barn's entrance. She *was* surprised that Jamie possessively tucked her hand into the crook of Trip's elbow when Virginia undressed Trip with her eyes. "Hi, Virginia. This is Jamie Grant, and that's Petunia at her heels. We were on our way to dinner when the service let me know you called. Your new stallion causing trouble already?"

Virginia's face darkened and her eyes raked over Jamie's striking contrast of hazel eyes against her Hispanic coloring. "It's that man you made me hire. He let Cirino into his paddock while Beltran was also out."

Trip examined the bite on Beltran's jaw, then the three-inch rip and hanging skin on his shoulder. "That shouldn't have been a problem. There's an empty paddock between them and the fences are five boards high. They're both Friesians, not jumper breeds."

"Edmundo let Cirino get through the gate, and he went straight for Beltran's paddock. I ought to fire him."

"I'll talk to Edmundo about what happened before we leave. The bite isn't bad. It'll heal if it's kept clean, but the shoulder will need to be stitched so it won't leave a bad scar." Trip glanced toward her truck, then held out the shiny steel bucket to Virginia. "Can you get a couple of clean towels and fill this about a third full of warm water?"

Virginia took the bucket, frowned at Jamie, and sashayed into the barn for Trip's benefit.

Jamie stared after her. "What a piece of ass. And I don't mean that in a good way."

Trip grinned. "A pain in the ass is more like it." She wasn't going to elaborate by recounting her last encounter with Virginia. "But a lucrative pain in the ass." She led Jamie to the back of the truck where Edmundo was waiting. "Edmundo. It's good to see you, my friend." She said this in Spanish, then switched to English. "May I introduce you to another friend, Jamie Grant, and her dog, Petunia."

Jamie offered her hand. "Que tal, Edmundo?"

Trip's ears heated. "Sorry. I don't know how I forgot that Spanish is your mother's first language."

Edmundo smiled. "I am fine, thank you, Jamie. My English is fine, too. Dr. Beaumont and I speak in my native tongue when she visits to help her keep up her skills."

Trip grinned and switched back to Spanish. "And because Virginia can't understand a word we're saying." She began gathering supplies and handing them to Jamie. "So, Mundo, tell me what happened."

Edmundo snorted and shook his head. "The new stallion was restless and unhappy when he arrived. He called out night and day, so I phoned his old groom. The man said their studs are always raised with a companion animal since they can't be let in with mares or other stallions. Most pair off with a goat or a barn cat, but this horse took up with a dog that protected the barn. He said the dog ate and slept with Cirino, but it was old and died a few months before Cirino was sold and shipped here. I talked to the mistress about this, but she said it was ridiculous, that the horse would settle soon. And he did. Not long after he settled, I discovered a skinny beagle bitch hanging around Cirino's paddock. She had squeezed under the fence and he was licking her from head to tail. I began to leave food and a water bowl for her in his paddock shed. Yesterday, Miss Virginia found the dog and took her to the county pound. Cirino immediately began to run the fence, and when I went to check on him this afternoon, he ran me over as I opened the gate and searched all between the barns and paddocks, calling for the dog. When he couldn't find her, he challenged Beltran through the fence."

"Do I need to look over Cirino after I stitch up Beltran?"

"No. I checked him good, then saddled him for a long ride to wear him out. He's tired and back in his paddock, but still staring into the woods, looking for his dog."

"I'll take care of this." Trip patted his shoulder. "Stay out of Virginia's sight, then come take Beltran to the stallion barn when I signal you. He'll need to stay in the barn for a few days until the skin begins to knit. I don't need to tell you the rest, but I will. Start with a few hours and increase his time out each day until you take the stitches out in ten days. Call me if you see any problems at all."

Edmundo nodded and disappeared around the barn.

Trip sighed and looked at the ground. "This isn't working out like I planned." Hope flickered and caught when she looked up to find Jamie's expression soft and curious. She gathered her courage. "I hope you aren't starving, because we need to go to the shelter from here and find Cirino's beagle."

"The shelter closes at six."

"I have a key."

"Of course you do." Jamie smiled. "If you're going to play Supergirl swooping in for the rescue, I get to be Wonder Woman."

Trip laughed. "Deal."

❖

The small beagle was anesthetized and sprawled on the table. But before Trip neutered her, she scanned her for a microchip. She grimaced when the scanner produced a number.

"That's good, isn't it?" Jamie hovered over her shoulder.

"It might mean we'll have to see if Cirino will bond with another dog. Depends on whether the number traces back to an actual owner." Trip went to a computer sitting on the lab bench along the wall and pulled up the website to check.

Virginia had pouted, but caved when Trip insisted the stallion absolutely must have his dog returned, then they'd easily located the beagle at the shelter and Trip left the necessary paperwork registering the dog to herself on the director's desk. When they arrived back at the vet clinic, Trip's kennel help, George, was still taking out trash and cleaning floors, so he offered to give the pup a bath while they scrounged for food at Trip's house.

Essie had shooed them away from the fridge and toward the butcher block kitchen table while she filled two plates with mouth-watering country fried steak, rice and gravy, green beans, and a huge fluffy biscuit each. When they shoved their empty plates away, she handed Trip a paper grocery bag packed with a third plate for George.

"Shit." Trip swore at the address the chip number produced. She braced her hands on the operating table and stared at her patient, anesthetized, intubated, and hooked to an IV. Was this dog worth what she was about to risk? Her career, her fragile second chance with Jamie? The beagle's ribs showed through her skin. Her sagging teats were typical of an overbred female. Her coat was dull and thin. Before her bath, she was crawling with fleas, her ears filled with ticks. Yes. Dogs and kids didn't get to pick their owners or their parents.

"Did you see the address on the screen?" Trip didn't lift her gaze from the dog.

"Yeah." Jamie's answer was cautious.

"Without looking again, can you recall it?"

Jamie recited it perfectly.

"That's unfortunate." Trip closed her eyes and took a deep breath, then opened them and turned to Jamie. "Because I am about to commit a crime, and if you stay, you will be a witness. If I'm caught, you're already subject to subpoena for the claimant."

Jamie's gaze bored into hers while Trip held her breath. "And what do you risk?" Her question was soft and unexpected.

"A lawsuit, a fine, my veterinary license suspended or revoked." Trip's throat tightened, and her traitorous eyes teared. She blinked several times and cleared her throat "And I could lose a very valuable friend I'd just found again."

Jamie cocked her head. "Why would you risk all that?"

Trip looked to the table again, clamped her jaw down on the venom she wanted to spew about the man to whom the dog was registered. She spoke only after she'd thought out her answer. "Because I've seen how the man who owns this dog treats his animals. He overbreeds to sell packs of beagles to hunters who want to run deer—something honorable sportsmen won't do—and to supply medical labs. He feeds a poor quality of food, keeps them in cramped pens, forgets to feed and water them when he's drunk, and shoots them when they get sick rather than call a vet. I've been sent out there a dozen times to investigate complaints about him beating dogs and shooting old ones. But he knows how to walk right on the legal line without crossing it so I can't shut him down."

Jamie's expression turned as grim as Trip felt inside. "The shelter might have already checked for a chip and let him know that they have her."

"They know about him, too. If they checked, then they've called Brenda to leave a message for me to come get the dog."

"So, you've conspired with county employees to do this on previous occasions?"

"I plead the fifth."

Jamie's jaw tightened. "I can't be a witness."

Trip nodded, despite her disappointment. "I understand you're a sworn police officer and have to leave." She stared at the floor because she couldn't bring herself to see what might be in Jamie's eyes. "Or maybe you have to turn me in. But I'm asking that you wait until tomorrow. Give this dog a chance for a better life like you did Petunia."

"You didn't let me finish. Could you use an accomplice instead?"

Trip's brain froze. What did she say? She searched Jamie's face. "Accomplice?"

"Don't you need someone to hand you instruments? Don't you normally have a vet tech to suction and stuff?"

Trip swallowed. "Uh, yeah. You won't get queasy when I cut her open?"

Jamie looked away, like she didn't want Trip to see in her eyes what she held inside. "It can't be worse than seeing your lieutenant's intestines hanging out of his belly or your buddy's head on the ground three feet away from his body."

Trip went to her without thinking, curling her hand around Jamie's nape to draw their bodies close and press their cheeks together. She wanted so badly to kiss her, to say that horrible images from the past couldn't be erased, but she wanted the chance to fill Jamie's head, her dreams, with new, beautiful memories.

Jamie brushed her lips against Trip's cheek as she withdrew gently. "We have a patient on the table, Doctor."

Trip smiled. "Yes, we do."

As in everything else, they worked together seamlessly, removing the dog's puppy-making parts and changing out the microchip in her neck. Then Trip tucked her into a pen to sleep for the night and entered a file for her as "female beagle, owner Edmundo Vegas."

They found Petunia in Essie's suite. The TV was turned down low and Essie was snoring in one end of her reclining loveseat.

Petunia sprawled across the other half of the loveseat with her head in Essie's lap.

"You get your dog, and I'll wake Essie and help her to bed," Trip said. She tugged Jamie to her for one last hug. She was addicted to Jamie's hugs now that Jamie was hugging back. "I'm sorry about tonight. It wasn't at all the relaxing dinner staring out over the river that I had planned."

Jamie's hug tightened. "Rescuing the little amiga was a perfect evening."

"I think you just named her," Trip whispered. "Amiga. I like that."

Jamie pulled back and smiled as she nodded. "Amiga." She signaled a few silent commands to Petunia, who was awake now and watching them. Then Jamie waved as the two departed quietly down the hallway.

CHAPTER SIXTEEN

"Grace, you in there?" Trip pounded on the door to Grace's cottage again. This had better be good. She'd just sat down to one of Essie's pecan waffles and thick, crispy bacon when Clay had stormed in, shouting about Grace being missing. To make things worse, she snagged Trip's second waffle and half her bacon to make a waffle rollup and ate it while Trip drove.

"Come on, Gracie, stop fooling around and open up." Clay sounded a little scared, so Trip decided to forgive the waffle theft.

"Grace, open the door or we're coming in." Mary Jane joined the chorus. "I left plarn weaving to check on you, so let us in."

Trip looked at Clay, then they both looked at MJ. "What the hell is plarn weaving?" Trip asked.

MJ just shook her head at them and yelled at the door again. "Gracie, honey, this is your last warning." When no response came, MJ dug into her pocket for a key and unlocked the door.

Clay and Trip shoved to be the first to get through the door after her, then stopped cold at the foot of Grace's bed.

Jamie cruised the highway, then steered her patrol car toward town. She had hoped to dream about little Amiga being reunited with the beautiful stallion, but flashes of the pup's surgery mutated to bloody wounds in the desert, then Adder's tormented eyes. She'd checked in with Toby and Pete, but Toby said last time they'd seen him, Adder looked real bad. She'd seen plenty of soldiers return with the ghosts from their tour of duty haunting them. They sometimes still haunted her. Like last night when she woke up shaking and sweating, a silent scream lodged in her throat.

She shuddered and began to count. Ten utility poles, twelve, sixteen, twenty-three goats, ten, fifteen, twenty fence posts and a cat sitting on the twenty-first post. Three rural mansions, two ranch-style houses, ten houses on the first block as farms gave way to neighborhoods.

Jamie was jerked from the distraction she'd learned to stave off those memories when Petunia barked an alert from the rear seat. She sighed when she spotted a gray-haired woman blatantly taking a hit from a one-shot pipe as she rocked on her porch. Grace had warned her to leave Old Lady Jackson alone and concentrate on the drug runners passing through to the interstate. She only smoked enough to ease her arthritis, Grace explained. She bought a bag of weed every six to eight weeks—depending on the weather—with money she made writing smutty romance novels. Nothing was gained by busting every artist, writer, or old farmer who self-medicated with what was once a common pain reliever for poor people. Jamie privately agreed, but rules were rules, and ignoring them didn't sit exactly right with her.

"Stand down, P," Jamie said as her attention drifted to the other side of the street to a woman wearing fuzzy orange slippers and one of those thin, cotton shifts her grandma used to call a "housedress." She was so focused on the huge, hideous flowers adorning the housedress and the ceramic angel holding a brightly colored "Thank You, Jesus" sign in the yard, she didn't immediately realize the woman was waving both hands over her head in a frantic "stop" gesture.

Jamie released her seat belt and reached to open the cruiser's door as she steered over to the curb. "Do you need assistance?" she asked, slamming the car into park and jumping out onto the sidewalk with her hand on her service weapon.

"It would take God's army to save this town, but you can start by arresting that heathen over there—Agnes Teresa Marie Jackson. She sits there every day, using drugs right out in the open."

Jamie followed the woman's pointing finger to Old Lady Jackson, who pointed back with her middle finger. "You're just mad, Clarice, cause John White retired and that new pharmacist won't refill your valium prescription that expired twenty years ago," Old Lady Jackson yelled.

"I need those pills for my nerves. You're just a flat-out criminal," Clarice shouted back. She turned pleading eyes on Jamie. "I can't even have my grandchildren come to my house because I'm afraid the wind might blow some of that vile smoke this way, and next thing you know, they'll all be in a drug rehabilitation program."

Petunia stuck her head through the open window of the cruiser and yipped her "need to pee" bark. Jamie sighed and released her from the car.

"Lord almighty, what's that smell?" Clarice drew a handkerchief from one of the large pockets on her housedress and flapped it in Petunia's direction. "Don't let that dog do her business in my yard."

Jamie didn't answer. Petunia had been doing really well until last night when her flatulence problem had begun to resurface. MJ had admitted feeding Petunia a bit of the ice cream that Trip hadn't cleared yet, so Jamie was hoping that was the cause. At the moment, she had a truce to negotiate between a crusader and drug offender. She crossed the street with Petunia on her heels. Old Lady Jackson took a deep drag from her pipe and looked Jamie over as she and Petunia approached.

"Um-um," Ms. Jackson said, her voice deep and a bit dreamy. "Grace must be doing the hiring these days." She pushed off the arms of the rocking chair to stand, slowly straightening her legs and back, then sauntering smoothly to the top of the steps. She leaned casually against the white column that supported the roof. "Our police force is looking better and better."

Jamie smiled down at the brick sidewalk and shook her head. Old Lady Jackson wasn't all that old, now that Jamie had a closer look. Age had sagged the skin some around her eyes, and the joints in her fingers were thick with arthritis, but her broad shoulders and surgery-scarred knees spoke of a former athlete. Her lazy grin and shameless flirting told Jamie this woman might have been a player in her prime. "I'm Deputy Jamie Grant, and I appreciate the compliment, Ms. Jackson. But I need you to cooperate with me a little."

"You can drop the Ms., Deputy Jamie Grant. My friends just call me Jackson, but when I was a teen some of the girls started to call me ATM and that stuck, too."

"Ah. Agnes Teresa Marie?"

"That's what I told my dear old mother, but the girls said it stood for All That and More." She winked. "So, ATM Jackson at your service." She shifted her gaze from Jamie to Petunia. "And so is my yard, if your partner needs to make use of it."

"Thanks." Jamie struggled to keep her expression neutral. Seriously? Did lesbians Jackson's age really pick up women with silly come-ons like that? She signaled release and Petunia jetted to the side of the house.

Jackson laughed. "Grace told me she was hiring a deputy with a drug-sniffing dog, but that one is way off base if she thinks I'm growing something besides azaleas in that flower bed."

Jamie's smile slipped away as her face heated. She didn't like people who laughed at her dog. "She's shy about relieving herself." She crossed her arms over her chest and gave Jackson a hard stare. "And she already alerted to the marijuana smoke as we were driving up. I told her to stand down."

"Why, I don't know what you're talking about, Deputy." Jackson held up a zippered pouch. I was just smoking a little of this special blend from the tobacco store downtown. It smells a little sweet, but it isn't marijuana." She pushed off the post she was propped against, spread her stance, and lifted her arms. "Go ahead, search me. It'll be the biggest thrill I've had all month. Probably even top that morning last week when Clarice was chasing a cat out of her yard and the automatic sprinkler switched on."

Jackson's cocky grin sealed Jamie's decision. Petunia rounded the house and sat at Jamie's heel. "P. Go find."

The little dog sprang up the steps, pausing to sniff Jackson's legs, then nudging her hand before sitting and staring at it. Jackson held up the pipe cradled in her hand, and Jamie flicked her fingers in a silent command. Petunia went to the end of the porch and began to work her way back toward them as Jamie moved up the steps to watch her dog work.

Petunia sniffed around the three rocking chairs lined up on the porch, then tracked to the railing at the front of the porch. She stood on her hind legs and scratched at the thick top railing that was mostly hidden from the street by large, blooming rhododendrons, before sitting, looking at Jamie, and giving several decisive barks.

Jamie gave Jackson a sharp look, and Jackson shrugged.

"I set my pipe there earlier. That's probably what she smells."

Jamie stepped over to Petunia. "Good, girl, P." She rewarded Petunia with an ear scratch before knocking her knuckles along the banister. When the solid sound turned hollow, she felt along the unusually thick board. There—a slight edge on the outside lower lip and perpendicular lines at either end of that edge. Jamie pressed against the underside of the top rail, then slid back the cover of the concealed compartment. A plastic bag of marijuana dropped into her other hand cupped under the rail.

Jamie tossed the bag and Jackson neatly snatched it out of the air. "This was really too easy for her."

Jackson eyed her. "Are you going to arrest me?"

"Nope. Sergeant Booker told me about you. I'm after bigger fish. The guys who pump this stuff and worse into urban areas where people use it to forget their circumstances rather than treat their aches. But P enjoys the practice."

Petunia wagged her tail at the sound of her name, and a high-pitched "pssst" was followed by an eye-watering odor.

Jackson coughed and stepped back, pulling the collar of her shirt up to cover her nose. "Damn, that's foul. Did something die inside that dog?"

Jamie glared at Jackson from where she'd moved to the bottom of the steps. "If you don't stop antagonizing your neighbor, we'll have to come back. I think P might like to sit with you on the porch for a while."

Jackson backed up against her front door. "No, not that. Please, Deputy. I'll be good."

Jamie shook her head at Jackson's clowning, then pointed at the empty flag pole holder nailed to the porch support. "I want you to put an American flag out and be nice to your neighbor if she comes over." She slapped her thigh. "Heel, P. Let's go smooth things over with Miss Clarice."

❖

"Well, I'm pretty sure what's going on right now, but are you okay, Gracie?" MJ stood with her hands perched on her hips, eyes politely glued to the ceiling. Trip and Clay, however, stared while Trip reached behind MJ's back to lightly punch Clay on the arm. Grace wasn't missing. She was busy. Like Clay had been busy with River lately. Mmm. Trip frowned. Like she wanted to be busy with Jamie. Her mind jumped to their college locker room…no, the shower in the locker room. Jamie asking for her shampoo. The punch to her shoulder from Clay brought Trip back from naked Jamie to the bed in front of them where naked Grace and…holy crap! Was that Dani?

Grace pulled the blanket tighter around her and Dani. "What are y'all doing here? It's early and I'm…we're busy."

Too busy. Trip had expected Dani to court Grace like she meant something. Not jump her like a softball tournament fling.

"We've been calling your cell and no one in town has seen you since Wednesday," MJ said. "What else could we do but launch a full-on search?"

"What's up, Grace?" Trip frowned. Something was off here. Had Grace drunk so much that she was still slurring her words this morning? In all the years they'd been friends, she'd never seen this happen.

"Seriously, dude?" Clay apparently read the same tea leaves and was using her laser vision to burn a hole in Dani, the person she judged responsible.

Dani jumped up, clad in boxers and sports bra. "I don't know what you think is going on, but I'm pretty sure you're wrong."

"And I'm pretty sure I'm smart enough to figure out what's going on, and I don't like it, not one little bit, sport." Clay eyed Dani hard.

Trip wasn't so sure. If something was going on, Dani definitely lost points for still having clothes on...or maybe it was Grace who should lose points. There must be a lesbian Miss Manners rule book on all this.

"Trip, Clay—"

"Hold on, Grace." Clay stalked Dani like a hunter on safari. "Did you or did you not throw Grace over your shoulder and haul her out of a bar Friday night in Savannah?"

"Well, I—"

Now they had Trip's full attention. She should have listened while Clay talked on the way over instead of plotting revenge for the waffle theft. She moved next to Clay and they advanced on Dani.

"Just answer the question," Clay said.

"Yes, but—" Dani's escape route blocked, she raised her hands in surrender.

"We spent the whole day together yesterday, and you didn't say one word about...this." Trip shook her head. That was it, wasn't it? She'd liked and trusted Dani. Now, doubt was already creeping in. What else was Dani hiding?

"I never pictured you as that type, Dani," MJ said.

"Stop it!" Grace screamed from the bed.

They all turned to her.

"I never figured y'all as the lynching type either. Get away from her."

Was that what they were doing? Jamie had assumed a lot of things about Trip. Was she doing the same to Dani? What Clay was insinuating didn't match up with the woman Trip had been working with over the past few weeks.

"I mean it. Move. *Now*." Grace tried to stand up, then slumped back on the bed and grabbed her head. "Oh crap."

Trip and Clay instantly turned away—because Grace was naked—but MJ ran to Grace's side and handed her a robe. Trip lost her focus on their conversation when Clay tapped her and jerked her head toward Dani, who had continued to stare at Grace. Did the woman have no decency? Had she been raised by goats?

Clay was reaching to push Dani's shoulder to twirl her around when a change in Grace's voice broke through their preoccupation with Dani.

"I'm not really sure what happened the other night myself, but I do know Dani is the only reason it wasn't a lot worse," Grace said.

"What?" Trip grimaced. She and Clay sounded like a Greek chorus.

Grace nodded to confirm it. "She basically rescued me from some pervert."

Dani pushed past them to pull on her jeans, grab her shirt and boots, and start toward the door. "That's my cue to leave."

"No way, dude," Clay said.

"Maybe we should let Dani tell her side," Trip said, ushering Dani and Clay out of the room. "We'll wait out here until you're ready. Take care of her, MJ."

On their way out of the room, Trip rested her hand on Dani's shoulder and gave it a squeeze to let her know she wasn't going to throw her under the bus. Then she thumped Clay in the back. "You owe me ten bucks, Cahill."

"Your sidekick here says nothing happened. You owe me a Hamilton."

"I need to wrap this up and go to work," Dani grumbled.

"Yankee-doodle-doo," Harry called from the sunroom when he spotted Dani.

"Well, aren't you going to arrest her?" Miss Clarice glared at Jamie, then across the street at Jackson, who wiggled her fingers in a flippant wave.

"I'm sorry, but I can't do that, ma'am."

Miss Clarice put her hands on her ample hips. "And why not? She doesn't even try to hide her drug addiction."

"She's not an addict. She's part of a government project, but it's top secret."

Miss Clarice frowned. "Is that what she told you?"

"No, ma'am. I've checked her out. But I can't tell you more than that."

Miss Clarice squinted one eye. "Is she some special undercover cop or something? No. That can't be. She's lived here all her life. I don't know that she's ever held a proper job. Everybody says she runs one of those porn websites on the internet."

"No, ma'am. She doesn't run a porn site. I can promise you that."

Clarice's small eyes lit up. "There was that time she joined the military and went away for a while. They said she was one of those medics. When she came back, none of her family would talk about why she quit the army or why she didn't ever get a job."

Jamie nodded. Got her. She let Petunia into the squad car, then lifted her hat to scratch her head like she was trying to make a hard decision. After a few seconds, she glanced back at Jackson, then stepped close to Miss Clarice and lowered her voice to a whisper. "Will you swear you won't repeat a word of what I tell you? Somebody needs to know in case something goes wrong."

Miss Clarice leaned even closer. "Pinky swear."

Jamie almost burst out laughing at Clarice's extended pinky finger, but the military had taught her how to remain stoic no matter how loud and how close the sergeant got to your face. "I could get into trouble for sharing top secret information. Will you swear on the Bible?"

Miss Clarice's eyes widened. "I don't—"

"I shouldn't ask that." Jamie stepped away. "Forget I said anything."

"No. Wait." She pointed to the angel yard ornament. "With this angel as my witness, I swear on God's holy word that I won't repeat anything you say."

Jamie squinted and studied Clarice's face as if she were struggling with the decision. After a long moment, she stepped close and lowered her voice. "When Ms. …Major Jackson was in the army, she was part of a secret unit trained by the CIA to respond in the event of chemical warfare. There was an accident. I can't go into details, but those who survived—Major Jackson was one—were medically retired from service."

"I suppose that could explain her, um, aberrations." She leaned close and spoke in an even lower whisper. "She beds women, you know."

Jamie frowned at her. "You know that's not abnormal, don't you?" She knew it was a stupid question to be asking this woman.

Miss Clarice stiffened. "The Bible says she's an abomination."

"Major Jackson is a patriot." Jamie scowled and turned as if to walk away. "I don't think I can trust you with the rest."

"Wait. I'm sorry. God should strike me for judging another. Please tell me the rest."

Jamie crossed her arms over her chest, then relented. "Cannabis was used long ago as a poor man's medicine, just like the original Coca-Cola contained cocaine and was sold as a headache remedy. Medical researchers already know the chemicals in marijuana can be used to treat seizures and a variety of illnesses. The military is exploring its potential for treating battle trauma and chronic pain from war wounds

"The preacher said that's just liberal propaganda."

"It's not." Jamie cast furtive glances as if checking to make sure no one was lurking behind a tree or in Miss Clarice's azaleas to hear her next words. Miss Clarice's eyes followed hers, then the two of them put their heads close together. "Now, they believe a buildup in your system might lessen the effect of radiation poisoning...you know, in the event of nuclear war. So, the CIA has recalled what's left of Major Jackson's unit to test it. If the researchers are right, she and the others might be the only people who will be able to man our defenses in the event of nuclear war."

"No-o-o, you don't say." She cast a glance across the street where Jackson still had a shoulder propped against the porch support, watching them.

"Yes." Jamie straightened. "Her taunting you from across the street is just part of her CIA cover. She's actually very nice. So, I'm asking you to respect a patriot. She's already risking her life by inhaling those chemicals. She'll risk it again without hesitation if nuclear war happens. She and the rest of her unit will be our front line."

Miss Clarice's mouth was a perfect O. "Why, I had no idea."

"It's okay. She understands. But this has to be kept secret. The CIA doesn't like leaks. I'm only telling you so this doesn't cause a fuss and compromise the project."

"I understand." Miss Clarice crossed her heart and pantomimed twisting a key to seal her lips.

Jamie grasped Miss Clarice's forearm and gave it a squeeze. "I thank you, and our government thanks you." She dropped her chin to her chest in a brief show of grateful acknowledgement of Miss Clarice's sacrifice for her country. Then Miss Clarice turned her eyes skyward and, for a moment, Jamie thought she was humming "America, the Beautiful" while watching Old Glory wave in the rockets' red glare as bombs burst in the air. When the humming stopped, Miss Clarice snapped to attention, looked across the street at her new shero, and snapped a salute that would make a five-star general proud.

CHAPTER SEVENTEEN

The big fluffy Maine coon cat snuggled into Trip's unbuttoned lab coat to leave another layer of hair on her dark green Beaumont Veterinary polo shirt in his journey to rub the scent glands in his cheeks against her chin. The breed was typically affectionate, but Romeo was aptly named. He had purred through his vaccinations, barely flinched and instantly forgave Michelle for taking his rectal temperature, but had to be distracted with a feather toy to make him stop purring long enough for Trip to listen to his heart and lungs.

"I'd say you have a very healthy, handsome fellow here, Taylor." Trip handed Romeo over to the eighteen-year-old waiting at the end of the exam table. "When do you head off to Emory?"

The girl made a face. "I want to go to Georgia Southern so I'll be closer to home." She stroked the big cat and he raised up on his hind legs to rub his face on hers, too. "I just know one of my stupid brothers is going to leave the door open while I'm gone, and Romeo will get out in the street, or they'll do something mean like tie a firecracker to his tail."

Trip could sympathize. Boys in their early teens could be careless, insensitive, subject to peer pressure and, well, just stupid. Not to mention they usually smelled really bad when they sweated or took their shoes off.

"I'm sure your dad will keep an eye on Romeo. He says they like to watch those fishing shows together."

Taylor hugged Romeo to her. "What if he isn't home when they do something stupid?"

She propped against the exam table and studied Taylor. Blond and pretty, she was the type every Emory sorority would rush. And while Taylor might join one, Trip knew she would choose wisely. She'd look for the one that produced the highest number of undergrads that went on to medical school, law school, or other professional schools. Taylor had the grades and IQ to be accepted into any of those programs after three years of undergrad work, but she was most interested in environmental science and astrophysics. She wanted to be in the first group sent to establish the first colony on a new planet. Taylor had confided that her plan was to go to Emory her first year and transfer to MIT her second year when she was old enough to get an apartment and keep Romeo with her.

"You tell your two brothers that if anything happens to Romeo, even if he's okay later, they will have to deal with the three amigas. That means they'll have to drive clear to Alabama to buy a decent hunting dog, once I put the word out on them. They can forget ever getting a tow from Clay when they end up in a ditch because they're drag racing. And Grace will have her new deputy on their bumper every time they look in their rearview mirror. Officer Grant loves to write tickets. Already busted the Pine Cone record after only a few months."

Taylor smiled. "Thanks, Doc. I'll tell them."

Trip nodded. "Tell your mama and daddy I said hello."

"I will."

Michelle appeared in the door the moment Taylor exited. "That's it for today. It's noon and I just put the 'gone fishin' sign on the door."

"Hallelujah."

Michelle followed Trip to her office. "Tell me again why Dani isn't working today."

God, that girl was nosy. Trip shucked off her lab coat and tossed it into the laundry hamper in her office, then peeled off her hair-coated shirt. "Don't know. Said she had to tend to something out of town and should be back tonight. I don't pry into people's personal stuff." She had promised Grace that she'd stay out of it, and so she would. She still wasn't sure she could trust Dani, but she had to trust Grace. She opened the closet in the corner of her office.

"I wonder if Grace knows where Dani's gone."

Crap. Empty hangers and nothing on the shelves. She hadn't restocked her emergency supply of clean clothes. She pointed at Michelle. "Whether Grace knows where Dani has gone is their business. Stay out of it."

Trip glanced in the full-length mirror on the inside of the closet door. Her dark sports bra did have racing stripes. Maybe she'd start a new fashion trend. She trotted down the hall toward the back door. "Put me on pager, please. Today's my volunteer day."

"Do you need some help?" If Michelle could have unbuttoned jeans with her eyes, Trip's would have been around her ankles.

"Nope." Trip turned to her and grinned. "I'm expecting a new volunteer to help out today."

Michelle averted her gaze and her face flushed. "Oh, right. Okay." She stared at the floor, refusing to look at Trip again. "I wasn't...I mean, you're my boss. I can't help if I haven't had a real date in a month and you're running around here half dressed. I'm not dead, you know. But I wasn't flirting. I was really offering to help because I don't have any plans for tonight."

Trip put her hand on her shoulder. "Michelle. There are plenty of women more your age. If you're looking for a party girl, go to the Savannah bars. If you're looking for a serious girlfriend, go to the colleges and hang out in the student center or the library. Check their intramural sports calendar and look for softball, basketball, and rugby schedules."

Michelle's smile was small and tentative. "I'm pretty good at softball."

"There you go. Go watch a few games in Statesboro or Savannah, and you'll have them swarming around you like mosquitoes before you know it. It's Saturday afternoon. I'll bet the fields at Georgia Southern are humming right now."

Her smile broadened. "I think that's exactly where I'll go." She grabbed her purse and followed Trip out.

"Don't go alone, and don't drink and drive. If you do drink too much and don't have the money for a motel room, go to a reputable hotel and have the desk clerk call me for a credit card number."

"Yes, Mom."

Trip pointed her middle finger toward the sky as she trotted toward the house and a change of clothes.

Millicent Williams, the Boys and Girls Club director, wasn't a short woman. She just wasn't tall like Trip. And what she lacked in height, she normally made up in bulk. But the cancer she'd been fighting had taken its toll. She looked weary and forty pounds lighter than the last time Trip had seen her.

Trip bent to hug her. "You look like hell, Millicent."

When Millicent laughed, her face came alive and her whole body shook with it. She patted Trip's arm. "The doctor says he's done all he can do. My time has come. But I told him it's not over until I hear the good Lord calling me home." She peered up at Trip with that somebody's misbehavin' expression. "I don't know why you're out here, though. She's inside with the kids."

"I thought we'd play basketball." Trip held up a bag of new basketballs. She'd called Millicent to find out which day Jamie was scheduled to volunteer. She'd been looking for a way to get Jamie on a court and remind her how well they fit together. But Millicent shook her head.

"Our usual problem beat us to the court."

Trip followed Millicent's gaze. The neighborhood small-time drug dealers and corner bullies were playing two-on-two, producing more profanity than they were points. She handed the bag of balls to Millicent. "Can you manage that?" Trip asked. "I'll bring the shoes inside."

"I don't know why you asked me for shoe sizes again. You know what happened last time."

"I think I have a solution for that."

She managed to gather up two tall stacks of boxes and balance them in both arms while Millicent held the door open. She barely made it inside when her boxes went flying as the children rushed past her with cries of "Miss M" and tussled over the ball bag to carry it in for her. Jamie turned from the computer where she and a girl were working and laughed when Trip stumbled over a small boy, lost her balance, and landed on the floor among the boxes. Petunia rushed over and licked her face.

"That was graceful," Jamie said.

Trip started to rise, only to be pounced upon by a bright-eyed eight-year-old.

"Doc, are you going to show us how to faint today?"

She rolled onto her back and tickled Jamal's ribs. "No, but I might show you how to fake when you're coming down court."

Darius—probably around twelve but at the age when his attitude was growing faster than his body—drew a new basketball out of the bag Trip had brought. "Ain't you got eyes? We can't play today. Jubal's boys is playing." He threw the ball hard at the younger boy's face and Trip put up a hand to block it. But the ball never met its target.

Jamie snatched it midair and spun the ball on one finger. Then she tossed it up to spin it on the index finger of her left hand. "*Don't* you have eyes? Jubal's boys *are* playing."

"My brother says that's white talk," a girl said, then glanced at Trip. "Sorry, Doc."

"Then I must speak brown talk," Jamie said in Spanish.

Jamal eyed her. "Are you from Mexico?"

"No," Jamie answered in English. "I'm from Atlanta. I grew up in the projects there with black kids and brown kids." She put some more spin on the ball, executed a few lunges to pass it under her thigh or bounce it on her knee, and caught it again on her fingertip. "And a few white kids, too. My mother is from Central America."

The children drifted over, mesmerized by Jamie's ball work, so Trip grabbed a second ball and spun it. They tossed the spinning balls between them, each catching the other's on fingertips. For their closing trick, Trip took both balls, and Jamie turned her back, closed her eyes, and pointed index fingers shoulder high toward the ceiling. The children gasped, then applauded when Trip tossed the balls and they landed neatly onto Jamie's fingers and continued to spin.

Trip wanted to applaud, too. The little display was a show they'd sometimes treat the crowd to during pregame warm-ups. It took precision and trust, but they still had it. The precision, at least.

She pointed to the bench that ran the length of the room. "Okay. Everybody have a seat and Miss M will hand out your new basketball shoes." She caught Jamie's eye and nodded toward the door. "Let's go do a little reconnaissance."

Jamie followed without question, and they stood against the building to watch Jubal and his friends play. Jubal was the star of his high school team, but was thrown off his college team for selling drugs out of his dorm room before his freshman season even started. Neither his grades nor his game was good enough for any other college to invest the time needed to straighten him out. Trip's grandfather had tried, too. He got Jubal to enlist in the army, but drugs washed Jubal out of the military after two years.

"Think we can take them?" she asked Jamie.

Jamie snorted. "You and me against those guys? Sure. They're all mouth and no finesse. But you've been in the heat too long if you think they'll be honorable enough to just walk away after we embarrass them in front of their hombres."

"I might have another card up my sleeve. Come on." Yep. Just like old times.

Trip strode onto the court, right on the edge of their play. "Hey, Jubal."

Jubal ignored her and laid in a jump shot when the other three paused to look at her. Jubal got his own rebound and slammed the ball into the stomach of another guy. "Play ball."

"Your dyke sister wants to talk to you, man," a guy shouted from the sideline, and the others laughed.

"She ain't my sister."

"I thought we were friends, Jubal."

Jubal stared at the ground. "This ain't your neighborhood, Trip. Things are different down here."

"You're wrong. The rules for honorable men are the same no matter where you are. Right now, we're on public property that's currently leased to the Boys and Girls Club. You should be showing the children how to play, not running them off their court."

"What do you want, Trip?"

"I want to play for the court. Me and Jamie against you and your next best guy. Full court, first team to reach twenty-six points."

Jubal's boys hooted. Trip knew Jubal couldn't back down now without losing face in front of his guys. "What do we get when you lose?"

"The court," Jamie said. "But we won't lose."

Jubal laughed. "We already have the court."

"The puppy they wouldn't let you adopt from the shelter last week."

Jubal stopped laughing and stared at Trip. "How do you know about that?"

"The director told me when I went by to look at another dog for them. You get the puppy or we get the court. Go pick your other player."

While Jubal huddled with his guys, Trip discussed strategy with Jamie, and the kids crept out of the building and sat along the brick wall on the sidelines.

Jamie and Trip stretched while Trip talked. "Let them score first, then we'll match them point for point unless they come on strong. They're already warmed up, and we aren't. But they're also tired and we aren't. So I don't mind giving them a little early lead, then winning it back when they tire. After we see how good they are and how quickly they tire, we'll decide whether we can risk letting them lose by just one point. I don't think we'll gain any ground in the neighborhood by embarrassing them today."

"Sounds like a plan," Jamie said.

Jubal won the coin toss, and brought the ball in from under Trip's basket. His fake was easy to read when he reached half-court, but Trip took it anyway and let him lumber past her and muscle Jamie out of the way to score. He would have been called for the offensive foul of charging if they'd had a referee, but Trip was okay with letting it go.

Jamie grabbed the rebound, and the men trotted downcourt to wait for her and Trip to cross the half-court line.

"Your pal is slow. I could have easily blocked that."

"He's put on a few extra pounds since high school."

Trip picked up speed to join Jubal under the basket. Jubal had chosen wisely from his ranks. Blueberry, dubbed that after he was sent to juvie for stealing blueberry pies from the neighborhood convenience store, bested Jamie's height by a few inches and was fast and lean. But while he had a physical advantage, Jamie had better game skills. She gave up a few turnovers, testing his reach and quickness, but Trip or Jamie would recover the ball each time until Trip gave a nod and Jamie let Blueberry past her for a showy dunk that brought cheers from Jubal's gang and groans from the children.

"Time out." Trip walked Jamie to the end of the court where the children sat, ignoring the wide smiles from Jubal and Blueberry. She noticed they didn't protest the timeout and shooed a few guys from the bench so they could sit and wipe the sweat pouring from their faces. "What do you think?" she asked Jamie.

"I think you're toast." Darius crossed his arms over his slim chest. "I think we're never going to play basketball on this court again."

Trip grinned at him. "Remind me to take you down to the river, young man, and show you how to tickle the bait to lure the big fish before you set the hook to haul him in." She turned to Jamie. The point guard always ran the game.

"Blueberry is fast, but easy to read. Jubal's skills are good under the basket, but he has no shot outside the arc. All he knows how to do is dunk or hook. I say we lay back like we're tired and let them get ten ahead, then turn it into a running game and light up this dog and pony show."

"You got it."

Darius's frown indicated he was skeptical, but the game unfolded exactly as Jamie planned.

The catcalls from Jubal's gang turned to groans when Jamie swished in one almost from half-court. Then they fell silent when Trip streaked along the sideline toward her goal as Blueberry dribbled into his offensive half-court. Her movement distracted Blueberry a millisecond, which was long enough for Jamie to cleanly swipe the ball from his hands and fling a pass that Trip leapt up to intercept and dunk into the basket. The children were on their feet cheering until a glowering look from Jubal silenced them.

The next twenty minutes was filled with behind-the-back, no-look passes, hook shots, fast breaks, reverse layups, and fakes that left the guys staring at empty air. Jamie and Trip flowed up and down the court like they were one brain operating two bodies. In the end, they won twenty-seven to twenty-five.

Jubal doubled over to catch his breath, hands on his knees and sweat dripping onto the pavement.

Trip went to him and offered a handshake. "Good game, Jubal."

He swatted it away. "Fuck you." He headed for the street and his guys gathered to follow.

Trip followed, too, and touched his shoulder. He whirled on her, and she backed up a step, her hands up, palms out. Jamie and a growling Petunia were instantly at her side. Jubal's gang surrounded them, but Trip touched Jamie's arm while she held Jubal's angry gaze. "Jubal and I are just talking."

Jamie flashed a signal and Petunia sat and quieted, but her lips still curled up to show her fangs. Jubal's gaze flicked down to take it in.

"I just wanted to tell you to come by the clinic tomorrow morning and pick up your pup. He's going to be a big boy, but a real sweetheart. I already neutered him and took care of his first shots for you."

He glared at her. "I didn't win."

"But this pup can win if you come get him. I told the lady at the shelter about Buster, how you took great care of him for fifteen years until he passed in his sleep a few months ago. She thought you would chain him in the front yard and make him mean. I told her that you and I had fenced your entire yard years ago for Buster. I explained to her that you only needed a dog that looked fierce to protect your mother when you were out. This pup needs you, Jubal."

He rubbed the back of his hand against his chin for a moment, then looked up into her eyes, and she saw the man she knew as a friend. "You still open at eight thirty?"

Trip smiled and held her hand out for a fist bump. "Yeah, but bring Brenda a ham biscuit from the diner and she'll let you in at seven thirty."

Jamie elbowed Trip to take the center of attention. She made a show of scanning the young men surrounding them, then pointed to the kids who were waiting by the building to see if they needed to run or stay and play basketball. "These kids need all of you like that pup needs Jubal," she said to them. "This is your neighborhood and those are your neighborhood kids."

"Nobody protected me," one guy said, spitting on the ground. "What's in it for me?"

"I want a dog like Jubal," another said.

"Me, too." Seemed everybody wanted pups.

"Okay," Jamie said. "A hundred hours of volunteer work here at the club for a pup and veterinary care for the lifetime of the animal."

Trip sputtered. "Lifetime?"

Jamie smiled and nodded.

Trip looked around her. The men's faces filled with distrust a second ago had turned hopeful. "Okay, but I don't crop ears, and Jubal has to vouch that you'll provide a good home before I'll hand over a puppy." She slung her arm over Jamie's shoulder. "Also, Deputy Grant will be holding puppy training classes here each week. I'd suggest that you take advantage of them because once you get your pup, she'll pop by your home periodically to check that you're taking good care of your animal and to help you with any training issues you might be having."

It was Jamie's turn to sputter, but her glare held little heat.

"A hundred hours is a lot. And I ain't cleaning no toilets," Blueberry said.

"A full-time job is forty hours, so it's just like two and a half weeks of a full-time job," Jamie said. "And I promise no toilet duty."

Their lure was working, so Trip decided to set the hook to haul them in. They put the guys and kids to work stripping rust and old paint from the goal posts, then spraying them with bright white paint and hanging new orange nylon nets. They sprayed the weeds that were pushing up through almost every crack in the concrete, but she'd send a contractor out later to see if the court could be repaired or would need to be replaced. The kids were collecting empty paint cans and sweeping up paint chips while Millicent was getting contact information from Jubal's gang. Trip tensed when an arm went around her waist, then relaxed when Jamie's voice filled her ear.

"The puppy card you had up your sleeve was the game changer," she said.

Trip sagged into Jamie. Even though she was a few inches taller, Jamie was solid and strong. "You had the winning game plan on the court." Trip smiled at the instant replay in her head. "Our old mojo came back like it was yesterday that we wore college uniforms."

Jamie pushed her away playfully. "You think so? You're a little slower, Beaumont. But I was able to adjust."

"Slow?" Trip put her hands on her hips. "If I was slow, it was to allow you to keep up."

Jamie snorted. "In your dreams."

"How about you prove it with a little one-on-one. First to reach twenty-one."

"You're bluffing. You know the paint on the backboards won't be dry enough until tomorrow."

"Not here. I know where there's another court, a better indoor court. Just us."

Jamie hesitated, her eyes searching Trip's. They both knew the powder keg waiting for them to light.

Please, Jamie. Take this chance with me.

Jamie nodded.

"Follow me."

Trip slid the door to the barn back, and Jamie stepped onto the gleaming court. "My grandfather built it," she said, "but I've recently updated everything and put in a new floor and goals. This is where he taught me to play."

"No wonder you were so good when you showed up for our freshman year."

Trip shook her head. "I got the basics from him, but he only knew old style. When I began to play with you, a whole new world opened up for me. Those first few months at school, I stayed a lot of evenings to study the film our recruiters had of your high school games. I learned so much from you."

"I thought your late nights out were because you were changing the definition of "sorority rush." Jamie shifted her feet and scanned the building. Or was she avoiding Trip's gaze? After a minute, she strode over to the rack of balls and bounced a few before choosing one and snapping a pass to Trip's belly. "You have first in."

Apparently, Jamie wasn't ready for verbal exchange, so they'd fall back to the language that had always worked between them.

They measured each other during the first ten minutes, testing fakes, rolls, and fading jumpers, then the play became more physical. They bumped to create space, spun around each other, clashed under the basket, raced and dove after each ball. Trip matched her to protect the goal side as Jamie streaked down the court, but found herself defending empty air when Jamie spun at the last minute and laid the ball in on the opposite side.

"You didn't learn some things from me." Jamie scooped up the ball and slammed a pass at Trip's gut.

"Like what?" Trip took the ball out and back in quickly and fired off a long three-point shot as soon as Jamie cleared the foul line. Jamie whirled, waiting for the first indication of where it would bounce if it wasn't true, but Trip already knew it wouldn't go in. She'd intentionally shot it too hard and spun it so that it should bounce off the rim to the left side of the court. By the time Jamie read its direction Trip was already there, catching the rebound and sinking a short jumper.

"Like bedding the entire volleyball team."

Trip stared while Jamie took the rebound back to half-court. "They were on target to win a national championship, and the coach asked me to tutor them in math. I'm good in math, but that's not a character flaw last time I checked. Who told you I was sleeping with them?"

Trip moved to thwart Jamie's drive toward the goal, then blocked her shot. They both scrambled for it, but Trip snatched it away when Jamie's foot slipped. She took a few steps and cocked her arm to shoot, but Jamie had recovered and swatted the ball out of Trip's hands from behind, followed it, and threw in a reverse layup. She trotted to half-court to wait for Trip to pick up the ball and bring it out to reintroduce it.

Trip fumed over her unanswered question. "Who told you I was sleeping with the entire volleyball team?"

"And the tennis and rowing teams," Jamie said without turning to face Trip.

Trip crossed the half-court and turned to face Jamie. "I wasn't a virgin when I arrived on campus and I dated, but I can count on one hand the number of women I slept with the three years I went there." She turned her back and worked her way down court moving left and right, pushing Jamie back with small bumps. "Who told you I was sleeping with half the campus?" Trip switched into high gear with a double fake and dunked the ball. Jamie was too far under the basket to defend the shot and had to jump back when the ball slammed through the net.

"Suzanne. My girlfriend who you were always flirting with." Jamie snatched up the ball and stalked toward half-court.

"She was always flirting with *me*." Trip's frustrated response echoed in the cavernous building.

The score was tied at nineteen-all. Jamie turned when she reached half-court and faced Trip. "I guess that's why you jumped at the chance to climb in our bed. Because she was chasing you? Why should I believe that for one second?"

Before Trip could reply, Jamie executed a triple fake and broke free. Trip scrambled to catch up, then reposition for a block when Jamie pulled up at quarter-court and rose to fire off the winning jump shot. Off balance and too late, Trip crashed into her midair and they fell to the floor. Trip took advantage of her momentum and rolled them to lessen the impact, but they slid the last couple of feet before coming to a stop with Trip's weight pinning Jamie.

Trip rose to her elbows and searched the hurt, anger, and something else battling, swirling in Jamie's eyes. "It was a poor decision made by an immature teen. But I didn't know what else to do. I was desperate to get you to look at me as something other than a friend and teammate. I knew Suzanne was sleeping around on you, but not with me. I was never interested in her. I wanted you, Jamie. I only ever wanted you. And after all these years, I still want you."

Trip lowered her head to rub her cheek against Jamie's, then closed her eyes and took a chance. She caressed Jamie's lips with hers, peppered Jamie's neck with small kisses, then returned to her lips. When Jamie didn't respond, Trip withdrew. She rolled off and onto her feet. "Lock up when you leave, please." She strode out of the barn and was almost to the pool when Jamie called out.

"Trip, wait."

Trip stopped and, after a heartbeat, turned. Jamie had closed the barn door, but stood there uncertainly.

"You know what else hasn't changed, Jamie? You've never wanted me the way you wanted Suzanne. Don't worry. We'll still be friends. I just…I just need a few days." She turned before she further embarrassed herself by breaking down into tears and continued toward the house. She'd taken only a few steps when Jamie slammed into her back, propelling them both into the pool.

Trip was struggling to orient herself under water when Jamie's hands grasped her T-shirt and yanked her to the surface. Trip coughed, then sucked in air, but Jamie didn't release her hold.

Jamie shook Trip. "Let me tell you what hasn't changed—you are wrong. You've always been wrong. Suzanne was who I settled for." She yanked Trip to her and took her mouth with a hunger that left Trip reeling. When neither had a wisp of breath left in her lungs, she reluctantly withdrew, soothing Trip's ravished lips with gentle kisses. "You were the one I really wanted. Suzanne convinced me that you were out of my league."

"I don't want to talk about her anymore," Trip said, grasping Jamie's face. Jamie's mouth was so sweet as Trip explored it, her tongue so gentle as it roamed Trip's mouth. The spotlight over the barn clicked off, and Trip slid her hands under Jamie's basketball shorts and underwear to caress her smooth hips.

Jamie's hands caught Trip's. "Wait. Where's P?"

"Essie just let her in the house. Didn't you see the spotlight go out and hear the door close?" Trip nuzzled Jamie's neck.

"I thought it must be a motion light, and I can't hear anything but…uh…the fireworks in my head."

Trip scooped Jamie up and sat her on the lip of the pool, then pulled off Jamie's water-filled shoes and wet shorts. Jamie's shirt and sports bra were next, then all of Trip's clothes quickly followed. She groaned when she drew Jamie into the bathwater-warm pool again, their slick skin sliding together, nipples touching, hips pressing, legs entwining. Jamie was long, smooth muscle under caramel skin as soft as down.

Jamie closed her fingers around Trip's nipples and squeezed while guiding her back against the pool's side. Trip gave herself over, letting Jamie explore with hands and mouth. She needed to be Jamie's, maybe even more than she hoped Jamie would be hers. She pressed her thigh between Jamie's legs and urged the thrust of Jamie's hips. Trip gasped when Jamie's deft fingers found her begging clit and stroked it with a rhythm that matched her thrusts. Trip called to whatever gods would listen when Jamie slid inside to claim her. But when years of contained emotions exploded free to wash through her, and Jamie's soft cry of release joined hers, Trip held back the tears of surrender she feared would scare Jamie away. Instead, she let Jamie hold her until she could breathe again, until the shuddering aftershocks of her orgasm faded.

Trip nipped at Jamie's ear and whispered into the stillness. "Come inside with me." When Jamie didn't immediately answer, she added persuasion. "You might as well stay. Essie has your dog. Do you want to face her right now after we've just been howling at the moon out here?"

Jamie dropped her head to Trip's shoulder. "Christ. I'll never be able to look her in the eyes again."

Trip squeezed her and stood, lifting Jamie off her feet and setting her down on the first step to get out of the pool. "Essie knows how I feel about you. She's known since I came home with my tail tucked between my legs after you joined the service." *And left without saying good-bye.* She shook her head. "If it hadn't been you out here, she would've flipped on all the yard lights and yelled, 'Tripoli Miranda Beaumont, quit acting like an alley cat in heat...we've had indoor plumbing for years so if you want a bath, drag yourself inside like decent folk instead of flashing your possibilities for the entire countryside to see.'"

Jamie held her sides, she laughed so hard at Trip's very authentic imitation of Essie's voice. "Tripoli Miranda?"

Trip nodded solemnly. "TM. Trademark Beaumont. Tall and blond. That's what Daddy said. Grandpa is responsible for the Tripoli, though. Everybody thought it was because of his family's military service in either the marines or navy, but he told me his favorite dog from his childhood had been named Tripoli."

Jamie smiled. "That sounds like something you'd say."

Trip forgot to breathe for a second when she realized the college student she had loved no longer existed. Before her was a woman she wanted to know. Jamie was stunning in the pool lights, with her raven hair slicked back and her latte skin and contrasting hazel eyes. Even as they stood together naked and Trip reveled in Jamie's beauty, she knew that wasn't what drew them together. The irresistible pull between them was something soul deep. They could have both been men or a heterosexual pairing in some other life. It wouldn't have mattered. She would never worry that she'd lose interest if Jamie suffered a disfiguring or disabling disease or accident. Jamie would always be at the root of her heart. They were alike, yet so different. Two parts meant to fit together. It was true in college, and no less certain now.

Trip took Jamie's hand and tugged her up the steps and into her arms. "Stay tonight. Please. I want my mouth on you."

"I have to work tomorrow."

"We'll set an alarm, but I usually get up at five to run before breakfast at seven thirty."

Jamie kissed her. "That's perfect if you loan me some clothes to run with you."

Trip stopped Jamie when she reached to gather some of their wet clothes. "Leave them or you'll ruin some of Essie's fun. If you think I'm kidding or just being a princess, wait until morning and you'll understand."

They crept into the house and found a note on the kitchen table.

The dog is sleeping with me. Try to keep the noise down and use those towels. I don't want to find water tracked all over my floors when I get up. And don't make me drag you out of bed naked for breakfast. You know I will.

Trip grabbed one of the big, plush towels and began to dry Jamie's shoulders and back. When Jamie turned, Trip gently dried her breasts and stomach, then knelt to dry each leg. She brushed her nose and lips through the curls at the apex of Jamie's taut thighs. Jamie's legs trembled, but a towel dropped to cover Trip's head. "You better dry off fast because I'm not going to wait for you long, and you will *not* track water on Essie's floors."

Jamie was already halfway up the stairs by the time Trip had the towel off her head and one leg dry.

❖

Jamie took advantage of Trip's delay to use the facilities and finger-comb her hair. She felt Trip's presence before she saw her in the doorway watching her. They'd been naked together many times in many locker rooms, but this felt different. You never devoured your teammates with your eyes like Trip was doing now. Jamie turned to her as Trip pushed off the doorframe and moved toward her.

Trip's hands were warm where they cupped her buttocks and lifted so that Jamie instinctively wrapped her long legs around Trip's hips. Then they were in the bedroom and Trip lowered her onto soft white sheets, followed her downward, and mapped Jamie's mouth with her tongue. Jamie stroked Trip's silky locks, brushed along the buzzed hair at her nape, and then she closed her eyes to focus on the wonderful things Trip's mouth was doing to her right breast, no her left breast...both breasts. She couldn't decide because she was distracted by the maddening fingertips alternately rubbing and tweaking her left nipple while others stroked lightly up and down, up and down her leg, then tickled the back of her knee—a move that surprisingly made her belly clench and roll in a tiny pre-orgasm—before moving up the inside of her thigh. She wanted to grab that hand in frustration when it diverted to trace the crease where her leg joined her torso and along her hipbone.

She was so intent on the path of that hand, she hadn't felt Trip's shoulders slip under her thighs, lifting and parting her. "Please. You're killing me." She caught Trip's hand in hers. "We can go slow later."

The promise of later proved to be the gate Trip was waiting to open. She swiped the flat of her tongue over Jamie's turgid flesh, then sucked Jamie into her mouth as she filled her with one, then two fingers. The slight scrape of Trip's teeth as she sucked matched the thrust of her fingers and Jamie fought to extend the crest of her pleasure as she rode it impossibly higher and higher until she could hold back her orgasm no longer and snatched up the pillow beside her head to muffle her scream when it all shattered into a million electric shards that tore through her and left her gasping and weak.

After a while, Trip tugged the pillow from her grasp, and Jamie realized her whole body was shaking and her face was wet with tears. Trip hovered over her, her blue eyes full of agony and self-recrimination.

"Jamie, I didn't mean to…I would never…did I hurt you?"

Jamie shook her head to stop Trip's distress. "No." Her answer was more of a croak, so she cleared her throat and looked away, embarrassed, before she tried again. She was sure she would have blushed if she wasn't already flushed from that screaming orgasm. "It's just been a while, you know? Too busy in the desert, then I was in the hospital, then trying to get resettled—"

Trip's finger on her lips stopped her excuses. "Me, too…but we were in the pool and already wet so you didn't notice what I couldn't hold back." She grabbed Jamie's hand and held it to her lips, which made Jamie want to cry again, then rotated them both to pull the sheets up.

Jamie reached for her clock and set it for five. She normally woke at four thirty anyway, but her body might take longer to recover after tonight's activities. She laid her phone on the bedside table, and Trip drew her down for another kiss. Jamie's sex impossibly pulsed to life again, and she rolled to cover Trip's long body with her own, pinning Trip on her back.

"If you keep that up, we might never sleep tonight." Jamie nipped Trip's earlobe and slid under the covers to kiss a path down her smooth belly. Her turn for a taste.

CHAPTER EIGHTEEN

Jamie's internal rooster was crowing for her morning run, but her body was arguing that the soft cotton sheets, the pleasant hum of central air, and the warm body at her back was too comfortable a nest to leave just yet. Then light kisses along her neck and fingers lightly stroking her lower belly were persuading her libido that waking up, and rolling onto her back would be an excellent compromise. She smiled. She could compromise. She rolled over and looked up into summer sky eyes.

"Hi," Trip said softly.

"Good morning."

Propped on her elbow, Trip dipped her head to place a soft kiss on Jamie's lips. Her smile widened when she moved back again. "You don't snore anymore."

Jamie barked a laugh and stretched her arms over her head. "The army fixed my deviated septum."

Trip cocked her head. "I sort of miss it."

Jamie snorted. "Only you. Suz—" Trip's hand covered her mouth.

"I don't want to hear that woman's name ever again. Nod if you agree." Trip removed her hand when Jamie nodded.

Jamie cleared her throat and searched for something different to say. "Stick around. I'm sure I'll start snoring again by the time I turn sixty. You'll be snoring, too." Did she just say that? Insinuated that she'd still be around, that when they were old, they'd...no, no, no.

She was not a U-Haul kind of lesbian. One night in bed didn't mean…
Trip hadn't said, Jamie wasn't sure—

"Relax, Jamie. We have all the time in the world to figure this out." Trip must have realized her panic. Her hand stroking Jamie's side was likely meant to sooth, but inflamed instead.

Jamie pushed Trip onto her back and began a little stroking of her own. "How much time do we have?"

Trip's chest flushed an attractive pink that traveled upward to color her cheeks. Her eyes glinted in the morning sun. "Not much. You turned off, uh, turned off your alarm…oh, yeah." Trip opened her legs wider to give Jamie easy access and moved her hands along Jamie's back, unconsciously conveying the pace she desired from Jamie's hand. "…because we didn't go to sleep until three."

Jamie groaned when Trip's fingers found and slipped over her dripping sex. She struggled to form coherent words. "I set my clock for…God, that feels so good." They each thrust against the other's fingers, driving themselves to the point of release.

"Jamie, I can't hold on." Trip massaged Jamie's clit firmer, faster.

Jamie could feel the pressure gathering in her belly with each stroke…almost, almost. "Yes, come with me. Come with me now."

Trip's body bowed a split second before hers, and Jamie collapsed on top of Trip when the orgasm released its grip. They both panted while their hearts slowed.

Jamie rested her head between Trip's breasts. "Better than a morning run," she told the erect nipple that filled her vision.

"That's good. Because we don't have time for one," the nipple's owner answered lazily.

Oh, yeah. They'd been talking about time when they got sidetracked. "What time is it?"

"Seven. If we're not downstairs in thirty minutes, Essie will be up here dragging us out of bed whether we're naked or dressed."

Jamie pushed up from where she'd been listening to the steady thump of Trip's heart. "You didn't lock the door?"

"Wouldn't matter if I did. She has keys to every room in the house." Trip sat up, planted a quick kiss on Jamie's lips, and scooted to the edge of the bed. "Come on. Shower with me. I promise to be good. You don't want to miss the Essie show this morning."

❖

Trip couldn't resist helping Jamie wash her hair and soap that gorgeous body, but she kept to her promise, and her touches were as chaste as was humanly possible. Even though it did sorely test her resolve. In the end, it was worth her restraint. Essie was in rare form.

Trip settled in her usual chair at the end of the kitchen table with her back to the patio door and indicated for Jamie to sit on her left so she'd have full view of Essie's performance. Amani, the niece who managed the house now, was cracking eggs into a blender while keeping an eye on sausage links and bacon sizzling in a cast iron skillet.

"What are you doing here on a Sunday?" Trip grabbed the Sunday newspaper that was still folded on the table and began sorting the sections.

"Girl, Jerome called me first thing this morning to tell me Aunt Essie was up at daybreak, buzzing around like a bee and talking nonstop to some little dog that was following her around." Amani flashed a huge smile of perfect white teeth, but kept her voice low.

Trip kept the comics for herself and handed Jamie the news and sports sections. "Put that news section in your chair and sit on it. We don't let Essie see the front page before church unless you want a sermon with your breakfast."

Amani shook her head to confirm nobody would want the aforementioned sermon, then continued. "Jerome said, 'Amani, she won't let me in the house. You need to come on over and get a front row seat.' He's promised to hang my new porch swing if I report back."

Jamie flinched, but Trip grinned at the sudden repeated slamming of cabinet and appliance doors in the adjoining laundry room.

"I swear, you'd think a band of gypsies camped in our yard last night. Clothes everywhere. I pick up one thing and I see another," Essie fussed into the kitchen without acknowledging Trip or Jamie. "A pair of shorts here, a shoe there." She checked the skillet.

"I just turned those," Amani said. "I'm about to pour the omelets." She added egg whites from a carton into the blender.

"If you don't know how to separate fresh egg whites—"

Amani pushed a button on the blender, drowning out the rest of her aunt's complaint. "I'm not going to throw away good yolks, Aunt Essie," Amani said when she switched the blender off. She looked over her shoulder and winked at Trip and Jamie. "Besides, the gypsies can't tell the difference."

Essie threw her hands up. "You're right about that. Act like they was raised in a barnyard. Clothes flung from here to Atlanta." She finally looked their way, glaring at Trip. "Don't think I didn't recognize those unmentionables hanging from the diving board. I had to call Jerome over from the barn to crawl out and retrieve 'em. Just cause they call them bloomers doesn't mean a lady should plant them outside for everybody to see."

"Trip wouldn't let me—"

Trip cut Jamie off. "I'd like one of your pecan waffles with strawberries and whipped cream."

Essie picked up the remaining sections of the newspaper and slapped Trip on the head. "You want a short-order cook, you go on down to the diner and sit at Bud's counter. In my kitchen, you eat what I cook for you."

Jamie frowned at Trip. "I'm sure whatever—"

"But I told Jamie that nobody cooks waffles like you. And I had Toby pick some strawberries especially for you. I put them in the fridge yesterday."

Essie considered this, then went to the huge refrigerator and took out a bowl of huge red strawberries. She bit into one and nodded, then placed the bowl on the counter. "Get my flour down, Amani."

"Yes, ma'am." Amani flashed another smile at Trip and began pulling ingredients from the cabinets for her slight, stooped-back aunt.

Essie walked back to the table and reached across to pat Jamie's hand. "Don't mind me, honey. If I didn't fuss at that wild child sitting next to you, she'd think I didn't love her anymore."

"Yes, ma'am. I'm Jamie."

Essie smiled. "I know who you are, honey. You and your cute little dog are always welcome."

"Uh, where is P exactly? We have to be at work by ten."

"She's in the barn with my grandson, Jerome." Essie turned back to the kitchen counter and began measuring out ingredients when Amani slid two plates laden with neat omelets, sausage, and bacon in front of Trip and Jamie. "You've got time to enjoy your breakfast. He'll be back with her soon, so I guess I'd better make a waffle for him, too."

Jerome did appear as if conjured at the very moment they finished their omelets, Petunia was at his heels but ran to plant her feet against Jamie's leg, her tongue lolling from her mouth and tail wagging. "Hey, P. Have you been having fun?"

Petunia replied with a sharp yip. Happy was written all over her little doggy face.

"She caught a mouse in the feed room," Jerome said.

"She didn't eat it, did she?" Jamie asked. "Because she's on a very strict special diet."

"Funny about that," Jerome said. "I know a lot of horse people who keep terriers because they're better than cats at catching mice. Cats are lazy and only hunt when they feel like it. Most terriers gobble down what they catch, but Petunia brought it to me after she killed it."

"Special diet?" Essie asked. "Is that because she's a police dog?"

"No," Trip said. "Petunia has some stomach issues." She put down her fork and folded her fingers around Jamie's hand that rested on the table. "She had surgery a couple of weeks ago to fix it, but some of her symptoms seem to be returning."

Essie nodded. "Trip will fix her up. She might be my wild child, but she's a right smart one."

Amani placed beautifully arranged Belgian waffles, piled with plump strawberries and whipped cream, in front of Trip and Jamie. Essie brought two more for her and Jerome, then Amani returned with one for herself. The waffles were gone so fast, there was little time for small talk, and Essie rose to put her dish in the sink.

"I'll slip on my dress and get my hat, then Jerome and I can go so he'll have time to get dressed. Amani?"

"My dress is in your room. I brought it so I'd have time to clean up and go to services from here."

Essie nodded and toddled off toward her suite of rooms. She barely rounded the corner when Jerome and Amani scooted down to huddle at Trip and Jamie's end of the table.

"Damn, girl. I haven't seen Granny that happy since the day I announced her first great-grandchild was on the way," Jerome said, poking Trip's shoulder. "She could have preached today's sermon when she spied your drawers hanging from the diving board."

Trip grinned and glanced at Jamie, who wasn't smiling. She was silently staring down at the table. She realized Jamie hadn't said much throughout the meal. Stupid, stupid. She'd screwed up again. She'd talked about Jamie so much, she already felt like part of the family here. Only she'd forgotten that Jamie never had a real family and didn't know how to interpret Essie's fussing, and Jerome and Amani barging in on their morning-after. What an idiot. She should have planned a private morning for them.

Trip glanced at the clock. She'd run out of time. "I guess you and P better get going if you're going to have time to get changed and make it to the station by ten." She wished Jamie didn't have to leave, that she could have the rest of the day to make up for this blunder.

Jerome was still laughing, but Amani was studying Jamie. She laid a hand on Jerome's arm to silence him. "You've been very quiet, Jamie, and I'm afraid we've offended you by barging in on your private time."

Jamie didn't look up. "I'm sorry. I'm not used to having people… this is kind of different for me." She glared at Trip. "I don't leave my clothes for someone else to pick up and launder." She ducked her head and stared at her plate again. "Breakfast was delicious, but I'm not used to having someone come in and cook for me. I take care of myself."

This was worse than Trip thought. Jamie's impression was completely wrong. "Jamie, no. It's not like that."

"Would you even be able to manage if you didn't have money to hire people to take care of you?"

Jerome shook his head. "Nope. If it doesn't go on the grill, she can't cook it. The woman can't even pop popcorn."

"I only burned that one bag."

Amani shot Trip a "for real?" look. "He's right. Her cabinets would be empty and laundry stacked clear to the ceiling."

"Quit, you guys. This is serious." She grabbed Jamie's hand again. "They're ribbing me because they're being bad, nosy siblings this morning."

Amani closed her hand over Jamie's other hand. "She's telling the truth, Jamie. We should apologize. Here's the truth. Trip was overwhelmed when her grandfather died and left her this place. She left a good position in Atlanta and came home to start a practice here, mostly because this is the only house Aunt Essie has ever lived in since she was twelve years old and her mama came to work for the Beaumonts."

Jerome nodded. "It was clear right off that she couldn't manage the farm and her practice, so we worked out a deal. I negotiated a really good contract to manage the farm for my best childhood friend."

Trip bumped fists with Jerome. "And Amani isn't my housekeeper. Essie thinks she is, but Amani owns several companies that provide a range of cleaning, rental management, and maintenance services for businesses and households."

"I mostly do just enough around here to keep an eye on Aunt Essie and stop her from doing too much, but several of my employees do most of the real work." She gave Jamie's hand a shake. "Trip wouldn't let you pick up those clothes because picking up after Trip and swatting her with the newspaper is what keeps that old woman's heart chugging along. When she saw those clothes strewn across the lawn, she was like a kid at Christmas."

Jerome nodded and laughed again, then glanced at the doorway to make sure Essie wasn't standing there. "I wish I'd had my phone so I could've made a video."

A door closed in another part of the house, and Amani began to gather the rest of the plates. "I hope we haven't scared you off. Please, accept our apology."

Jamie shook her head and smiled. "No, you haven't. Thank you again for breakfast, but I really have to go."

"I'll walk you out." Trip stood. "I'll come back and help with the dishes."

"You better," Amani said. "I don't want to be late to church."

Trip walked Jamie to her truck parked by the barn. She was relieved that Jerome was parked by the front door, so he'd take Essie out that way and she could have a moment alone with Jamie.

Jamie hoisted Petunia into the truck and climbed in, but lowered the window.

"I just can't seem to stop screwing things up with you," Trip said, bracing her forearms against Jamie's door so their faces are close together. "I should have gone downstairs and brought something up for a private breakfast on the balcony outside my room. Something romantic."

"It's okay," Jamie said. "I need to learn to stop being so prickly." She looked into Trip's eyes. "This is hard for me, too. I've always been on my own, and you're surrounded by people who love you."

"That's true, but there's still a missing piece in my life. A big one, and I think that piece might be you."

"What if it's not?"

"I want to find out. I'll try to do a better job of showing you that we're the right fit."

"Then I'll try to be less prickly…as long as I can get a rain check on that balcony deal."

"Absolutely." Trip cupped Jamie's face and kissed her with every ounce of hope in her heart.

Trip bit into her thick burger and hummed her satisfaction while she chewed. After Amani left for church, Trip had tried to update some files for the clinic, but her thoughts kept straying back to the night before—Jamie hovering over her, Jamie under her, Jamie curled around her. So, she was contemplating saddling her favorite gelding for a long ride to fill the hours until Jamie finished her work shift when Grace called with an invitation to grill burgers at her place. The B and B was exactly where Jamie would go to change when she got off shift, and Trip would be waiting for her. Everything felt perfect until Dani showed up and introduced a nervous tension into their casual cookout.

"Sorry I haven't been around the last couple of days. Hope I didn't leave you in trouble at the clinic, Trip." Dani toyed with her fork. "I had business back in Baltimore."

Trip put down her hamburger. She glanced at Grace, who was staring at her food, her smile gone. No sense dancing around the issue. "Job interviews?"

Dani nodded as her face reddened. "They made me an offer I couldn't turn down." She reached for Grace's hand. "I apologize for my delivery."

Grace pulled away. "Your delivery? Just to be clear, you're not apologizing for keeping this from people who were depending on you? Not for leaving your employer in a lurch for two days? To say nothing of practically jumping from my bed and into your car without a word." Grace rose from the table, plate in hand, but stopped beside Dani. "You really are something, Dani Wingate."

"Grace, can we talk about this later, please?" Dani glanced toward Clay and Trip.

Trip felt Clay tense beside her. Grace, however, seemed to consider it, studying Dani for several long seconds. "I don't think that's necessary. I heard you perfectly the first time. Congratulations on finally getting what you wanted. I'm happy for you."

Trip suddenly lost her appetite. This felt too much like when Jamie left her in college without even a note of explanation. No, she and Dani were colleagues. She wasn't crushing on Dani. But her stomach didn't seem to know the difference. She grabbed her plate, still heaped with food, and tossed it in the garbage. "I took a chance on you, Dani, and you pull this crap." Her head knew Dani was not likely to stay, but her heart had become convinced that Dani would stay. Like Jamie would stay. She knew there was no reasonable connection, but what she and Jamie had started last night still felt very fragile. Would Jamie leave, too, if she and Petunia got a better job offer... maybe from the state or federal government?

"I can work a notice, if you need me," Dani said.

"Probably best for Grace if you leave right now, but it will take me two weeks to restructure the schedule so I can handle the clinic and the farm calls again. Right now, you can handle calls and treatments today since I worked in your place yesterday. Clay and I need to take care of Grace." Without another word, Trip followed Grace into the house.

❖

Cruising her usual route through town, Jamie alternately hummed and quietly sang the '90s tunes that played in her head, along with the good memories of her college days with Trip—fooling around at basketball practice, the team singing in the locker room shower together, Sunday afternoon challenges to see who could run the most steps in the football stadium or hit the most fast balls in the baseball team's batting cage. She didn't want to think about being with Trip last night or she'd end up with a giant wet spot in the crotch of her uniform pants. Acknowledging that, of course, sent her traitorous mind in that exact direction. Thankfully, her daydream was interrupted by the chiming of her cell phone.

"Jamie Grant."

"Ms. Grant. This is Victor Helms. I'm calling you on behalf of the Strange Foundation."

Jamie held out her phone and stared at the number calling her. She recognized the Albany, New York, area code. "What can I help you with, Mr. Helms?" She pulled the cruiser into the Piggly Wiggly shopping center and parked so she could concentrate on the phone call.

"The Strange Foundation is interested in developing and supporting a program I believe you helped pilot—the Shelter to Working Dog program."

"There were others in that pilot program. My dog and I dropped out."

"We are aware there was a health issue that disqualified your dog. That's exactly why you're the person we want to persuade to help us get this program off the blocks and moving. We need someone with your determination to overcome any obstacle. We want to talk to you about our plans and discuss a consulting contract or full-time employment with the program."

"I'm not job hunting, Mr. Helms. But I might consider a consulting contract if I can work it out with my current job."

"Good. As long as you keep an open mind. That's all I'm asking. Could you possibly meet our southeast director Tuesday? She'll be in Savannah on other business and could meet you around four."

Jamie calculated the time she'd need to drive to Savannah after her shift. "Four thirty would be better."

"I'm sure that will be fine."

Jamie wrote down the address he recited and thanked him before disconnecting. A nationwide program like this could mean a second chance for so many dogs. They could start with detection animals—drugs, explosives, cadavers, trackers—and branch into service dogs for the disabled and veterans with PTSD. Jamie smiled. She couldn't wait to give Trip her news.

The day turned out long with a major pileup on the interstate. Pine Cone was called to assist by setting up a detour route while highway patrol troopers worked to clear the wreckage and get traffic moving.

When she and Petunia finally made it back to the B and B, even the dog was tired and grumpy. She refused to eat and only drank a little water before climbing into her crate and closing her eyes. Jamie called Trip's phone again. It'd been going straight to voice mail, but Jamie figured she might be on a call and had left it in her truck while she was working with a patient.

"Jamie?"

Jamie's brain stuttered. "Uh, yes?" This sounded like Essie answering Trip's phone.

Oh, no. Her brain jumped to a hundred conclusions, all bad.

"This is Essie. I was just about to call you."

"Is everything okay? Has there been an accident? Is Trip okay? I've been trying to call her."

"The bonehead left her phone here in my kitchen. Must'a put it down when she was rootin' around in the liquor cabinet a few minutes ago. She's in a mood, sittin' out by the pool and sipping that fire stuff right out of the bottle. I think it'd help if you came over. Otherwise, Jerome is likely to find her sprawled out there on the grass when he comes to feed horses in the morning."

"I'm on my way over."

"You let that little pup in the house when you get here. I like her company."

"Yes, ma'am. Miss Essie?" Petunia's ears went up at mention of Essie's name.

"Yes, honey?"

"Does Trip drink a lot?"

"She works too much, but I can't say that she's that much of a drinker. She's just hit a muddy place in life's road. She's been hauling her wagon and everybody else's. Now, her wheels are mired in the mud, and she needs a reason to keep faith in her ability to get free of it."

A nose pushed against Jamie's leg. Petunia wagged her tail when Jamie looked down. "Okay. I'll keep that in mind." Jamie put Essie on speaker so she could throw some things in an overnight bag, then grabbed her keys. "We should be there in about fifteen minutes."

"Oh, and, Jamie?"

"Yes, ma'am?"

"I don't want to find clothes all over my yard in the morning."

Jamie felt her face heat. "N-No, ma'am. No clothes in the yard."

Essie's cackle rang out over the phone's speaker before she disconnected.

Jamie parked in front of the house and shook her head when she found the front door unlocked. Convenient for her, but the police officer in her wasn't happy. People in small towns were so trusting. Essie waved from her doorway down the left hallway, and Jamie released Petunia to go to her.

"She's still out back," Essie said before taking Petunia into her rooms and closing the door.

Jamie paused by the patio doors. Trip sat with her feet in the water, silhouetted against the pool's underwater lights. She shed her shoes in the kitchen and closed the door with a soft click to pad across the grass. Trip spoke when Jamie neared.

"Trying to sneak up on me?"

"As if. You need to oil the hinges on that door."

"Then I wouldn't know when Essie was headed out here to swat me with her newspaper." Trip didn't turn, but held up her hand for Jamie to join her.

Instead, Jamie straddled Trip and wrapped her arms around her from behind. The sudden change in their relationship still felt a little weird, but in a good way. A really good way. "Tell me what has you out here sipping whiskey?"

Trip held it up. "Fireball. Tastes like that hot candy we used to eat when we were kids."

Jamie sniffed it, then tasted. "It does." She coughed when the burn hit her throat. "Except for the afterburn." She set the bottle to the side, kissed Trip's neck, then began a gentle massage of her tense shoulders. "Now answer my question."

Trip heaved a huge sigh. "Dani's back. Her sudden need to take care of something was actually a job interview." Trip's barked laugh echoed across the pool. "Stupid, trusting me. I didn't even ask for details. I was sure it was some family issue since she asked at the last minute. But she had to know about the appointment days, at least a week in advance."

Jamie had gotten a call today for a meeting day after tomorrow. "You don't know that, Trip. Lots of things could have caused them to call her at the last minute. So, did she take the job?"

"Yeah."

"That sucks." Jamie stopped her massage and rested her cheek against Trip's when Trip sank backward into her embrace. After a long moment, she kissed Trip's temple and tightened her arms. "So, make a plan. You ran the clinic alone before Dani. You can do it again until you find another suitable hire. What about your second choice when you interviewed Dani?"

"He already had another offer and was holding them off while I made my decision. I'm sure he took that offer when I chose Dani because of her zoo experience. When I called to let him know I'd decided on another candidate, he said he was disappointed, but his wife and kids weren't excited about moving to the South and had been pressuring him to take the other offer anyway."

"Third candidate?"

"Nobody else I interviewed even made my short list."

Jamie couldn't believe Trip was this defeated. The woman she knew in college was a problem solver. In fact, she loved to solve problems. "You can make a new list after Brenda rearranges your schedule. Now tell me what's really bothering you."

Trip twisted out of Jamie's arms and jumped to her feet. "Grace has fallen in love with Dani." She began to pace the concrete poolside.

"I didn't know they were dating." Now that she thought back, there were some looks she'd noticed passing between Grace and Dani that made sense now, and some nights when she didn't hear Dani moving about in the room next door. Had she been in Grace's cottage?

Trip snorted. "I don't think they have dated." She stopped her pacing and held up a finger. "Oh, unless you want to count that lunch at the diner when Dani said the only seat open was the one at the counter next to Grace." She started to pace again. "So, Dani wastes my time settling her into my practice, beds one of my best friends, and then breaks her heart to run off after the first job offer that comes along." Trip stopped again and dropped her chin to rub her eyes with the heels of her hands. "Grace is crushed."

Jamie stood and tugged Trip's hands away from her face. "Grace will hurt, that's for sure. But she's a strong woman. She'll survive. Dani obviously wasn't the one for her."

Trip didn't meet Jamie's eyes. "We haven't really dated."

Finally, the heart of the problem.

Jamie smiled and let go of Trip's hands to cup her face and capture her eyes. "Sweetie, we slept within a few feet of each other for two years, ate most of our meals together, spent every afternoon together at practice, and showered in front of each other. That's got to be some kind of lesbian record."

Trip laughed and the spark Jamie loved returned to Trip's eyes. "I love it when you're right." She tugged Jamie close, then Jamie laughed when Trip lifted her off her feet to twirl her around. The world spun even faster when Trip claimed her with a kiss that warmed Jamie's mouth and heated everything else farther south. Maybe it was the remnants of Fireball on Trip's tongue. Nah. Jamie knew better.

❖

Jamie had insisted that no clothes come off until they crossed the threshold into Trip's bedroom, so shoes, shorts and T-shirts began to fly before the door clicked shut. They laughed as, naked, they playfully wrestled for dominance until Jamie yielded and Trip claimed victory with a long, hot dance of soft lips and probing tongue. Jamie had never wanted a woman so much…so much that her head was buzzing.

Trip cursed and drew back.

"What?" Jamie blinked. Did she do something wrong?

Trip grabbed her phone from the bedside table, and the buzzing stopped. "Beaumont."

A muffled voice sounded on the other end.

"No. I have the number in my contacts. I'll call them." Trip ended the call and glanced at Jamie. "Sorry. Essie must have brought my phone up here. That was my answering service." She put the phone to her ear again. "Hey, Will, it's Trip. What's up?"

More muffled words and Trip began to search around for her clothes, tossing items into a nearby chair.

"You have some of those pre-loaded doses of Banamine on hand? …Good. Give him one now, like I showed you. I'm on my way."

Trip tossed the phone onto the bed and flopped down next to Jamie. She brushed her fingers along Jamie's cheek. "I am so sorry, but I have an emergency colic. This client paid a ton of money for this horse. I might be all night."

Jamie kissed her. "It's okay. I understand. P and I can go home." She rose from the bed and looked to see where her clothes might have landed.

Trip pulled the bedcovers back and guided Jamie back to the bed, pushing her down and covering her. "Please stay. I'm sure Essie and Petunia are already tucked in bed, and I like thinking of you snuggled in my bed while I'm out sweating in a dusty barn."

Jamie shivered when Trip snuck her hand under the sheet and cupped her breast. "No fair. You're leaving me in a bad way as it is."

Trip smiled. "Hold that thought. I'll be back as soon as I can." Trip glanced at the clock and Jamie admonished herself for delaying Trip this long.

"Go. If I'm not here when you get back, it's only because it's after seven and I had to leave for work."

It was close to five thirty when Jamie woke to Trip crawling under the covers. She was very naked, but the tired lines of Trip's face stopped Jamie from doing more than rolling over to cuddle against Trip's back. Within seconds, Trip's breathing evened out and she was limp in Jamie's arms.

Jamie stared up at the ceiling. She hadn't told Trip about the call from the Strange Foundation. They'd gotten caught up in the Dani-clinic problem and then the Dani-Grace problem and she just forgot to tell Trip. No. That wasn't true. *We haven't really dated.*

Trip hadn't actually yet said the three no-going-back words—"I love you"—but she expressed it in a hundred other ways. Jamie hadn't ever come close to admitting how she felt. Not in words.

Was she afraid? Yes. She was afraid that when she told Trip about her meeting with the foundation, Trip would jump to the conclusion that she was going to follow Dani's example and chose a dream job over Trip.

Would she? Not even she could say for sure. One thing was certain—she would not sneak out of town like Dani did and come back to announce she was leaving. But she had only one day, and she needed a plan.

CHAPTER NINETEEN

Trip smiled without opening her eyes. This was a nice dream. Soft lips were planting little kisses along her backbone, then a tongue licked along her neck, and teeth nipped playfully at her earlobe. A shiver ran through her entire body when a warm hand glided over her naked buttocks and fingertips swirled along the back of her thighs. She moaned and opened her legs in invitation. "I thought about you all night and dreamed about you all morning."

A heavy weight covered in soft fleece pressed against her back, pinning her against the bed and the fingers sampled her arousal. "What did you dream?" The words were a warm, moist exhale in her ear that caused her belly and sex to tighten.

She scrunched her eyes more tightly shut so she wouldn't accidently open them and cause the dream to vanish. "I dreamed of your thumb inside me and your fingers around my clit, thrusting and thrusting, filling me, milking me...yes, like that, holy mother...yes." Trip screamed into her pillow. When she stopped jerking, she realized the touch that had pleasured her was gone. Had it been a dream? She opened her eyes to bright sunlight.

"Jamie?"

A playful slap to her butt prompted her to roll onto her back. "You'd be in a lot of trouble if it wasn't."

"I thought I was dreaming...a very, very good dream." Trip lifted the covers and grinned. "Get in here with me. I thought you had to work today."

Instead, Jamie stood and shucked off the soft robe she'd borrowed from Trip's bathroom. Trip frowned. Jamie was fully dressed underneath. She was just trying to fool Trip with the robe.

"Nope. I went in and swapped a shift with one of the guys, and Brenda has cleared your afternoon. I've got plans for us today, so get up and go shower."

"Plans?" She liked Jamie's plan so far. What else did she have in mind?

"You said we haven't really dated, so I want a date. Several dates. One right after another. Today." Jamie's expression softened.

Trip took the hand Jamie extended and let Jamie tug her into a loose embrace. Jamie kissed her, just a caress of her lips against Trip's. "Will you go on a date with me today, Trip Beaumont?"

Trip tilted her head. "Why, yes. I think I will." She batted her eyelashes, which made Jamie laugh. "I just need a few minutes to wash off my perfume de whorehouse."

As soon as Jamie heard the shower come on, she opened the bedroom door and ushered Amani's wait staff in to quickly set up a brunch of crepes, fruit, ham and potato fritters, fresh orange juice, and coffee on the bedroom balcony.

Trip's smile was almost as bright as the sun-filled morning when Jamie revealed their feast. They had nearly polished off every bite when Trip looked up, smiling. "So, what's next?"

"When we're almost finished, I'm supposed to text Jerome. He's standing by to saddle a couple of horses so you can give me a tour of your property."

Trip looked surprised, but pleased. "I didn't know you could ride." She grinned. "Not horses, anyway."

"Pervert." Jamie poked her leg under the table. "Jerome said he'd saddle one that even a beginner like me would be comfortable riding."

Trip nodded. "Two of my personal horses are Missouri fox trotters. Very smooth." She took Jamie's hand, her expression turning uncharacteristically shy. "I'd love to show Grandpa's land to you. Do you want to text Jerome now?"

Jamie shook her head and plunged in. "No. I want to tell you about a phone call I got yesterday." Jamie held her hand up when Trip's expression turned instantly sour and guarded. "No, don't do that. Can you just listen without deciding it's bad news before I even open my mouth?"

Trip had the decency to look chagrinned. "Sorry. I'm sorry. I'm listening."

"I tried to track you down several times yesterday as soon as the guy contacted me because I was excited and wanted to know what you thought about it. But my calls kept going to voice mail. I trusted that you were out on an emergency, not out playing call girl to Virginia what's-her-name."

Trip's face clouded. "If you think—"

Jamie held her hand up again. "No, I'm saying I know you well enough that I didn't think that, and I'm asking you to give me the same trust."

Trip's face flushed and her jaw worked—not like she was angry, but like she was holding back tears. Jamie kissed the hand that held hers. "Then I ended up working late because of a big pileup on the interstate, and Essie answered when I got off shift and called you again. She said you were here and upset. So, P and I packed an overnight bag and came right away. When we started talking about the Grace and Dani thing, I forgot about my news until after you had to go out on that colic call."

Trip held Jamie's hand to her chest, and Jamie could feel her heart thumping like a slow, steady drum. "You have my full attention now. Tell me this amazing news."

Jamie explained the call, emphasizing that she told the man she wasn't job hunting but would talk with them about some consulting work if it could be worked around her regular job. She was pleased that Trip asked some good questions and seemed to share Jamie's enthusiasm for the program.

"Maybe somewhere down the road, you could figure out how to rescue young men like Jubal and his pals, the same way this program would rescue shelter dogs," Trip said.

"I'm only one person, Trip."

"And every successful company begins with a single great idea and builds from there. Go to your meeting tomorrow. Essie and I will watch Petunia."

"Thanks." *I love you.* The words almost popped out of Jamie's mouth. They'd broken free from her heart and were poised to leap from her tongue, but fear held her back. Too soon, she told herself.

Trip wished she hadn't slept the morning away because the rest of their day felt like…well, like one of those sappy romance stories she secretly liked to read. They rode the horses along shaded tractor paths to every corner of the Beaumont estate, enjoyed a playful swim, dined by the pool and made plans for the Boys and Girls Club. They schemed, they laughed, and they shared.

Trip closed her eyes and tried to burn into her memory the feel of Jamie's naked body cuddled against her side, Jamie's dark head resting in the well of her shoulder, and Jamie's slow breaths warming her breast. She'd wanted to tell Jamie that the day had been the best she could ever remember. She wanted to confess she was falling more deeply in love with every smile Jamie turned her way, every word Jamie spoke to her, every touch of Jamie's skin against hers. She wanted so badly to vocalize what she'd tried to convey by making slow, sweet love when they'd come upstairs.

Even as desperate as she was to gaze into Jamie's eyes and say *I love you*, the only words her mouth would form were *Don't leave me.*

CHAPTER TWENTY

Trip watched Jamie stand in front of the dresser mirror in her uniform pants and a white T-shirt while she combed her hair. Trip liked that she'd hung her uniform in Trip's closet the day before, and wondered when the time would be right for her to suggest that Jamie bring more, then all her clothes to hang in *their* closet. Maybe she'd talk to Amani about doing something fancy with the walk-in closet and storing some of Trip's seasonal stuff in another closet. Jamie strapped on the Kevlar vest she wore under her uniform shirt, jerking Trip's thoughts from her remodeling plans. She went to Jamie and watched her fasten the straps so she could help or do it for her next time.

"You'll be careful today, won't you?"

Jamie smiled. "Always." She gave Trip a quick peck on the lips. "You never know when Bud might run short of hush puppies and a riot might break out."

Trip frowned. "I'm serious."

"I know you are." Jamie put her arms into her uniform shirt and tugged it over her shoulders before turning to Trip. "You be careful. I worry every day that you could get kicked in the head or crushed under a horse."

Trip frowned and began buttoning Jamie's shirt for her. "You chase down drug runners and answer domestic calls, the most dangerous call for police officers in any town. I know how to google things."

Jamie unbuckled her belt and opened her trousers to tuck her shirt in while Trip continued buttoning. "Let's talk about dangerous. You doctor alligators, snakes, and buffalo."

"I take precautions."

Jamie stilled Trip's hands. "I do, too. How about we both agree to be careful?"

This was hard. Trip thought that once they were more than friends, everything would be perfect. Oh, she knew they'd probably argue over her tendency to leave the cap off the toothpaste and eat cookies in bed, but that was minor stuff.

Amani was in the kitchen. "Y'all are moving as slow as Aunt Essie this morning. She said her arthritis is acting up, but I don't need to know your excuse." She pointed to two brown paper bags on the table. "When I packed the kids' lunches this morning, I made some extra breakfast burritos and wrapped up one for each of you. There's a doughnut in each one, too, because Aunt Essie said her sweet tooth was also acting up."

Trip grinned and gave Amani a quick kiss on the cheek. "You're the best."

"Thanks, Amani," Jamie said, grabbing her bag. "Where's P?"

"She's cuddled up with Aunt Essie. I let her out earlier, but I don't think she likes that food you have for her. She didn't even sniff it when I put it down. Just drank a little water and went right back to Aunt Essie. She didn't seem too perky either."

"Drinking water is good, even if she isn't eating. Give her the day off. It'll keep you from having to drive out here to drop her off before you head to Savannah." Trip checked her watch and tapped a quick text message on her phone. "I'm already going to be a bit late to my first appointment, but I'll get Dani to come check on her before she starts office hours. If she's still refusing to eat tonight, I'll ultrasound her belly."

Jamie hesitated, staring down the hall for a moment, then nodded. They were crossing the yard when Amani called after them.

"I gave Jamie two doughnuts for a little extra energy in case you kept that poor woman up all night, Trip Beaumont."

Trip whirled and opened her bag. She also had two doughnuts.

Amani laughed. "Made you look."

Jamie stopped beside her truck and shook her head. "They are like family, aren't they?"

"I can't imagine siblings being worse." Oh, yeah. She had blood siblings. She kept forgetting about those. "I mean, ones who actually like you and hang out with you."

Jamie gave her one last peck on the lips. "I'll call you before I hit the road to Savannah this afternoon."

"Please do."

Jamie turned to get into her truck and the clarion rang loud in Trip's head. Say it, say it, say it.

"Jamie?"

Jamie glanced at her watch before glancing back at her.

She was going to make Jamie late. Trip knew how obsessive Jamie was about being punctual. She should wait for a time when Jamie wouldn't feel trapped to say it back. That's right. Later would be better. Trip heaved a mental sigh. Truth? She'd lost her nerve.

"Good luck in Savannah."

Jamie smiled. "Thanks."

❖

The day was nonstop.

Spring was birthing season, which overlapped with breeding season as the mares came back into heat. Show season started up before school even let out, and there were always accidents and injuries when young equestrians gathered to compete for ribbons and breeding stock were trailered from show to show to rack up points proving the strength of their bloodlines. Sprinkled into the mix were the farms that wanted mares checked and ultrasounds performed to confirm pregnancy or send them back to the breeding charts to order another sperm shipment for when the mare went back into heat.

She was now in those peak weeks when she was still birthing a few late babies, neutering colts born late last year, inseminating mares, treating show season injuries, and performing follow-up visits on mares and their foals she'd helped birth earlier that year. Dani leaving now was going to put her back to working sixteen-hour days.

It would be more manageable if Trip limited her practice to horses, like some vets. But small animal clinics were bread-and-butter in the veterinary world. An equine vet could travel to only so many farms in one day, which limited the number of patients they could see. A small animal vet could treat the same number of clients and bring in the same amount of revenue in an hour or two with no downtime for travel since the client came to them. They could double their efficiency by seeing a second patient while blood was being drawn or anal glands cleared on the first patient.

Besides, who would take care of Big Wig, Jawbone, Kiki, and her other unique clients if she wasn't willing to do it? And to keep her income level vetting only horses, she'd have to range a lot farther than four counties. She'd spend her life alone, traveling from farm to farm.

She didn't return to Pine Cone only for Essie. She did it for herself, too. She didn't want work to be the only thing in her life. She wanted to bargain with Pete and Toby, Jubal and his guys. She wanted to save Grandpa's woodlands and enjoy them. She wanted to eat at the diner where she knew almost everyone and they knew her. She wanted to surround herself with longtime friends who really cared about her.

Pine Cone was her heart...and her entertainment. Where else would an old widow call an ambulance for a pig?

Trip had to park behind three police cars and two ambulances and push past a crowd of neighbors to get to Mrs. Ludwell's front yard where an emergency medical technician was trying to hold an ice pack to the back of Mrs. Ludwell's neck and another was pleading with her to move from her seat on the steps to their stretcher. She was waving her arms to fend them off and talking a million words per minute. All Trip could understand was "snake," "Annabelle," and "Beaumont." Deputy Thompson waved Trip over.

"What's going on?" Trip asked.

"Mrs. Ludwell has fainted twice, but she refuses to get on the stretcher. She said she called the ambulance for somebody named Annabelle because she was bitten by a snake. But we've searched the house but didn't find anyone. The medics want to tranquilize her and haul her to the mental ward, but she keeps asking for you. Is she a relative of yours?"

Trip shook her head, reaching into her pocket when her phone vibrated against her leg. "Beaumont."

"Hey, just letting you know I'm on Ninety-five, headed to Savannah."

Mrs. Ludwell spotted Trip and jumped up, sending both EMTs sprawling. "Dr. Beaumont, thank God you're here to save the day."

Jamie chuckled on the other end, apparently overhearing Mrs. Ludwell's exclamation. "Wearing your Superwoman cape again?"

Trip turned and stepped away from Thompson's big ears. "You know I only wear that for you." She looked over her shoulder. Mrs. Ludwell was barreling her way. "Gotta go, babe. Mrs. Ludwell is about to run me down. A snake bit her pet pig and she wants the ambulance people to put it on a stretcher and take her to my clinic. The whole neighborhood has turned out to watch."

"Do you need help with crowd control?" Jamie was suddenly serious.

"No, no. Thompson has it under control. Go to your appointment. I'll talk to you tonight."

"Okay."

"Love you." It was out of her mouth before Trip had time to think about it. But the call had disconnected. She almost smacked into Mrs. Ludwell when she turned around.

"Dr. Beaumont. A snake bit Annabelle. She screamed so loud, poor baby. I killed it with a hoe, but I can't get these men to take her to your hospital. She must be treated right away." Tears welled in her eyes, and she dabbed at them with a ball of tissue wadded in her hand. "I don't know what I'll do if I lose Annabelle. She's been such a comfort since Mr. Ludwell passed."

Trip took Mrs. Ludwell's hand in hers. "Mrs. Ludwell, I want you to sit on this stretcher and listen to me." Trip guided the now sobbing Mrs. Ludwell back to the medical people. Mrs. Ludwell's face had turned an alarming gray and she'd begun to hyperventilate.

Thompson bent close to Trip's ear. "I'm telling you there's nobody in the house, just a pig in the backyard."

Trip ignored him. "I'm going to take care of Annabelle. Snakebites are rarely serious for pigs. They have very thick skin, a thick layer of fat, and few blood vessels near the surface. In fact, pigs in the wild sometimes kill and eat snakes."

The medic looked wary when Trip signaled for him, but he approached slowly.

"Now, I need to ask you a few questions before I check Annabelle, but you're not looking so good either. You're going to lie back and let this medic put an IV in your arm while we talk."

"But Annabelle—"

"She seems fine, Mrs. Ludwell. Ran me right out of the yard when I went back to see if anyone was back there," Thompson said.

"And I'll check on her next. But you must let these guys take care of you first. I've heard of pigs grieving themselves to death over an animal friend or beloved owner. You wouldn't want that to happen to Annabelle, would you?"

Mrs. Ludwell shook her head emphatically and her eyes locked onto Trip's face like she was a lifeline. "I know it's silly to love a pig, but I do."

"It's not silly," Trip said, helping Mrs. Ludwell lie down on the stretcher. "Now, do what these guys ask and I'm going to get Annabelle so you can see that she's okay."

Trip went through the house to get Annabelle's pink harness, then brought her around so Mrs. Ludwell could watch her clean the tiny puncture wounds. Turned out the real victim was an unfortunate nonpoisonous rat snake that probably bit because the pig stepped on it. When it was all sorted, Mrs. Ludwell was transported to the hospital for an overnight stay to stabilize her heart rate, and a neighbor's fourteen-year-old grandson, who loved Annabelle, came to pig-sit until Mrs. Ludwell was released to come home.

One more stop, then a mound of paperwork back at the clinic. Trip's mind drifted back to Jamie. Had she arrived in Savannah yet? Her truck indicated an incoming call.

"Essie? Are you okay?" Essie never called since her grandkids taught her how to text from her iPad.

"Miss Petunia is real sick, Trip. I called over to the clinic and Dani's here."

"Is she there now? Put me on speaker."

"Trip?"

"Give me the bottom line, straight up."

"Heart rate up, respirations shallow. She's in a lot of pain. Her belly is tight as a drum. Essie said she hasn't eaten anything since yesterday morning, but threw up food about an hour ago. If we don't drop a gastric tube quick, her stomach could burst. After we do that, it looks like we'll need to open her up and see what else is going on."

"Take her to the clinic and prep her for surgery. I'm going to call Jamie, then see if we can get Professor Harrell to join us via the web. He's still out of the country."

"You can do this yourself, Trip. I've seen your surgery credentials. I also saw the MRI report. This has to be a complication from the first surgery or a new tumor."

"This one's extra special, Dani. I want Petunia to have every chance possible."

"You are her best chance, Trip. Because she and Jamie are more than an interesting case to you."

❖

Jamie was glad she'd arrived early because she had to drive around for thirty minutes just to find a city parking deck that wasn't full. The address was one of those old buildings on River Street in downtown Savannah that had been renovated for boutique shops on the first floor, then twenty or so additional floors were divided between professional office space and upscale apartments. The top floor was a popular restaurant and pub. Jamie was sure the property was worth more than the whole town of Pine Cone, but she wouldn't give a rusty penny for it.

The river was scenic if viewed from inside an air-conditioned building, but outside, the humidity coming off the Savannah River was so thick you could almost drink the air. She grimaced at her reflection in the shiny metal lining of the elevator. The collar of her white shirt had wilted and even her navy suit showed a hint of the sweat that soaked her armpits and back. She hoped their office was super cold because she wouldn't dare take her jacket off. Her shirt felt like she'd been caught in a rainstorm. As it was, she looked like a half-drowned river rat.

The elevator opened and she stepped out to look around. These doors didn't look like offices. They looked like residences. She checked the address again. Maybe it was a business suite the foundation kept for executives who landed in town periodically for business meetings.

She knocked on the door, then cursed herself for not seeing the doorbell inlaid in a swirl of scrollwork engraved into the door. She was about to push the bell's button when the door opened. A young blond man, shirtsleeves rolled up his forearms and tie loose, stared back at her. "Can I help you?" he asked.

"I'm sorry. I must have the wrong address," Jamie said.

"Jamie, it's so good to see you after all these years. Eric, don't leave her standing in the hallway."

The man stepped back and Jamie froze in disbelief. "Suzanne?"

Suzanne had grown even more attractive with maturity. Physical maturity. She hadn't lost that edge Jamie labeled "high school mean girl." Suzanne wrapped Jamie in a hug, then stepped back. She patted her cheek that had touched Jamie's sweaty one with a tissue. "I'm so sorry. I'm sure you don't feel like hugs after being in that god-awful heat outside. Sit and give yourself a chance to cool off."

This was too Twilight Zone for Jamie. "I have an appointment with the Strange Foundation. Obviously, I wrote the address down wrong. I'll go back to the lobby and call the man I spoke to before."

Eric opened the door with a smile and bowed when she started to make her exit. Suzanne's terse snarl stopped her.

"Not funny, Eric."

His smile vanished. He closed the door and returned to the sitting area.

"You have an appointment with me, Jamie. I'm the southeast director for the Strange Foundation."

Jamie leveled a hard gaze at Suzanne. "Then I'm definitely in the wrong place." She started for the door again.

"Wait, please." Suzanne gestured weakly to Eric and a brunette version of Suzanne he sat next to on the sofa. The coffee table in front of them was covered with coffee cups and official-looking papers. "This is Eric and Lisa. The Strange Foundation is serious about the Shelter to Working Dog program. We were just discussing it and want to talk to you about our plans. We can save a lot of dogs, Jamie."

Jamie knew how manipulative Suzanne could be, but what did it matter if some deserving dogs got a second chance instead of the euthanasia chamber? "May I use your restroom? I got here early, but spent the entire time looking for somewhere to park."

"Of course. Down the hall, first door on the right. Can I get you something to drink?"

"Soda. I'm not picky as long as it isn't something weird like grape or orange."

Suzanne pointed to the granite-topped island that separated the kitchen area from the rest of the living space. "You can leave your things here, if you want."

Jamie nodded and left her sunglasses and phone on the counter. The phone needed a code to open the contacts, but she wanted to see if Suzanne would try to snoop through her text messages.

The phone was still there when she returned, but not lined precisely with the edge like she'd intentionally placed it. And Eric and Lisa were gone.

"Where are your friends?"

Suzanne shrugged and smiled as she handed Jamie a glass of soda. "I told them I could pitch the program better alone, since we're old friends."

"We're not friends, Suzanne. You knew I thought Trip was too blueblood for me and you used that, making up lie after lie about her. Bedding the entire volleyball team? She was tutoring them in math."

Suzanne threw her head back and laughed in an overacted display of disbelief. "Is that what she told you?"

"I checked it out. One of those players works for the Georgia Bureau of Investigation now, so I called her. She was happy to tell me about how she'd never have stayed qualified to play in the national championship if Trip hadn't helped her understand algorithms. She also offered to give me the phone numbers of some other players she'd kept in contact with."

Suzanne shrugged. "Whatever. That's old trash, Jamie." She moved into Jamie's personal space and trailed her fingers down Jamie's neck and the vee of her shirt front. "Let's just throw it out and start over. I can offer you the job you've always wanted." She moved closer, her lips inches from Jamie's. "And special perks you only dreamed of before."

Jamie grabbed Suzanne's shoulders and shoved her back. "I have everything I want already, more than I ever dreamed possible."

"I'm sorry, Dr. Beaumont. Professor Harrell can't be reached by phone. He checks his email every three days, but he just responded to some messages yesterday. We don't expect to hear from him again for another couple of days."

Trip silently cursed. "Thank you. I'll email him about the case we've been working together."

Even if today's surgery was successful, Trip would want to keep him as a consultant on the case. An ultrasound of Petunia's belly revealed another tumor blocking the small intestine. It must have grown very fast because it hadn't shown up on the MRI several weeks ago. What on earth had that lab been researching? If she removed this tumor, would another grow just as fast?

Not that there was any choice to make, but she'd feel better if she could talk to Jamie before starting the surgery. Every time she tried, her call went to Jamie's voice mail. Petunia had been sedated to insert the gastric tube and complete the ultrasound, so there was no reason to delay the surgery. Petunia wouldn't survive without it.

Jamie fumed as she drove down the interstate. Suzanne was some piece of work. Part of her was disappointed that the offer had been bogus. It was just Suzanne popping into their lives to mess things up again. Not this time.

Her thumb had already been in motion to touch the "end call" icon when Trip's voice came through once more. *Love you*. Those words made her response to Suzanne instant and easy. Trip would no longer hold back. Well, Jamie was done holding back, too.

She glanced at her speedometer and backed off the accelerator. She smiled to herself. Trip would never let her live down a speeding ticket.

Jamie was one county away from Pine Cone when the police scanner in her truck lit up with traffic. Body. By the river. Homeless men. She listened, but the traffic was overlapping until a highway patrol sergeant ordered all discussion pertaining to that case moved to a different channel. But she missed the channel number. God, why did men mumble into their mics? She hated that almost as much as the ones who talked super fast, like they were practicing for their auctioneer's license. She keyed the mic on the police radio lying on the truck seat.

"This is Pine Cone unit twelve. What's the ten-twenty on that ten-one hundred?"

"You can relax, Pine Cone twelve. HP is handling this. We have two suspects already in custody."

Jamie growled under her breath at the young trooper's smug report. "Arrogant son of a bitch."

"Pine Cone twelve, you copy?"

Jamie smiled at the familiar sound of her dispatcher's voice. "Pine Cone twelve, ten-four."

"I had a ten-five for you earlier. You might want to check your messages."

"Ten-four. I'll do that."

Jamie pulled off at the next exit and groped for her phone. "Damn it." She didn't remember turning it off. Suzanne. You didn't need a security code to turn a phone off. She waited impatiently for it to boot up. Several missed calls and two messages from Trip. Jamie would listen to those later. Trip was probably anxious to find out how the meeting went. She kept scrolling until she saw a message from an unfamiliar number.

Miss Jamie, it's Toby. Pete and I found your soldier. It's not good. We're down by the river.

Jamie scribbled as she listened to him drawl out the directions, then spun tires as she flew down the ramp to merge back onto the interstate.

Trip carefully lifted the tumor into the lab dish.

"As much trouble as that tumor was causing, you'd expect it to be larger," Dani said.

"Didn't need to be because it was situated in a very bad place," Trip said, examining the edges of the tumor. The tumor looked exactly like the one she'd removed with Dr. Harrell, and she'd bet the farm it was also benign. Still, they'd let the lab confirm it. She turned back to the operating table. "Let's take a good look at everything else in here to see if we can spot any more of these tumors waiting to blossom."

"Good idea. How's our patient doing?"

"Vitals are still good," Cindy said.

Almost an hour later, Trip straightened to stretch her back while Dani hovered a moment more over the sterile field. "She looks clean as a whistle, but there's never a guarantee."

Trip held out her hand. Michelle laid the first suture in Trip's palm, then began preparing the next. "When I was trying to decide at one point what direction to take my life, my grandfather told me there are no guarantees, except death and taxes. He said, 'Trip, if a guarantee is what you're holding out for, death and taxes might be all you have when you reach the end of the road.' So, if she grows another tumor, we'll take that out, too, and keep looking for new solutions until Petunia has no options left. I'll never give up just because there's no guarantee."

The road down to the river was little more than a wide path and so completely blocked by multiple law enforcement vehicles that Jamie had to skirt a tree to keep going. The scene was lit by the headlight of the first two cars.

A long, thick branch of a huge oak stretched out over the water. Someone wearing a dark vest with bright yellow letters proclaiming Forensics was perched on the limb and sawing at a rope. Two men in fishermen's waders stood below, waiting to catch the body that hung from the rope.

"Miss Jamie, she knows us. Miss Jamie, over here."

Jamie turned and saw Pete poking his head around a huge state trooper who had Pete and Toby spread against his cruiser and was in the process of searching them. The trooper stopped and turned to her.

"And who are you?" His chubby, peach-fuzz-covered cheeks made his scowl look more like a pout.

"That's Deputy Grant, sir. She knows us." Toby spoke, but remained in the search stance since the trooper hadn't released them.

"Shut up," the young trooper said. "You aren't allowed to talk unless you're ready to tell us what happened."

"We been trying to tell you," Pete whined.

"I'm thinking that y'all are running drugs and crossed somebody you shouldn't have," the trooper said. "That what happened to your buddy?"

"Who's in charge here?" Jamie asked.

"Who wants to know?" The trooper sneered at the Pine Cone Sheriff's Office badge she held out to him.

"Deputy Grant, what brings you down here?" A trim man with a graying crew cut strode toward them. His handshake was warm when Jamie walked forward to greet him.

"Good to see you again, Captain." Jamie was relieved to see the higher-ranked trooper she'd met while working the big drug bust. He'd done time in the desert too.

A small splash drew everybody's attention, and they watched the body be carried to the black zippered bag laid out on a stretcher.

"Are there drugs tied up in this?" He looked around Jamie's feet. "Where's your partner?"

"She's off-duty. I was just coming back from a meeting in Savannah when I got a message from one of the suspects your trooper is searching over there."

"Suspects?"

Jamie pointed to where the trooper had resumed his search of Toby.

"Aw, hell." He waved his trooper over to join them. "Smith, you dumbass. I told you to ask them to stick around so I could talk to them. They're not suspects."

"Just look at them, sir. I'm betting they have a dozen warrants out on each of them."

He shook his head and turned to Jamie. "Can you vouch for these men, Grant?"

"Yes, sir. They've been helping me look for a young veteran that hasn't been doing well. They called to say that they'd found him." A forensic tech was blocking her view of the body, but she recognized Adder's duffel on the shore. "I'm pretty sure all three of us can identify the deceased, or at least give you enough information to track down his identity. But I want to talk to my friends first. It might not be good for Pete to see the body. He's already pretty wound up."

Pete was as agitated as she'd ever seen him, bouncing from foot to foot. Toby had finally turned and propped against the trooper's car. He was quiet and did not look up when she went to them. She gave him a one-armed hug. "Tell me."

"We don't usually come down this far, but we heard from someone else that Adder had been seen around here. This is how we found him." He finally met Jamie's eyes. "I'm so sorry, Miss Jamie. I know you wanted to help him."

"You're sure it's Adder?"

"I seen him," Pete said. "I shimmied up that tree to get close. I was going to cut him down and let the river take him, but Toby said no. We should call you."

"Toby was right, Pete."

She asked a few more questions, then clasped Toby's arm and gave it a squeeze. "Thanks for calling me. You guys wait here while I straighten this out."

"I don't know his last name," Jamie said. The captain nodded and a technician zipped up the body bag. She'd watched army medics close zippers over the boyish faces of young recruits and hardened soldiers alike. "He told me his first name was Francis. He's a vet. Couple of tours in the desert. They called him Adder over there. That's what he liked to go by. I'm betting you'll find his DD-two-fourteen and dog tags in that duffel over there. It looks like the one he always carried. If not in the duffel, Toby said Adder kept a locked metal box stashed somewhere in the old train depot. He never showed them where, but told Toby it was there in case something happened to him."

The captain nodded. "We'll look for it. If we can't find it, we'll call you and see if your partner can track it down."

"Only if he put drugs or explosives in it. Otherwise, you'll need a bloodhound."

He nodded. "You think this is self-inflicted?"

"Yeah. I was looking for him because the last time I saw him, he seemed to be losing his struggle with PTSD, but wasn't ready to accept help."

The captain shook his head. "We ought to be doing more for these soldiers coming back wounded worse inside than out." He searched her face. "You still have dreams?"

"Yeah." *Never lie to a fellow vet.*

"Me, too," he said softly.

"My dog seems to sense when I go back there in my head. She helps," Jamie said.

They stared out over the river until Pete added arm swinging to his nervous foot shuffling.

"These guys are not homeless, just restless," Jamie said. "I think Pete is a bit autistic, but Toby looks out for him. Right now, all these people milling around after them finding Adder is straining Pete's limit. All right for them to go?"

"Yeah. I'll call you if we need more information from them."

She returned to Toby and Pete. "You've answered all the questions the captain has right now. He'll call me if he has any more for you later. Need a ride back to Pine Cone?"

"Toby's truck is down the road. I can find it. I can find anything no matter how dark."

"You're a good man, Pete," Jamie said. "Thank you for finding Adder. I guess his burden was too heavy for him to carry, but he's in a better place now."

Pete nodded and swung his arms. "Better place. He's in a better place."

"He's got somebody, somewhere who must be wondering where he's gone," Toby said. "You find them and send his things to them."

"I will, Toby. I promise."

❖

The phone rang and rang.

"This is Jamie Grant. I'm not currently available. Please leave a message."

Trip ended the call. She'd already left a dozen messages. Her gut churned with a sense of foreboding, but she shook it off. She was being silly. Maybe Jamie dropped her phone and it broke. Hell, Trip dropped hers in a toilet once and no amount of time in a bag of rice could dry it out. Jamie might've simply run the battery down and didn't have a charger with her. She glanced at her watch. It was ten o'clock. *Where are you, Jamie?*

Accident scenarios rolled through her head. Assault possibilities formed in her mind—Jamie beaten unconscious and doctors working frantically over her while Trip stood helplessly in the corner. Geez. She'd been watching too much television.

Didn't Jamie say these people called her from New York? She'd heard those New York City types lived their work. They probably trapped her into a working dinner, which meant cocktails, several courses, and dessert. Jamie probably was itching to get back on the road while they chatted on and on.

Trip checked again on Petunia. She was snoring softly. A little swelling, but only what should be expected. She decided to pass the time by browsing the web for playground equipment. She and Jamie wanted to work up a proposal to turn the trash lot across from the Boys and Girls Club into a clean, safe playground.

She checked a few wholesale sites. Wow. This stuff was expensive, but it looked like it wouldn't be hard to build for a fraction of the cost. She bookmarked a few sites, then searched for grants that could help.

Then, on a whim, Trip typed STRANGE FOUNDATION into the search engine. A fancy website flowed onto the page and Trip began to read. The board of directors and the causes they supported were impressive. So was the amount of money they handed out. No wonder Jamie was sticking out the evening with them.

Ah. A list of full-time staff. Trip scrolled down the list until she reached the southeast region. She stared at the name. No. It couldn't be.

Every insecurity buried in Trip's subconscious came bubbling to the surface.

Jamie's gone, Trip. She left because of you. I told her that you seduced me, then dumped me. You were supposed to be her best friend, but you went after me anyway. She was never going to be yours. You are way too butch for her. She likes femmes. Even if you two got together, all I'd have to do is crook my finger and she'd come running back to me.

"No. I don't believe it. Jamie knows not to believe Suzanne's lies anymore. There's a good reason she's not back yet."

Maybe saying it a hundred more times would help her believe it.

Twenty-four poles, thirty-five cars, ten exits, fourteen light poles, seven houses, two dogs, twenty-six fence posts, four horses, six porch supports.

The sharp rapping startled Jamie. When had the sun come up? She was in her truck, sitting in front of Trip's clinic. She didn't dare close her eyes. When she did, she saw Adder hanging from that tree. She saw raw meat on desert sand but couldn't tell what part was her leg and what was her flayed canine. She even saw Suzanne touching

Trip, smiling at Jamie while she brought Trip to orgasm. Then she began to count. She didn't know how long she counted, but it was dark when she started.

She flinched when a second round of rapping jerked her into the present.

"Are you all right, hon?" Brenda looked worried. "Aren't you coming inside?"

Jamie opened her door and climbed out. She was stiff, but numbly followed Brenda into the clinic.

"Do you want some coffee?"

"Bathroom." Her throat was sore and her eyes felt gritty.

"Down the hall."

Jamie felt more alert after washing her face and hands with cold soapy water, but still bone-tired and resigned. She'd been so wrapped up in the excitement of this new, more exciting relationship with Trip that she'd forgotten that she was damaged. Or maybe she'd unconsciously blocked it out. The support group she'd been forced to attend before her discharge was filled with guys facing divorce because their wives couldn't deal with their mental issues. Last night was a rude notice that her new happiness hadn't magically cured the flashbacks, and Trip deserved to know. She trudged out down the hall to the reception desk. "Thanks, Brenda. I guess I'll go over to the house and see if Trip is there."

Brenda gave her an odd look. "She's right here, sacked out in her office." Something changed in her eyes. "Oh, honey, didn't she ever reach you last night? I know she called and called."

Trip's messages—had she listened to them? Had she returned Trip's calls last night? All she could remember was pulling back onto the dark highway. Then the flashbacks started.

"She had to operate on Petunia," Brenda said. "She's been up almost all night."

Jamie stopped breathing. One, two, three pictures on the wall, one bench, five chairs, one flower pot, one coffee maker. "Petunia."

"She's going to be fine."

Jamie whirled. Trip looked as tired as she sounded. Jamie could feel her mouth working, but no words were coming out. When Trip gestured to the doorway where she stood, Jamie wasn't sure her wobbly legs would hold up. But they did, and then she was standing in Trip's office by a large dog crate where Petunia was resting on a soft blanket. There seemed to be tubes everywhere. Jamie wanted to cradle Petunia in her lap, stroke her rough fur and tell her it would all be okay. Instead, she poked a tentative finger through the wire cage to touch Petunia's furry paw.

Trip opened the crate's door. "She's still pretty groggy, but you can pet her."

Jamie reached in and stroked Petunia's head. "Hey, P. I'm here now. You sleep as long as you need. I want you to get all better. I'll be here when you wake up, so don't worry about anything. You're not alone. I'm not leaving you. This is a good place, not a bad research lab." Her throat closed around the last words, but she added a final loving stroke before withdrawing.

"A second tumor had developed, just like the last one. That's why she stopped eating and was getting sick again. Dani and I had to remove it last night when her stomach got backed up and started swelling. This time, we opened up the abdomen and did a thorough search for any other suspicious cells that could grow another tumor as fast as that one. She appears clear, so I would say her prognosis is very positive."

Something in Jamie snapped and she began to cry. She was so tired and so, so broken. Maybe Petunia was broken, too, and would never be free of the tumors. She sank to her knees, her face in her hands.

Then strong arms wrapped around her, holding her tight, holding her up. It seemed like forever before she could gather herself enough to talk.

"We need to talk."

Trip didn't answer at first, but dropped her arms, stood and moved away. "You took the job and you're leaving." Her voice was flat.

"No, no, no." She shook her head as she rose and turned. "Why would you think that? We talked about it before I went to the appointment."

Trip stared at the floor. "Did you know you would be meeting Suzanne?"

"Is that what you think?"

"No." Trip rubbed at her face. "I don't know. Maybe. I was trying to pass the time and was shopping for playground equipment, then decided to look up this foundation. I saw her name. Southeast director. When you didn't answer your phone and it got later and later—" Trip shrugged. "I imagined all kinds of things...like she offered you a dream job...like maybe you decided you were still in love with her after you saw her."

"She did offer me a dream job and herself as a perk, but I told her to go fuck herself."

Trip's eyes were pleading. "Then where were you all night, Jamie? I've been crazy with worry."

Jamie's throat tightened as the desert invaded the edges of her vision. Five short bottles, two tall bottles, three glass canisters, six cabinet doors. "I was counting. Driving and counting."

Wordlessly, Trip sat at the end of the sofa and tugged Jamie down to sit between her legs so Jamie could see the rest of the office and things to count. Jamie began to shake so hard her teeth chattered. Trip's arms squeezed her like a vice. "When you're able, tell me about it."

"Puh-P-tuh-T-S-da-D," Jamie stammered out. "Four letters. Sta-stamped uh-eight times on my medical discharge." Two stacks of paper. One file cabinet, four drawers. Eight pencils in one cup.

It took the better part of an hour and half a box of tissues, but Jamie managed to explain about Adder, and how his death triggered the worst episode of PTSD she'd experienced since rehab. When she finished the story, she was no longer counting, her stutter subsided, and they were both fighting sleep. Trip slid down and Jamie rolled over to cuddle against her side. Still, Jamie wasn't done.

"Two words. I heard them. It should have been three."

Trip blinked. "Is that a riddle?"

Jamie rose up on her elbow. "You said, 'Love you.' I heard it on the phone."

"Ah. I'll give you more than three." Trip's gaze grew soft. "I love you, Jamie Grant. I have loved you since our first year together in college."

Even though Jamie was confident Trip would say the words she longed to hear, even though the past days together had erased her doubts about Trip's desire for her, the unguarded trust in Trip's eyes was new and daunting.

Jamie was the one mired in the mud now by the weight of this moment. She didn't doubt her attraction, her affection for Trip. Was she worthy of Trip's trust? Her willingness to accept Suzanne's lies about Trip had been the real problem between them. And she wasn't stupid enough to believe Trip's insecurities wouldn't resurface occasionally, just like her PTSD. Was she strong enough, whole enough, to accept Trip's love? Petunia had still another chance. Was it possible that she could, too?

Jamie scanned the shelf next to Trip. One stack of eight magazines, five books.

"Come on, Jamie," Trip said softly. "Let's erase the past and start clean. I want to count you as one...my only one."

Jamie stopped counting and looked down into eyes as blue as a cloudless summer sky, then took the biggest chance of her life. No. This wasn't chance. It was sure, solid ground.

"One. You're my one. I love you, Trip Beaumont."

EPILOGUE

Jamie slowed and peered at the porch of Old Lady Jackson's house. Unable to resist, she turned into Jackson's drive, climbed out of her truck, and helped Petunia down in time to enjoy the final verse of the national anthem.

"Well, if that doesn't put you in the mood for the Fourth of July weekend, I don't know what will," Jamie said, eyeing Clarice's bright red stretch pants and blue pullover with huge white stars. She looked ready to run up a flagpole.

Jackson and Clarice grinned happily from their rocking chairs... and from behind extra dark sunglasses. It was a sure bet she'd find very dilated pupils behind those glasses.

"We're just taking a break from our baking and the day is so pretty, we just burst into song," Clarice said.

"I'm happy you two are getting along so well."

Clarice waved a dismissive hand. "It was a big misunderstanding. She brought over some of her special brownies the very next day."

Jackson nodded. "And she baked lemon bars for me the day after that. I love lemon bars."

Clarice stopped rocking, sat forward in her chair, and stage whispered. "I volunteered and ATM got me in the program. We're baking enough brownies to fill the freezer in my bomb shelter out back of the house."

Jamie figured it would take a while to fill the freezer because they appeared to be eating most of what they baked. "ATM?"...*the girls said it stood for All That and More.*

Clarice nodded. "Agnes Teresa Marie. That's her name, but when we were buying brownie mix at the Piggly Wiggly, I heard one of her friends call her ATM. Jackson said I could call her that, too." Clarice beamed and Jackson grinned, but not for the same reason.

Petunia stared at the plate of brownies resting on the porch railing.

"I think she wants a brownie," Clarice said, reaching for the plate.

Jackson stopped her. "Uh, no. She has a sensitive stomach." She wrinkled her nose. "Gets gas really bad." She grinned at Jamie. They both knew why Petunia was staring at the brownies.

Jamie cleared her throat. "Well, her stomach problem has been fixed, but the chocolate isn't good for dogs."

Clarice grabbed on to Jackson's arm. "Oh, no. Are they bad for pigs, too? Mrs. Ludwell came by on her daily walk and Annabelle ate three brownies."

Jamie chuckled. "I'm not sure, but I think a pig would have to eat a whole lot of brownies for the chocolate to make them sick. But I'll ask Dr. Beaumont just to be sure. She's volunteering at the Boys and Girls Club today, and I'm headed over there, too."

"Annabelle has such a pretty pink harness." Clarice wasn't listening because her "special brownie" buzz was still focused on her memory of the pig.

Jackson slid her dark glasses down her nose and squinted. "I heard you and the doctor are bumping boots now."

Heat crawled up Jamie's neck, but she wasn't going to deny it. She was still a private person, but this was her home now and she wouldn't hide her relationship with Trip, or ask that of Trip. "We loaded up my U-Haul last weekend and emptied it out at her place."

"Well, congratulations." Jackson laughed at Jamie's use of lesbian code and sat back in her rocking chair. "You might want to watch your back for a while, though. There's going to be a lot of unhappy women around Pine Cone now that you've taken Fast Break off the market."

Jamie replied with a mock salute and a signal for Petunia to heel. "Y'all have a good day now."

Clarice's wavering soprano started up the first verse of "America the Beautiful" as Jamie backed her truck into the street, and ATM Jackson's smooth alto joined in as she pulled away.

❖

Trip held the leveling tool against the metal post that would support one side of the arched bronze sign announcing MISS M'S PLAYGROUND.

"That's good. Shovel in the concrete," she told Jubal.

"I can't believe you got all this done so quick," he said, carefully spading wet cement around the base of the pole while Trip continued to check it.

"I had a lot of help from people you wouldn't imagine. How's that pup doing?"

Jubal smiled. "Bruiser's chill. He's already graduated from puppy class, and Jamie is teaching us hand signals now. Bruiser's really smart. He's just a pup, but he figured out right off to be careful around Mama."

"That's great, Jubal. You've done a good job with him." She tamped down the last of the concrete. "I guess that does it. These posts will need a few days for the concrete to set before the men come out to install the sign. Looks like they need some help with the playground equipment over there. I'll wash out the wheelbarrow for you."

Trip paused and watched Jubal join the group that was unloading bulky playground equipment parts from a flatbed trailer Jerome had conscripted from the farm. Amani stood in the middle of the organized chaos, holding a master plan for the playground and pointing to where each part should be left for assembly.

An arm slid around her waist, and Trip smiled when a wheat-colored blur streaked past on a direct path to where Essie sat on a newly installed park bench, handing out cups of flavored water and snacks.

"Everything going okay here?" Jamie asked.

"Perfect. We've got so many volunteers, they'd be falling over each other if Amani wasn't such a great organizer."

The lot was filled with Jubal's gang, a few men and women from the police and fire departments, Toby and Pete, Edmundo and a few cousins, and several men from both the Baptist and Methodist churches. Trip and Jamie had intentionally arranged a diverse group, and Jamie had prepared the kids at the Boys and Girls Club with a talk about seeing people as individuals rather than making assumptions from their clothing or hairstyle or skin color. And about ways to get people to see them as individuals, not just as minority kids from a poor neighborhood.

"So, are you helping or just watching other people work?"

"Oh, crap. I need to wash the cement out of this wheelbarrow before it hardens. Can you grab that shovel and bring it?"

Jamie followed Trip across the street to an outdoor spigot and hose behind the Boys and Girls Club building. Trip set the wheelbarrow down and took the shovel from Jamie's hands.

"First things first." She tugged Jamie into her arms and kissed her. "I missed you."

"You just saw me a few hours ago," Jamie said. Still, she punctuated that statement with another kiss, this time lingering with a bit of tongue that made Trip's belly tighten…in a good way.

"How'd your meeting go with the contractor?" Trip was very excited about the new business Jamie would be starting soon.

"We agreed on a schedule. He's had another project delayed by some new city regulations, so his crew can get started as soon as he gets the building permit from the county. He estimates six weeks to two months, maybe less if the weather holds up and there are no surprises when they run the water and electrical lines out from the road."

An apologetic phone call from the director above Suzanne—now unemployed Suzanne—was indeed the consulting offer of Jamie's dreams. It didn't take much to persuade Jamie to ask Amani's advice on starting a business, but convincing Jamie to let Trip help finance the start-up took a lot more convincing. Trip knew Jamie wanted to rescue shelter dogs by turning them into valuable working dogs, but she also wanted to explore the use of therapy dogs for soldiers dealing with PTSD. The Strange Foundation was only offering seed money for the detection dog training program, so the PTSD program was the ace Trip played to deal herself in.

Grace was trying to be a good sport about losing Jamie, but was happy after Jamie promised to continue with the department until she could train a replacement. Turned out, Jamie already had her eye on Anderson. The rookie couldn't seem to remember to put his squad car in park, but had a way with dogs.

"That's great news." Trip tightened her arms around Jamie and sighed. "You're going to be really busy for the rest of the summer, juggling your deputy job and getting your new business off the ground."

"Probably as busy as you're going to be until you find another veterinarian to hire."

Trip nodded. "Let's make a pact now that we'll never be too busy with our own stuff that we neglect the kids down here."

"Deal, and I'm sorry I'm late today." Jamie stepped out of Trip's embrace to turn on the water. "I thought I was having some kind of strange flashback, and I had to stop for a few minutes."

Trip tilted the wheelbarrow and studied Jamie while she hosed it off. "You okay, babe?"

"No. I might have to wash my eyes out."

Trip relaxed at Jamie's teasing tone. "Why?"

"When I drove past Old Lady Jackson's house—"

"Only Grace calls her that. She's not that old."

"I know, but you're interrupting."

"Sorry. I'm working on that."

Jamie smiled and shared everything—the songs, the special brownies, the dark glasses, and the new friendship. By the time she'd finished, Trip was bent over and clutching her sides.

"Stop, stop. My stomach is going to be sore tomorrow from laughing. We have to go past there on the way home to see if they're still there."

"Only if you promise not to eat any food they offer you." Jamie's grin faded, and her expression turned serious. "Trip? Is it okay for pigs to eat brownies?"

Trip's throat constricted around the first gasp of laughter and she choked when she tried to swallow. Trip coughed and wheezed, trying to draw in a full breath while Jamie pounded on her back.

"Are you okay? Can you breathe? Are you choking?" Jamie's voice rose a few octaves with each question.

Trip tried to answer the rapid questions with nods and shakes of her head, but she couldn't keep up. Just as Jamie was moving behind her for what Trip feared was to be a Heimlich maneuver, her throat relaxed a bit and she gasped out a few words. "Image...Annabelle... on porch...in pink—" Her throat finally relaxed enough for a deep cough to clear it. "I had a flash of the three of them—Jackson, Clarice and Annabelle—lined up on the porch in their rocking chairs, the pig dressed in one of Clarice's pink housedresses, and all of them wearing dark glasses like they're the Blues Brothers."

Jamie stared at her. "You've already been by there, haven't you?" She grabbed Trip's jaw. "Open your mouth. I want to see if there are brownie crumbs in there."

Trip laughed even harder when Jamie joined in and they walked arm-in-arm back to the playground in progress. Life was good. Turned out that settling in Pine Cone hadn't been a gamble after all, because they'd both come in first in this winner-take-all adventure.

About the Author

D. Jackson Leigh grew up barefoot and happy, swimming in farm ponds and riding rude ponies in rural south Georgia. She is a career journalist, but has found her real passion in writing sultry lesbian romances laced with her trademark Southern humor and affection for horses.

She has published 11 novels and one collection of short stories with Bold Strokes Books, winning a 2010 Alice B. Lavender Award for Noteworthy Accomplishment, and three Golden Crown Literary Society awards in paranormal, romance, and fantasy categories. She also was a finalist for four more GCLS awards, and a finalist in the romance category of the 2014 Lambda Literary Society Awards.

Friend her at facebook.com/d.jackson.leigh, on twitter @ djacksonleigh, or learn more about her at www.djacksonleigh.com.

Books Available from Bold Strokes Books

Exposed by MJ Williamz. The closet is no place to live if you want to find true love. (978-1-62639-989-1)

Force of Fire: Toujours a Vous by Ali Vali. Immortals Kendal and Piper welcome their new child and celebrate the defeat of an old enemy, but another ancient evil is about to awaken deep in the jungles of Costa Rica. (978-1-63555-047-4)

Holding Their Place by Kelly A. Wacker. Together Dr. Helen Connery and ambulance driver Julia March, discover that goodness, love, and passion can be found in the most unlikely and even dangerous places during WWI. (978-1-63555-338-3)

Landing Zone by Erin Dutton. Can a career veteran finally discover a love stronger than even her pride? (978-1-63555-199-0)

Love at Last Call by M. Ullrich. Is balancing business, friendship, and love more than any willing woman can handle? (978-1-63555-197-6)

Pleasure Cruise by Yolanda Wallace. Spencer Collins and Amy Donovan have few things in common, but a Caribbean cruise offers both women an unexpected chance to face one of their greatest fears: falling in love. (978-1-63555-219-5)

Running Off Radar by MB Austin. Maji's plans to win Rose back are interrupted when work intrudes and duty calls her to help a SEAL team stop a Russian mobster from harvesting gold from the bottom of Sitka Sound. (978-1-63555-152-5)

Shadow of the Phoenix by Rebecca Harwell. In the final battle for the fate of Storm's Quarry, even Nadya's and Shay's powers may not be enough. (978-1-63555-181-5)

Take a Chance by D. Jackson Leigh. There's hardly a woman within fifty miles of Pine Cone that veterinarian Trip Beaumont can't charm, except for the irritating new cop, Jamie Grant, who keeps leaving parking tickets on her truck. (978-1-63555-118-1)

The Outcasts by Alexa Black. Spacebus driver Sue Jones is running from her past. When she crash-lands on a faraway world, the Outcast Kara might be her chance for redemption. (978-1-63555-242-3)

Alias by Cari Hunter. A car crash leaves a woman with no memory and no identity. Together with Detective Bronwen Pryce, she fights to uncover a truth that might just kill them both. (978-1-63555-221-8)

Death in Time by Robyn Nyx. Working in the past is hell on your future. (978-1-63555-053-5)

Hers to Protect by Nicole Disney. High school sweethearts Kaia and Adrienne will have to see past their differences and survive the vengeance of a brutal gang if they want to be together. (978-1-63555-229-4)

Of Echoes Born by 'Nathan Burgoine. A collection of queer fantasy short stories set in Canada from Lambda Literary Award finalist 'Nathan Burgoine. (978-1-63555-096-2)

Perfect Little Worlds by Clifford Mae Henderson. Lucy can't hold the secret any longer. Twenty-six years ago, her sister did the unthinkable. (978-1-63555-164-8)

Room Service by Fiona Riley. Interior designer Olivia likes stability, but when work brings footloose Savannah into her world and into a new city every month, Olivia must decide if what makes her comfortable is what makes her happy. (978-1-63555-120-4)

Sparks Like Ours by Melissa Brayden. Professional surfers Gia Malone and Elle Britton can't deny their chemistry on and off the beach. But only one can win... (978-1-63555-016-0)

Take My Hand by Missouri Vaun. River Hemsworth arrives in Georgia intent on escaping quickly, but when she crashes her Mercedes into the Clip 'n Curl, sexy Clay Cahill ends up rescuing more than her car. (978-1-63555-104-4)

The Last Time I Saw Her by Kathleen Knowles. Lane Hudson only has twelve days to win back Alison's heart. That is if she can gather the courage to try. (978-1-63555-067-2)

Wayworn Lovers by Gun Brooke. Will agoraphobic composer Giselle Bonnaire and Tierney Edwards, a wandering soul who can't remain in one place for long, trust in the passionate love destiny hands them? (978-1-62639-995-2)

Breakthrough by Kris Bryant. Falling for a sexy ranger is one thing, but is the possibility of love worth giving up the career Kennedy Wells has always dreamed of? (978-1-63555-179-2)

Certain Requirements by Elinor Zimmerman. Phoenix has always kept her love of kinky submission strictly behind the bedroom door and inside the bounds of romantic relationships, until she meets Kris Andersen. (978-1-63555-195-2)

Dark Euphoria by Ronica Black. When a high-profile case drops in Detective Maria Diaz's lap, she forges ahead only to discover this case, and her main suspect, aren't like any other. (978-1-63555-141-9)

Fore Play by Julie Cannon. Executive Leigh Marshall falls hard for Peyton Broader, her golf pro…and an ex-con. Will she risk sabotaging her career for love? (978-1-63555-102-0)

Love Came Calling by CA Popovich. Can a romantic looking for a long-term, committed relationship and a jaded cynic too busy for love conquer life's struggles and find their way to what matters most? (978-1-63555-205-8)

Outside the Law by Carsen Taite. Former sweethearts Tanne. and Sydney Braswell must work together on a federal task force to justice served, but will they choose to embrace their second chance love? (978-1-63555-039-9)

The Princess Deception by Nell Stark. When journalist Missy Duke realizes Prince Sebastian is really his twin sister Viola in disguise, she plays along, but when sparks flare between them, will the double deception doom their fairy-tale romance? (978-1-62639-979-2)

The Smell of Rain by Cameron MacElvee. Reyha Arslan, a wise and elegant woman with a tragic past, shows Chrys that there's still beauty to embrace and reason to hope despite the world's cruelty. (978-1-63555-166-2)

The Talebearer by Sheri Lewis Wohl. Liz's visions show her the faces of the lost and the killers who took their lives. As one by one, the murdered are found, a stranger works to stop Liz before the serial killer is brought to justice. (978-1-635550-126-6)

White Wings Weeping by Lesley Davis. The world is full of discord and hatred, but how much of it is just human nature when an evil with sinister intent is invading people's hearts? (978-1-63555-191-4)

A Call Away by KC Richardson. Can a businesswoman from a big city find the answers she's looking for, and possibly love, on a small-town farm? (978-1-63555-025-2)

Berlin Hungers by Justine Saracen. Can the love between an RAF woman and the wife of a Luftwaffe pilot, former enemies, survive in besieged Berlin during the aftermath of World War II? (978-1-63555-116-7)

Blend by Georgia Beers. Lindsay and Piper are like night and day. Working together won't be easy, but not falling in love might prove the hardest job of all. (978-1-63555-189-1)

ou by Jenny Frame. Principe of an ancient vampire Debrek must save her one true love from falling into s of her enemies and into the middle of a vampire war. -63555-168-6)

Mercy by Michelle Larkin. FBI Special Agent Mercy Parker and psychic ex-profiler Piper Vasey learn to love again as they race to stop a man with supernatural gifts who's bent on annihilating humankind. (978-1-63555-202-7)

Pride and Porters by Charlotte Greene. Will pride and prejudice prevent these modern-day lovers from living happily ever after? (978-1-63555-158-7)

Rocks and Stars by Sam Ledel. Kyle's struggle to own who she is and what she really wants may end up landing her on the bench and without the woman of her dreams. (978-1-63555-156-3)

The Boss of Her: Office Romance Novellas by Julie Cannon, Aurora Rey, and M. Ullrich. Going to work never felt so good. Three office romance novellas from talented writers Julie Cannon, Aurora Rey, and M. Ullrich. (978-1-63555-145-7)

The Deep End by Ellie Hart. When family ties become entangled in murder and deception, it's time to find a way out... (978-1-63555-288-1)

A Country Girl's Heart by Dena Blake. When Kat Jackson gets a second chance at love, following her heart will prove the hardest decision of all. (978-1-63555-134-1)

Dangerous Waters by Radclyffe. Life, death, and war on the home front. Two women join forces against a powerful opponent, nature itself. (978-1-63555-233-1)

Fury's Death by Brey Willows. When all we hold sacred fails, who will be there to save us? (978-1-63555-063-4)

It's Not a Date by Heather Blackmore. Kade's desire to keep things with Jen on a professional level is in Jen's best interest. Yet what's in Kade's best interest…is Jen. (978-1-63555-149-5)

Killer Winter by Kay Bigelow. Just when she thought things could get no worse, homicide Lieutenant Leah Samuels learns the woman she loves has betrayed her in devastating ways. (978-1-63555-177-8)

Score by MJ Williamz. Will an addiction to pain pills destroy Ronda's chance with the woman she loves or will she come out on top and score a happily ever after? (978-1-62639-807-8)

Spring's Wake by Aurora Rey. When wanderer Willa Lange falls for Provincetown B&B owner Nora Calhoun, will past hurts and a fifteen-year age gap keep them from finding love? (978-1-63555-035-1)

The Northwoods by Jane Hoppen. When Evelyn Bauer, disguised as her dead husband, George, travels to a Northwoods logging camp to work, she and the camp cook Sarah Bell forge a friendship fraught with both tenderness and turmoil. (978-1-63555-143-3)

Truth or Dare by C. Spencer. For a group of six lesbian friends, life changes course after one long snow-filled weekend. (978-1-63555-148-8)